THE BEIJING CONSPIRACY

THE BEIJING CONSPIRACY

Shamini Flint

This first world edition published 2019
in Great Britain and the USA by
SEVERN HOUSE PUBLISHERS LTD of
Eardley House, 4 Uxbridge Street, London W8 7SY.
Trade paperback edition first published
in Great Britain and the USA 2020 by
SEVERN HOUSE PUBLISHERS LTD.

British Library Cataloguing in Publication Data
A CIP catalogue record for this title is available from the British Library.

ISBN-13: 978-0-7278-8942-3 (cased)
ISBN-13: 978-1-78029-620-3 (trade paper)
ISBN-13: 978-1-4483-0237-6 (e-book)

All Severn House titles are printed on acid-free paper.

Severn House Publishers support the Forest Stewardship Council™ [FSC™],
the leading international forest certification organisation. All our titles that
are printed on FSC certified paper carry the FSC logo.

MIX
Paper from
responsible sources
FSC® C013056

Typeset by Palimpsest Book Production Ltd.,
Falkirk, Stirlingshire, Scotland.
Printed and bound in Great Britain by
TJ International, Padstow, Cornwall.

For the Friday Football Dads and the Saturday Dilfs – Thanks for inspiring so many characters . . .

A revolution is not a dinner party, or writing an essay, or painting a picture, or doing embroidery. It cannot be so refined, so leisurely and gentle, so temperate, kind, courteous, restrained and magnanimous. A revolution is an insurrection, an act of violence by which one class overthrows another.

Chairman Mao Zedong

Our country is in serious trouble. We don't have victories any more. We used to have victories but [now] we don't have them. When was the last time anybody saw us beating, let's say, China, in a trade deal? They kill us. I beat China all the time. All the time.

President Donald Trump

MAJOR CHARACTERS

The Americans

Jack Ford – ex-Delta Force
The President of the United States
Elizabeth Harris – Vice President of the United States
Joseph Griffin – National Security Adviser
Andrew Bonneville – China expert reporting to NSA
Alberto Rodriguez – Secretary of Defence
Dominic Corke – Director of the CIA
Peter Kennedy – cultural attaché at the American Embassy in Beijing

The Chinese

Xia – student youth leader during Tiananmen Square protests
Fei Yen – Xia's daughter
Zhu Juntao – Secretary General-elect of the Communist Party
General Zhang – head of the People's Liberation Army
Liu Qi – member of the Standing Committee of the Politburo
EMPEROR – codename for a spy in the higher echelons of the Chinese government
Guo Feng – a colonel in the PLA, military adviser to Secretary General-elect Juntao
Tank Man – heroic figure from China's 1989 protests; identity unknown
Confucius – rebel and intellectual who befriends Jack Ford in Beijing

5 June, 1989
Beijing, China

A young man watched a column of tanks rumble down Chang'an Avenue towards Tiananmen Square. It was the day after the crackdown on student protesters and the sound of automatic gunfire had died away. The road was deserted except for a burned-out factory bus – and the tanks, with their distinct sound of heavy engines and the clank of metal tracks. The Chinese Type 59 tanks, pride of the People's Liberation Army, trundled along the broad avenue in single file as if they were participating in a military parade but there were no flag-waving spectators to line the streets.

The young man stepped out from the shadows and walked up the avenue towards the cavalcade. He wore a dark pair of trousers and white shirt and carried a shopping bag. He was a tiny figure compared to the iron behemoths. The cannon on the first tank was trained directly on him as they advanced towards each other. A red star emblem dazzled against the camouflage paint.

The stranger stopped directly in the path of the first tank.

It looked as if the tank would run the man over. He did not baulk or move. At the last possible moment, the tanks came to a halt, one behind the other, just a few short yards away from him.

The lead tank turned sharply in an attempt to go around the man. He stepped directly into its path again.

The armoured vehicle tried the same manoeuvre a second time, and then a third, but each time the man moved so that he was once more in its path.

The tank commanders switched off their engines and silence fell.

The man climbed on to the hull of the first tank, hauling

himself up using the cannon. He clambered over the gun turret and called to the crew inside. He had a brief conversation with the gunner and then jumped down. A commander appeared at the hatch, watched the young man take up his position in the path of the tanks and then disappeared back inside the belly of the beast.

The roar of engines broke the silence. The tanks inched towards the flesh and blood obstacle. The protester remained in their way, the exact opposite of an immovable object but determined to face down the tanks.

Suddenly, two men appeared out of a side alley and hurried to the protester. They each grabbed an arm. He struggled and then gave up the fight. They dragged him away and, in a moment, he was gone, disappeared, as if he was never there.

A foreign reporter taped the scene from his hotel window overlooking the road. The 8 mm reels, smuggled out of China, were the only proof of the Tank Man's lonely resistance.

ONE

J ack Ford woke up and flinched as the shafts of morning light stabbed right through his pupils. He felt like that old Greek guy – what was his name? – who'd put out both his eyes because he didn't want to witness the consequences of his own deeds.

'Oedipus,' he muttered, rolling his legs off the sofa. He propped himself up with an elbow until he was half way sitting up. 'Oedipus Rex.'

He shut his eyes against the glare and found himself back in the desert; Afghan red dust clogging his nostrils, the sun so bright it was like a weapon in the hands of the Taliban. He remembered young Private Whiteside sitting next to him in the armoured personnel carrier, hands clasped together, praying for deliverance from IEDs. Events after that were tattooed into his brain.

The explosion.

Being flung from the vehicle.

Complete silence. Blood trickling from his ears.

Screaming for help.

Puffs of dust from incoming fire.

Holding Whiteside down and tying tourniquets to stop the blood.

Jack took deep slow breaths until the visions receded and he was back in the present. He looked around and established that he was in his tiny Brooklyn apartment, in his own clothes, surrounded by empty bottles from the previous evening. What had he been trying to forget?

The letter.

The letter was still there, on the cigarette-scarred coffee table, tugging at the corner of his vision, like a migraine or a memory or a sniper's scope catching the light.

He reached for the nearest bottle, tipped it back, gulped and then spat the mouthful all over the front of his shirt. Shit tasted weird. He held the bottle up to the light, squinting and grimacing. Ashes. *Ashes.* He'd used the bottle as an ashtray. Way to go, war hero.

Jack wiped his mouth with the back of his hand and then rubbed his eyes with his palms. As recently as the previous afternoon he'd intended, he'd absolutely intended, to get on with the rest of his life as best he could, to look at the past only when he had no choice and then only through the bottom of a shot glass.

Until the letter.

It arrived in the post – which in itself was a surprise. When was the last time he'd received any mail other than an advert for real estate or a flyer for fast food? Usually, Jack gathered up the mail and chucked it in the trash. Anything that wasn't junk was likely to be a bill – he got around to paying those when they sent a collection agent to wait on his doorstep. But, the previous evening, protruding out of the assortment of crap, he'd noticed the letter. A real letter with those airmail marks on the envelope, a hand-printed address and a rectangle of Chinese stamps.

It was one of those moments which had fate written all over it, like when Sergeant Price stopped to pat the dog and got his head blown off in Fallujah.

Or when he'd been a young man in Beijing and met Xia for the first time.

She had smiled and asked him, 'Are you an American spy?'

He should have chucked the damned letter in the trash. He wasn't looking for trouble. Thirty years was so long ago that when he cast his mind back, it was like peering into the wrong end of a telescope. The images at the end were still as sharp as broken glass but so, so far away.

Instead, Jack opened the letter. He didn't hesitate or try and talk himself out of it. If you know you're going to end up doing something, you might as well do it right away.

It was from Xia.

I need your help, she'd written. *There is no one else I can trust.*

And her plea brought the past right up smack into the present; into this stinking apartment, so that it was sitting on the couch next to him like an old friend, asking why he hadn't kept in touch, where he'd been all this time.

He'd been to a lot of different places. Kosovo. Afghanistan. Iraq. But none of them, it would seem, quite far enough away.

Jack reached out, picked up the envelope again, and the photo slipped out. He stared at the studio headshot, close up, smiling. So very beautiful. He turned it over and there was an address on the back: Faculty of Law, University of Peking.

Suddenly, he was back in Beijing in 1989, around the corner from Tiananmen Square, crouched in the shadows along Chang'an Avenue. He could smell the petrol fumes and gunpowder. Xia and Peter were huddled next to him. Sweat stung his eyes and he clutched her hand, looking for courage. *Cowards die many times before their deaths.*

'We have to do something,' he said, his voice an urgent whisper. 'We have to save him.'

The man jumped in front of the lead tank for the third time.

Xia raised her head slightly to get a better view, peering over a temporary road divider. 'What the hell is he trying to do? He's playing chicken with a tank!'

'There's nothing we can do,' Peter said. He gripped Jack's arm. 'He's a dead man.'

The valiant never taste of death but once.

Jack Ford dragged himself back to the present with an effort that felt like pushing rocks uphill. He stared at the photo of the beautiful young woman again. *Please help her*, Xia had written. *If you won't help me, please help our daughter.*

Our daughter.

Her name is Fei Yen.

Jack reached for a vodka bottle and then hesitated. He looked at the photo again. A photo of the woman that Xia claimed was his daughter.

What's past is prologue.

He took a deep, slow breath and then shoved papers and bottles off the coffee table until he unearthed his phone. The past was calling. Maybe it was time he picked up.

'Soon you will achieve your dreams.' Yu Yan was in bed next to her husband, soon to be the most powerful man in China.

Zhu Juntao smiled. 'I could not have done it without you.'

He was in a generous mood because he too could sense that his time was at hand. He lay back against the heavy brocade bedding with the dragon motif, folded his hands under his head and stared at the ornate carved ceiling with the brass chandeliers. Even though he had not yet officially taken up his position as the Secretary General of the Communist Party (and, by implication, the next President of the People's Republic of China), his residence was fit for an emperor. He remembered the distant past when he had been a young man and an avowed communist, despising luxury as the corruption of capitalist running dogs. He would never have guessed that Party leaders lived in such opulence, and he wouldn't have approved if he had known. But times changed. People changed. It was necessary to have the trappings of power, both as a reward for the hard scramble to the top and to impress the citizens.

'Of course you couldn't have done it without me,' she said. 'It is as Mao said, women hold up half the sky.'

'Don't you go around quoting Mao. That man was a lunatic. His Great Leap Forward almost caused China to leap right back to the Stone Age.'

'The walls have ears,' she cautioned.

'You expect the Secretary General-designate of the Communist Party of China to be afraid?' He enjoyed rolling his new title around his mouth.

'I expect him to be careful, that is all.' She sat up on the bed and leaned her head against his shoulder. 'You have many enemies. The Politburo will fight your reforms every step of the way.'

He smiled but there was no humour in it. 'There are some who will support me.'

'Few speak truth to power.'

Her husband laughed. 'Some day, my dear, they will have your sayings in a Little Red Book!'

'And you will have your image in Tiananmen Square instead of . . .' She stopped, unable to finish the sentence. Chairman Mao, displayed in mummified splendour within his mausoleum on Tiananmen Square, haunted his successors like Hamlet's ghost.

'What are you looking forward to the most?' Juntao asked, keen to change the subject away from Mao. He turned over in the bed and sat up, reaching for his trousers. He was a tall, angular man who looked like a law professor.

'I hope the Americans give us a state dinner,' she said as she got out of bed and began to dress. 'I would enjoy that.'

'Consider it done. I will send word that my first diplomatic engagement upon being confirmed as Premier will be to make a state visit to Washington, DC.'

He leaned back on a pillow and imagined the President of the United States waiting for him at the end of a red carpet, the image beamed around the world. He hoped the buffoon they had elected wouldn't embarrass him with one of those power handshakes that became a tug of war.

His wife tried with moderate success to zip up her silk *qípáo*. He stood and assisted her, gazing at their reflections in the long mirror. She barely came up to his shoulder. Her face had fine lines but her body was slim and youthful. The mandarin collar and pearl buttons suited her delicate features. Her hair was cut in an old-fashioned bob that framed her face. Yu Yan would be an asset by his side. He would demand and she would charm. How could they fail?

'You must wear a red *qípáo* that shows off your legs when we meet the President of the United States,' he insisted, smiling. 'Or maybe not. That old lecher might grab you . . . and then I would have to start a war to avenge your honour.'

'I will have difficulty keeping him at a distance, but for the sake of world peace I will do so, my husband.'

Yu Yan sat down on the edge of the bed, knees together, back straight, and adopted a serious tone, all business now. 'Will the Politburo be happy if you go to America so early in your term?'

Juntao frowned and adjusted his spectacles, a nervous tic when he didn't like the way a conversation was going. 'You are right – they will want me to wander around the industrial belt admiring high-speed trains and factories. They are all backward isolationists.'

'Do not say such things to anyone except me,' she said.

'Someone like General Zhang would probably have you arrested for treason.'

'Zhang? He's nothing but a thug.'

'A powerful thug who has the loyalty of the People's Liberation Army,' she warned. 'You would be wise to see him as a threat. That is the way he sees you.'

'The PLA is supposed to be loyal to the Party and its leadership – that's me.'

'Don't be naive, Juntao. General Zhang made his way up through the ranks. He commands personal loyalty amongst the uniformed men.'

'That is why I need the people on my side,' he said.

'They do support you.'

Juntao walked to the window and shifted the heavy gold brocade curtain so he could look across the lakes that surrounded the Zhongnanhai complex, official residence and workplace of Chinese leaders. He smoothed down his hair with both hands and braced his shoulders.

'How do we know what the people want?' he asked. 'We never ask them for their opinion. We don't give them a vote. We just sit around in small rooms filled with cigar smoke and tell them afterwards who their next leader will be. And then we provide school children with flags so they can cheer our procession as we ride to power.'

'Sometimes we don't ask the question because we might not like the answer.'

'That is precisely why I waited so long to ask you to marry me,' said Juntao, turning away from the window and reaching for his wife. She allowed him to hold her for a moment and then stepped away and looked at him, not trying to disguise her worry.

'You plan to go ahead?' she asked.

'Of course! If I do nothing, I will go down in history as the Premier who presided over the disintegration of China.'

'Is the situation really that bad?'

'Worse. There is unrest and unhappiness everywhere in China. The people want change and they grow impatient at the snail's pace of reform.'

'What are you going to do?'

'Find a hero,' he said. 'In her hour of need, China needs a hero.'

The President of the United States of America crushed the empty can of Diet Coke and tossed it towards the bin. He missed. A few other misshapen cans on the carpet suggested both that POTUS enjoyed his Diet Coke and that his aim was rarely true. He made no attempt to clear the mess. The man at the global apex of power did not stoop to such things. POTUS looked around his Oval Office and tried to feel cheerful – nice digs when you considered it, although he personally preferred a more opulent style. But truth be told, the job was getting him down. He levered himself to his feet with the help of the *Resolute* desk, carved from the timbers of the ship *Resolute* and presented as a gift to President Hayes by Queen Victoria, and walked over to the big mirror hanging on the wall. Gilt-edged and antique, it had either belonged to one of the earlier presidents or been a gift from some foreign head of state trying to curry favour with the incumbent of the time. The President admired his reflection – the patrician nose, the wide shoulders, the carefully combed-over hair. He pulled the edges of his jacket together to try and disguise the paunch but fine tailoring could only do so much. The stomach and the watery blue irises, faded against the bloodshot whites, gave the game away. He was out of his depth.

There was a discreet knock on the door and it was pushed open by his secretary, Mrs Hibbert, built like a World War Two tank and with similar firepower. He was terrified of her. 'Mr Griffin and General Rodriguez are here to see you, sir.'

The President glanced at the diary on his desk, open to that day's page, and stifled a sigh. 'Yes,' he said. 'For my security briefing. Send them in.'

Joseph Griffin, the National Security Adviser – unkempt, with a moustache like an untrimmed hedge, spectacles so thick they looked like magnifying glasses and a spotted bow tie that verged on the ridiculous – walked in and they shook hands briefly even though they saw each other almost every other day. Secretary of Defence General Rodriguez followed and saluted smartly. The leader of the free world smiled. He liked that; the formality of the military always pleased him.

'What's happening in the big bad world?' POTUS asked, reaching into his desk and retrieving another Diet Coke.

'The North Koreans have threatened to resume nuclear testing, sir.' Griffin's tone was matter-of-fact.

'Nasty little Rocket Man. I thought he and I had a deal,' said the President of the United States.

'Yes, sir, but the North Koreans are notoriously unreliable.' General Alberto Rodriguez was in his uniform and looked the part of the old war horse that he was. His grave bearing and impeccable manners always suggested generations of breeding; no one would have guessed that he was the son of a single mother who cleaned hotel rooms to put him through school.

'Yes, but we made a *deal*!' insisted POTUS.

'Yes, sir,' the other men said, almost in unison.

'What can we do? Give me some options. I can't look weak.'

'I've just been debriefed by the CIA, sir, by Dominic Corke,' replied Rodriguez.

'And?'

'We still have time. According to his intel – which he rates as being of high quality – the North Koreans do not have an ICBM that can reach the continental United States.'

'How long do we have before they acquire the technology?' asked Griffin.

'Difficult to put a precise time frame on it but the estimate from the CIA is one to two years, especially if we toughen sanctions.'

'Doesn't mean they can't threaten our allies,' growled Griffin. 'What about Japan and South Korea?'

'They remain at risk,' agreed Rodriguez, 'but that was the case even with North Korea's conventional weapons.'

'It looks bad if North Korea gets the long range nukes. We don't want them to have any nukes that can hit us,' said POTUS.

He felt that Griffin and Rodriguez were making a huge effort not to glance at each other. The President hated it when these hawks in his administration treated him like an idiot.

'We need leverage against China so they cooperate with us to contain North Korea,' said Griffin.

'What about the trade war?' asked POTUS.

'It is possible that the Chinese see that as leverage over *us*,' said Rodriguez.

The President glared at him but could not read from his stern face whether sarcasm had been intended.

'So how do we do that? How do we pressure China?'

'Send a few warships through the Taiwan Strait; supply the Taiwanese with some weapons technology,' said Griffin, brushing down his moustache over his upper lip.

'We should just kill him.' The two subordinates stared at the President. He said, 'You know, Kim Jong-Un. We should send in a team. Like a SEAL team. Like Obama did with bin Laden.' The President's face turned red and made a sharp contrast to his straw-coloured hair. 'I could do a news conference and announce it.'

'US policy is not to assassinate the heads of state of other nations,' explained General Rodriguez, face impassive.

'I decide on the policy, right?'

'Yes, Mr President, but an assassination would risk destabilizing North Korea – we have no idea who would take over – and render the potential for first strike by them even more likely,' replied the general.

'I thought you just said they couldn't reach us!'

'Our allies, sir.'

'Allies in harm's way are an expensive nuisance,' complained POTUS. 'Why did we promise to provide military protection, anyway?'

When neither man responded he said, 'So we have to show the Chinese we mean business?'

'I believe we have time to explore a relationship with the new Chinese leader, Secretary General-elect Juntao.' Rodriguez did not make eye contact with the National Security Adviser as he contradicted his position.

'That tall chap with the great-looking wife?'

'Yes, Mr President, our information is that he might be willing to come to the table to do a deal. He will rein in North Korea in exchange for an end to tariffs.'

'He wants a deal?'

'That is what we have been led to understand, sir.'

'How do we know this guy will keep the deal? The North Koreans didn't! I can't look like a fool again.'

'My suggestion is that we send a few ships to convince them we mean business, and offer Taiwan missile defence tech. We can do this *while* responding to the overtures from the new kid on the block,' said Griffin. 'It was your tariffs, after all, that brought them to the table.'

POTUS beamed. 'America First,' he said. 'If the tariffs brought them to the table, then the warships will seal the deal. Send them.'

'Yes, sir,' barked Griffin. 'And the defence tech?'

'Sure, sure, whatever you think is best.' POTUS was bored now, and it showed as he hugged himself and stared at the ceiling like a sedated patient in a straitjacket.

'Shall we go over the rest of the security briefing, sir?' asked Rodriguez.

'Anything urgent?'

'No, sir.'

'Brief the VP then! What the hell is the use of having that dried-up stick on the show if she doesn't do anything?'

Jack was buckled into the window seat of a Boeing 777 on his way from JFK to Beijing, via Singapore. He was trapped in there by an American couple from the Midwest. They smiled at him and he smiled back. Jack knew they were affable because he looked so ordinary. Slightly below average height, about five ten, eighty kilos, the cords of muscle and the tracks of bullets both hidden under a loose T-shirt and windbreaker. His nose had a kink in it – but not so much as to say 'fighter'. More like that guy who walked into a door once after a few drinks too many at the office party.

A few drinks too many. That part was usually true.

'We're going to see our brand-new granddaughter in Singapore. How about you?' asked the woman in the next seat.

He was on his way to meet Peter Kennedy, former colleague. In a sense, there was a symmetry to this plan: if Xia was back in his life, then it made sense that Peter would have a role to play too. History was repeating itself. This was not, however, information he planned to share with these gregarious strangers.

When he didn't respond, they settled for colonizing the arm-rests. Jack shut his eyes, knowing that he needed sleep, knowing that the memories would keep him awake. It had been that way since he received the letter with the photograph of his daughter; the spitting image of Xia with maybe, just maybe, a little bit of him around her eyes and chin. Or was that just wishful thinking?

Jack had spent his days looking for information and drawing blanks. On the seventh day he called Peter and asked for assistance, even though each word caught in his throat like a fish hook.

And now, after thirty years during which they'd each done their best to pretend that the other didn't exist, Jack was on his way to meet Peter again. In Singapore.

Raking up the past was an all or nothing deal.

Jack remembered the second to last time he'd seen Peter, the day after the Tiananmen Square massacre, one of his eyes gummed shut with blood, the other focused on the street as the tanks rolled by. They'd met for the first time six months earlier at the US Embassy in Beijing where both were playing at being spies. Jack had been recruited from Georgetown when he finished his degree in English Literature; Peter Kennedy was from NYU. In their blue jeans and baseball caps they were young enough, cool enough, American enough to save the world from communism. Or so Jack had thought anyway. Peter didn't seem to care much either way.

The CIA station chief in Beijing arranged a 'chance' meeting with one of the student leaders, Xia.

'What do we do? What's our mission?' asked Jack.

The man laughed out loud. 'Nothing. You don't have to do anything. Make some friends. Keep your ears to the ground.'

Xia, the student leader, had been waiting for Jack at the South Entrance of the Temple of Heaven. Her slim figure was silhouetted against the carved wooden circular exterior of the building. The sun behind her head created a halo. *Who ever loved that loved not at first sight?*

'I'm Jack,' he said.

Xia smiled, revealing even white teeth and a dimple that hinted at mischief. 'Are you an American spy?'

Her English was flawless and he remembered his brief: that the rebellious students were the children of the well-heeled city dwellers.

'I'm an American student,' he answered.

'What do you study?'

'Post-graduate journalism,' he answered. 'I'm in Beijing doing an internship but I thought I could write you up for my college newspaper – generate some sympathy for your cause back home in the States.'

'We would appreciate the support of our Western counter-parts in the struggle for the liberty of the Chinese people,' she said solemnly.

Every statement of Xia's sounded like a slogan of the intended revolution. Later, Jack realized it was the way she had been taught to express political thought. The only problem for the Chinese authorities was that the students were quoting from Plato and Lincoln instead of Mao's Little Red Book.

'What are you hoping to achieve?' Jack asked.

'A government of the people, by the people, for the people,' she replied.

Peter, always the sceptic, said, 'Let us know what that's like when you get it.'

Within a few weeks, Xia and others had organized more than three thousand students from Peking University and Tsinghua University to set up camp in Tiananmen Square. Jack reported everything back to the embassy, was commended for his efforts, resented Peter when he tagged along and fell deeply in love with the youthful Chinese rebel.

'They will have no choice but to agree to our demands for greater freedom and democracy,' she said to him, bright-eyed, one day, clutching a flyer that had recently been distributed on the streets. It listed seven demands, including a free press and democracy, that had been cobbled together by the students.

There was a quote in the flyer from Jack: *The students of China may rely on the solidarity of their American counterparts – Jack Ford, American student activist.*

'No one in America sounds like that,' Jack said.

'No one in China knows that,' she replied.

Jack realized that Xia was aware of the value of propaganda. He admired her for it.

'The press is urging a hard line . . . and we all know what that means,' he warned, taking her hand in one of his. For once he'd been able to ditch Peter, so he was keen to make some real progress with the girl. She drew back but smiled at him to lessen the rejection.

'You're right,' she said. 'They are laying the groundwork for violence to disperse the protesters.'

'You have to stop! You're in danger.'

Her face grew hard.

'The numbers in Tiananmen are swelling,' he continued, as if she didn't know.

They'd been there earlier in the day. The atmosphere had been festive – the drums, the shared food, the colourful bandanas and the young Chinese men in their fake lumberjack shirts and bad haircuts flocking around Xia like bees around a honey pot.

'Do those kids realize the risk they're taking?' he asked.

'Sacrifices must be made,' she said. 'Did not your Thomas Jefferson say that the tree of liberty must be watered with the blood of patriots and tyrants?'

'You sound like you're hoping for bloodshed!'

'Don't be ridiculous.'

He must not have looked convinced because she reached for his hand and said, 'Come – let us go back to my place and prepare more flyers for the revolution!'

Jack hesitated for a second, still doubtful. And then she smiled at him and he was lost again.

Dragging himself back to the present, Jack leaned his forehead against the Boeing 777 aircraft window and slipped his hand into his jacket pocket. He felt the rustle of thin paper and the harder edge of the photograph. How different things might have been if he hadn't gone home with Xia that day to her tiny room in a maze within the old city. His lids flickered and he opened his eyes wearily. An air hostess pounced immediately. 'Sir, will you put your seat in the upright position and secure your tray table? We will be landing in Singapore shortly.'

When he fled Beijing after the Tiananmen Square massacre thirty years earlier, he'd stopped in Singapore. Jack looked out the window and took in the skyscrapers along the water's edge, their radio antennae lost in low clouds, the hundreds of ships anchored offshore and lined up with the tide, the golf courses dotted with sand traps on the approach to Changi Airport. Times changed. Places changed.

Did people change? That was what Jack wanted to know, needed to know. The plane touched down and taxied to the terminal. Jack unfastened his seatbelt, grabbed his bag from the overhead locker and checked for his passport. History was repeating itself. But he needed a different ending this time around.

TWO

'**S**uddenly, US security is less important than a game of golf!' Director Griffin was livid despite having more or less got his own way with the President.

He glared at his subordinate, Andrew Bonneville, China expert, as if daring him to disagree. He didn't. Those who worked for the National Security Adviser had learned the hard way not to contradict him when he was angry. Nor, for that matter, when he was calm. Turning him into a raging bull was as easy as pulling the pin on a grenade.

'Report to the VP! Who does he think I am? Fifty years serving my country and I'm sent to a woman who does not have America's interests at heart. Just because that fool' – Bonneville knew he meant the previous VP – 'had a heart attack and POTUS decided that his reality show presidency needed a plot twist. So he selects a bloody Democrat.'

'I'm sure the VP will follow your advice, sir.'

'Rubbish. She wants to replace me with some lily-livered do-gooder – I just know it. Someone like that asshole over at Langley.'

The other man in the room had no difficulty identifying the 'asshole over at Langley' as the CIA director, Dominic Corke.

'The President respects your judgement, sir.'

'That fool only respects shiny objects . . . lucky I gave him some to play with.'

'Sir, *should* we brief the VP?' asked Bonneville.

Griffin flung himself into a chair. 'I've sent Rodriguez,' he said. 'What did you want to see me about anyway?'

'This country is facing an existentialist threat.'

'So what else is new?'

'I don't mean ISIS or Al-Qaeda, sir. They are not a threat any more; at most we're talking about small-scale attacks, probably overseas targets.'

'I reckon that's true,' agreed Griffin. He added, 'Those are still Americans in the line of fire.'

'Yes, but not the American way of life!'

'What is the *existentialist* threat, then?'

'China, sir. This is the Cold War all over again, and we're being distracted from protecting our interests by a few mad mullahs.'

'I agree the Chinese are a formidable enemy. They own our debt, they make everything the American consumer buys in their factories, they're a nuclear power, they have a growing space program, the North Koreans dance to their tune and they have a culture and a philosophy that is the polar opposite of the US. But that's been the case for a while. What's changed?'

'There's no telling what's going to happen in this battle for control between the liberals and the hardliners; between the new Sec Gen, Juntao, and General Zhang's faction.'

'Whose side are we on?'

'The forces of reform have the upper hand right now. If China attempts to liberalize, it could be a mess. Pussyfooting down the reform path led to the fall of Imperial China. If it works, America's competitive edge – our status as a thriving democracy – will be lost.'

'And if the hardliners win?'

'It's hard to know what they'll do but it could involve a confrontation over Taiwan – they might force us to put up or shut up. Or, they might throw their weight behind North Korea and leave us and the South in a difficult position.'

'This President doesn't have the balls for a fight outside Twitter.'

'I'm not sure the American people have the appetite for confrontation either, sir. Not after Iraq and Afghanistan.'

'According to your analysis, we're screwed whichever side wins . . .'

'That's right, sir. In my view, now that the economy's slowing down and the Chinese have time to think, the only thing that's going to keep us ahead of the game is if neither side of the Chinese equation gains pre-eminence. We need a stalemate.'

'I see,' said Griffin. 'And how do we achieve this delicate balancing act?'

'I have an idea, sir.' Bonneville's glasses caught the light and hid his eyes, but not before Griffin caught a glimpse of single-minded determination.

'Tell me,' said the NSA. He suppressed a smile with some difficulty. This was probably not the time to tell his enthusiastic underling that he had the matter well in hand.

General Zhang, a stocky uniformed man with grizzled, closely shaved hair, sipped tea from a small china cup. His big fist clasped the fine crockery in a grip just shy of crushing it, like a gorilla with a daffodil. The general leaned over, sniffed the aroma, kneaded the bridge of his nose with the thumb and forefinger of his other hand and had another sip. This delicate routine did not indicate a lack of strength. It was often said of General Zhang that ten thousand bones had been crushed on his route to the top.

He sat the cup back down and looked around the massive glossy conference table at the civil servants, all men, all wearing dark trousers and white shirts, all terrified even though they met the general once a week to update him on the general situation in China.

'Report,' General Zhang snapped.

'This month alone there have been nineteen *thousand* incidents of civil disobedience.' The civil servant shuffled the papers in front of him to indicate that he was just the messenger.

'What sort of incidents?' he asked.

'Mostly protests against corrupt officials at village level. The taxi drivers in Nanjing are on strike for better wages. A factory owner suspected of selling adulterated baby milk was lynched in Guangzhou. CNN is reporting on this.'

'Was the baby milk adulterated?'

'Of course, sir.' The man looked surprised at the question and pushed his heavy black spectacle frames back up the bridge of his nose. 'The local government officer promised a full investigation but the townsfolk did not trust him. It seems that he was lucky to escape with his own life.'

'The people of the town know that he is in the pocket of the factory owners.'

'We have no information to that effect.' The skinny creature looked down at his notes, fearful that they contained some information he had failed to notice.

'How else did the factory pass its health and safety checks when it was packaging cement dust instead of baby milk?'

General Zhang pointed a thumb at the next in line until each of the rest of the men had delivered their summary of recent events affecting the various major cities and key provinces in China.

'Well? What do we make of it all?' he demanded.

'Economic growth in China has stalled, sir. There is widespread unrest. It is difficult to know where it will end.'

The man who answered was some bureaucrat from the finance ministry. A man who was not afraid to speak truth to power. He would learn soon enough, Zhang thought.

Zhang jerked his head, the signal to clear the room, and the minions gathered their papers and left. Only his aide-de-camp remained.

'It reminds me of the days before Tiananmen Square,' said General Zhang. 'Anger, unrest, rebellion . . .'

His aide was too young to remember the details but he was well briefed on the official Chinese line and he trotted it out without hesitation. 'The Party showed resolve to end that foolish rebellion,' he said.

'Tiananmen Square was easy – they were students. No organization, no high-level backing, no plan. Even so, every year, on the anniversary of the crackdown, we have to watch documentaries about so-called heroes on the Western fake news media. Like the one they call the Tank Man.'

The aide maintained a respectful silence.

'This time feels different,' the general continued.

'What do you mean, sir?'

'The middle class is greedy. The poor menace the cities. The drought is driving farmers to suicide. Social media means we cannot always control the news. One spark . . . and China will go up in flames.'

'I have faith that the Party will take the necessary steps to quell any unrest.'

'You are a fool. Party officials have their noses so deep in the trough they cannot see what is coming.'

There was a knock and Liu Qi, a powerful member of the Politburo and a Vice Premier, pushed the door open and marched in. General Zhang's nose wrinkled against the smell of sweat and hair oil as they shook hands. Liu Qi had been interested in the Secretary General's post but he'd never stood a chance against the photogenic Juntao and his beautiful wife, Yu Yan. He was resentful and therefore easy to manipulate.

Liu Qi indicated the exit and the aide left at a speed that was just short of a run. Liu Qi closed the door after him quickly, almost catching the man's heels.

'Has this office been swept for bugs recently?' Liu Qi asked.

'Just this morning.'

'You're sure?'

'Yes. You are jumpier than a cat, Liu Qi. What is the matter?'

'The memo is missing.'

General Zhang half rose to his feet. 'You were instructed to shred it.'

'I took it home to think about. Now it's gone.'

'You have been blindingly stupid,' bellowed Zhang.

'Things that are done, it is needless to speak about . . . things that are past, it is needless to blame.'

General Zhang despised his colleague's habit of quoting Confucius or Mao whenever it suited him. Half the time he was convinced the little bureaucrat made the stuff up.

'Who took it?'

'I'm looking into it,' Liu Qi replied.

'You have placed our entire mission in jeopardy.' General Zhang stepped forward until he was right in the face of the other man, close enough to see his pores, open and sweating. 'If this document falls into the wrong hands, I will make sure you are standing right next to me when we face the firing squad.'

'Can you make head or tail of this?' Dominic Corke, hands on hips and demanding answers of his number two, was head

of the CIA. A short, muscular man with a deep tan and bleached
hair, he didn't look like a desk jockey. He didn't even look
particularly smart; there was a Forrest Gump-ness about him
– maybe his eyes were too wide apart or the grey too faded
or he didn't blink quite as much as other men. But looks were
misleading: Corke was one of the smartest minds in the administration. Which, as he reminded himself sometimes, wasn't a
high bar. Confirmed by the Senate under the previous administration, he'd been kept on by the current president. Most of
the betting was that his days were numbered.

Now, however, he was worried. 'It doesn't make sense.'

He read the printout again as if repeated reading might make
its meaning clearer.

'This is definitely from EMPEROR? You're sure.'

Only Corke and Jackson Steward, not even the President of
the United States, knew the identity of their mole in the highest
reaches of the Chinese government. And there was no way
Corke was telling POTUS. He didn't want to read about
EMPEROR in a tweet. Corke suspected that the Vice President
too knew EMPEROR's real identity, had been briefed in her
role as Secretary of State in the previous administration, but
he hadn't asked in case it provoked awkward questions.

'Yep – usual channels. Verified.' Jackson Steward was a
man of few words. He was also the physical opposite of his
boss: long-limbed, smartly dressed, hair a touch too long. He
looked the part that his boss played.

'Any hint of what it's about? Any chatter?'

Corke meant electronic chatter. The US government had the
very best technology that smart men could invent and money
could buy. Every agency tasked with protecting the homeland
had the latest in listening devices, tracking devices, tracing
devices. The US Embassy in China was the hub for some of
the most powerful spy technology in the world. But – 'Not a
whisper,' replied Steward.

'Dammit – aren't we supposed to be spies?'

'We don't have boots on the ground.' Steward was a master
of understatement as well.

'Even fewer now,' said Corke.

He meant even fewer after the most recent purge. The Chinese had successfully turned one of their local agents and executed the rest, leaving only a few scattered men distant from the centres of power in Beijing, apparatchiks without access.

'Except for EMPEROR,' said Steward.

'Except for EMPEROR,' agreed Corke.

POTUS didn't know how much of the intel on China was received from this one uncorroborated source. But Dominic Corke believed in his man with the fervour of the religious. He knew EMPEROR's backstory. It had turned a patriot into a traitor and Corke could only thank his lucky stars that such an asset had fallen into his lap.

'A document . . .' he mused. 'EMPEROR wants to send us a *document*? A piece of paper? What is this – 1960?'

'The courier must be someone already travelling a route out of China – no changes of travel plans, no increase in electronic chatter, no redeployment of any personnel.'

'In other words, no red flags.'

Corke felt adrenaline form a starburst in his chest. He was old school too, like EMPEROR. Computers filtering electronic chatter and satellites looking into bedrooms from space hadn't been why he joined the spy game. This was more like it. Human intel being smuggled out the old-fashioned way. A document. A document so important EMPEROR thought the CIA had to see the original. Maybe something big on the new guy, Juntao, Secretary General-elect of the Communist Party. A little leverage would go a long way if POTUS planned to continue his trade war with China or start a hot war with North Korea.

'What do we do?' Steward asked.

'Exactly what EMPEROR wants.'

'It's a risk.'

'I don't see we have a choice. He's stuck his neck out. Whatever this is – it's big.'

'If we lose EMPEROR . . .'

'. . . we might as well just hand over the keys to the future to China.' Corke finished Steward's sentence for him. 'We really need him now too – the President is going to stumble into a confrontation if we are not careful. We need a backchannel to Chinese thinking . . .'

The CIA director leaned forward, elbows on his desk, and placed his palms together as if in prayer. 'We do as EMPEROR asks. Find someone. Find a courier for this goddam document.'

'I already have,' replied Steward.

A raised eyebrow and a half smile. 'Who've you got? We don't need some cowboy.'

'Peter Kennedy – Beijing embassy staffer and spook – due in Singapore on leave.'

'Never heard of him.'

'Old-timer. Mid-level. A nobody. Not the hero type.'

EMPEROR had been to Tibet. Unlike many of the top guys, he'd actually spent time in the mountainous country where the air was as crisp as a freshly minted yuan note and the population, in the thrall of that cult figure, the Dalai Lama, as rebellious as a gang of teenagers. He'd gone on a fact-finding mission early in his career and actually found the province rather charming and scenic – although he was careful to keep that opinion to himself.

Thus, every night when EMPEROR awoke screaming from his nightmares, he knew that his mental picture of the place – snowy ranges, craggy peaks and ornate temples – was accurate. As for the rest, his imagination filled in the detail with the care of a master brushstroke painter. Now, he lay unmoving in the bed, pillow and bedclothes damp with sweat, and did his best to remember the dream in all its bloody horror. He did this every night. It was not enough to suffer the nightmares; he wanted the pain of memory and imagination when awake too. It was his penance for not being there when his son needed him.

When his boy was first posted to Lhasa, the family cele-brated. Yongkang had been asked to command the military division there. As far as numbers went, it was a small command. In terms of its strategic importance and newsworthiness, though, it had been an important step for an ambitious young man. EMPEROR believed in the worth of his son. Rarely, even in the China which rigorously enforced its one-child policy and had a generation of Little Emperors as a result, was there a father as devoted to his son's interests.

EMPEROR remembered a conversation over a cup of fragrant tea on one of his son's infrequent home visits. They had sat together in the garden, watching the blossoms flutter off the trees in puffs of pink. His wife had been inside preparing a suckling pig to celebrate Yongkang's return. He had smiled at the irony. She looked forward to the boy's return with the same enthusiasm as he did but then spent her entire time in the kitchen. She believed firmly that the best way, the only way to show her love was through his stomach. EMPEROR had to admit that he did not know either how to lean over and clasp the boy by the shoulder or give him a hug. But he could play chess with him in the garden and listen to him as an equal.

'They are reluctant to accept our sovereignty, Father. Many of the people – led by the monks in their orange robes – believe that they should be independent.'

'But even that celebrity-chaser accepts that Tibet is part of China.'

'That is what the Dalai Lama says when he is issuing official communiqués – but we believe that he whispers quite a different message to the Americans when we are not in the room.'

'The Americans will not dare interfere in internal Chinese matters,' snorted the older man. He had very little respect for the decadent West.

'Father, your insight is always sound. However, they are happy to instigate civil unrest in Tibet – anything to cause us to lose face.' He laughed a little at the irony. 'We bring the Tibetans development – new roads and buildings and investment – and they complain as if we are slave masters, and the Western press make us out to be monsters.'

'How is the programme of resettling more Chinese residents there to dilute this problematic attitude?'

'The numbers are good but there is often tension between the newcomers and the residents. A lot of my job is keeping a lid on such animosity overflowing into the streets.'

'Eh? You are a policeman in Tibet now? Do you ride a llama to work?'

They had both laughed at this, although Yongkang sobered

quickly. 'These people do not know what is good for them,' he concluded.

'Do not worry, my son. I am sure you are just the man to show them the error of their ways.'

'Remember, Father – victory has a thousand fathers but defeat is an orphan.'

EMPEROR had heard that expression before – from General Zhang – and it left him with a sense of unease that a more superstitious man might have treated as a warning. But he wasn't a superstitious man so he ignored the feeling of foreboding and moved his rook instead. 'Check,' he said.

In the end his son won comfortably although, truth be told, EMPEROR let him win – just happy to have his son across the table from him again.

He wondered sometimes, as he lay in a pool of his own sweat, whether he would have said and done anything differently if he'd known it was the last time he would see Yongkang alive.

THREE

Colonel Guo Feng of the PLA, once the most loyal military adviser to the new Secretary General-elect of the Communist Party, was being blackmailed by General Zhang. And now he was forced to reveal the secrets of a good man to one whom he despised heartily. He had to inform Zhang that the mission the Secretary General-elect had given him was on the verge of a successful outcome.

Guo Feng remembered the scepticism when he said to his underling, 'We need Jack Ford back in China. It is the only way to deliver on the Secretary General-elect's wishes.'

'I don't see how that is possible. What do you expect me to do? Send out an invitation? Invite him for a ten-course Chinese dinner?' His colleague did not like the task he was being set.

'Whatever it takes! Without him, we do not have any leads. And Secretary General Juntao was quite adamant.' Guo Feng raised his voice to make his point.

'What about the other American? Isn't he easier to reach?'

'Yes, but my sources say Peter Kennedy knows nothing.'

'Well, if the order is from the top, surely it is better to send a crack team to Washington. It is much more practical to bring him by force than to find some way to entice him here.' Guo Feng's subordinate was still looking for an easier way.

'You have read his file and yet you can say such a thing? He is a decorated soldier with a stubborn streak as wide as the Great Wall. We do not want a botched mission like the Saudis with Khashoggi.'

Colonel Guo Feng's tone of admiration provoked a scowl from the other man. 'The Americans are not good soldiers. Capitalist running dogs do not have what it takes to be fighting men.'

Guo Feng looked pained. 'Must you trot out this communist nonsense?' he demanded. 'Not even the Politburo uses such Maoist language any more so there is no need for you to do it.'

The other man ignored the criticism. 'What makes you think we will do any better if we have him here? Have you perfected some truth serum previously unknown to science?'

'You're looking at this the wrong way,' complained the colonel. 'We do not have to torture this man, Jack Ford, to make him talk, or kidnap him to get him to Beijing. We just need to find the right leverage. What do we know about him? What are his secrets? Does he have a fondness for little boys or animals? Whom does he care about?'

'For a desk jockey, you definitely know how to fight dirty,' said the other man.

Guo Feng ran his hand in a caress down the other soldier's face. He had always had a soft spot for the craggy, sunburned faces of the men who fought on the front line – usually Tibet or the border with India. But this particular soldier was special. He was built like a tank, wore his uniform with pride, retained a spark of wit despite the PLA training regime and, when they had first met at a military function, had answered Guo Feng's admiring look with one of his own. One thing led to another and the colonel knew that he was putting his career and possibly his life on the line. Despite a long history of acceptance of gay relationships throughout China's history, neither the Party nor the PLA were tolerant of those with 'the passion of the cut sleeve'. A dark shadow filled Guo Feng's mind but still he smiled at his young lover.

'Why don't you run along and figure out a way I can get this decorated war hero to China?' he asked. 'And tell me tonight?'

This was a reference to their meeting that evening at an underground gay bar in Beijing. The soldier saluted smartly, turned on his heel and marched out the door. A new figure filled the space and walked in without pause.

'Good morning, Colonel Guo Feng.'

When he saw who it was the colonel's heart sank but he kept his expression impassive. He rose to his feet and saluted, allowing only the tiniest hesitation to convey his dislike of the man and his annoyance at the invasion of his private sanctum without the courtesy of a knock on the door. 'General Zhang, to what do I owe the pleasure of this visit?'

Zhang explained in no uncertain detail what he wanted from Guo Feng and why he expected to get it. It seemed that General Zhang had photos and was prepared to use them. Colonel Guo Feng had dug deep to find the courage to thwart the general but had not found it. He was the most trusted military aide to the Secretary General-elect and now, black-mailed by General Zhang, a traitor to him. But what choice did he have?

Colonel Guo Feng knew it was useless to regret the past. He was under the thumb of General Zhang and that was all there was to it. He rang the general on his private line and told him that the American, Jack Ford, sought by Secretary General-elect Juntao, was on his way to China.

An excuse. Manufactured.

In hindsight, it was obvious. Tibetans were restive. An international coalition of celebrities was waging a highly successful propaganda war. The Dalai Lama spoke of peace while fomenting rebellion. A crackdown was needed. Tibet had to be cut off from the outside world.

But Chinese control needed to be established away from the prying eyes of the Western press. Otherwise, every so-called outrage would be splashed across the front pages. If ever there was an organization that wanted to have its cake and eat it too, thought EMPEROR, it was the Standing Committee of the Politburo. They wanted total control of China and all its vassals, but they also wanted to bask in the approval of the people, thumb their noses at the West and its democracy and speak with confidence of the adulation of the people for the leadership.

EMPEROR gazed over the mound of his stomach and could barely see his cocked toes. He was lying on a wooden plank instead of one of the Italian mattresses favoured by his colleagues. His back hurt but physical pain was welcome; it disguised the pain in his heart.

Back in 2001, EMPEROR was not involved in dealing with the Tibetan problem. Although it was an annoyance to the

Chinese, it was not a threat. It was an issue with which lesser men could make their mark. He, as a senior member of the Politburo with major ambitions, had been handling Taiwan, a country and a subject much closer to the heart. He remembered the time well. He had been taken up in negotiations with the Americans over the spy plane that had made an emergency landing on Hainan Island after being rammed by a Chinese fighter jet. They had arrested twenty-four Americans and got their hands on sensitive data from the aircraft. It had come at the cost of the life of the pilot, Lieutenant Commander Wang Wei, but that was a very small price to pay. Looking back, he remembered his sense of intense satisfaction over the capture of the aircraft, his indifference to the fate of the young pilot. But Wang Wei had been someone's son too – it was just that the thought had never crossed EMPEROR's mind. Not until it was his own son in the firing line.

General Zhang, still eager to make a name for himself as a hawk in those days, had been determined that China should refuse to return the aircraft or the crew. 'Let them languish in a Chinese jail,' he had insisted. 'They are spies and deserve no mercy.'

'We cannot do that,' EMPEROR insisted. 'This is not the time or place to provoke an outbreak of hostilities with the Americans.'

'They will not dare to take us on.'

'Don't be ridiculous, General Zhang. They have a new president, George W. Bush, who needs to impress his father. You imagine he can afford to look weak?'

'Our pilot is dead. We must have our revenge.'

EMPEROR snorted out loud. Suddenly, General Zhang of all people gave a damn about the life of a soldier? They were all pawns in his personal Great Game.

'The black boxes of the aircraft show that Wang rammed the spy plane. Maybe he thought he was some sort of Chinese Top Gun. This was not an authorized act. It is a shame that he is dead but it was the outcome of his own foolish actions and should not affect our decision-making in this matter.'

'Perhaps it should have been an authorized act,' countered

Zhang. 'It has brought us good intel and humiliated the Americans.'

'I do not order suicide missions,' EMPEROR answered coldly. 'I value the lives of our young warriors.' He said it to put General Zhang in his place, but the truth was that he had already dismissed the young pilot as expendable. His focus was on drawing out the negotiations with the Americans so that he could obtain as much information as possible from the crew and the craft.

'What is your plan?' asked Juntao, a young up-and-coming leader at the time, already spoken of as a future Party Secretary General.

'I will demand an apology and compensation. I will send their crew back alive but their plane in boxes – after I have extracted every piece of technological information possible.'

'Your plan is sound – you have my support,' said Juntao in his crisp, carrying voice.

General Zhang gave him a look which suggested that he had the younger man marked down as a troublemaker and then added, determined to have the last word, 'At least this is an opportunity to deal with the Tibet situation, don't you agree?'

'What do you mean?' EMPEROR asked.

'The Americans and the rest of the world are watching Hainan Island. Their press is camped in Hong Kong. This is a good time to crack down on the insurrection in Tibet.'

Zhang was daring him to act the dove on two separate fronts, but EMPEROR was not so easily manipulated. He threw him a bone. After all, prudence dictated that he did not make a greater enemy of someone with a memory as long and unforgiving as that of General Zhang.

'That is a good idea, General Zhang. I look forward to hearing about your success in Tibet.'

Back in the present, EMPEROR turned over in bed and was aware that a tear had formed in the corner of his eye. He brushed it away. Grief was indulgent.

He had no one to blame but himself – and General Zhang.

EMPEROR looked at his alarm clock. Dawn. Another night survived. Another day in which to do everything in his power to avenge his son. Even if it meant being a traitor. Even if it meant disclosing state secrets to the Americans. He would do that so long as he had breath in his body. And so long as his double life was not discovered.

FOUR

The following day, Vice Premier Liu Qi sat in his favourite chair in his Spartan living room. He rocked gently back and forth, his eyes on the dead man on the floor. The small concentration of bullet holes in the chest of the body looked like a bouquet of roses, little bursts of red.

General Zhang marched in. Liu Qi had called him first. The police would have their moment, grovelling and scraping and assuring him, a senior member of the Standing Committee of the Politburo, that no blame could possibly attach to him for shooting a man dead in his living room. But his discussions with Zhang would determine how events in the real world, the world of high stakes and high politics, played out.

'What the fuck happened here?'

'I shot him,' said Liu Qi.

'He stole the memo?'

'Yes.'

Zhang prodded the body with the toe of his boot. 'Did you question him?'

'Yes.'

'Well?' The impatience, always so close to the surface in the powerful, barrel-chested general, was already spewing like an active volcano.

A shadow passed across Liu Qi's face. 'It seems that my aide was an American spy. Codenamed EMPEROR.'

General Zhang sat down suddenly on a facing chair.

'I don't understand,' General Zhang said. 'If the Americans know, surely they would have said something by now.'

'The document has not reached them yet. They are going to use a human courier to get it out of the country.'

Zhang nodded. The subject matter of the memo would probably be dismissed as the product of a rabid imagination or a clumsy plant if mere words of its contents were leaked.

'Who is the courier?'

'A cultural attaché at the American Embassy – Peter Kennedy. I've already alerted the intelligence services. And airports.'

Zhang rose to his feet and, without warning, rained kicks on the body on the floor. Bones cracked like distant gunshots, flesh split. The sudden surge of rage mottled Zhang's face; his cheeks and forehead turned red but the skin around his eyes and nostrils was bloodless.

'Control yourself,' Liu Qi yelped. 'I do not need to tell more lies to the police.'

'Why did you kill him?' asked Zhang, panting heavily. 'He might have had more to tell us.'

'He spoke freely – I became suspicious.'

'And?'

'He had a knife in his boot.' Liu Qi pushed away the lacquered coffee table with his foot and they both looked at the long thin double-edged blade. 'He came at me. I am fortunate to have escaped with my life.'

'It's a shame,' muttered Zhang. 'I would have liked an opportunity to question him . . . and then rip him into pieces myself.'

'It is better that no one knows how deeply the Americans had infiltrated the Politburo.'

'Better for whom?' Zhang had gone from blind rage to calmly calculating in the blink of an eye.

'Better for all of us. We are in the same boat, General Zhang, and don't you forget it.'

His phone buzzed. Liu Qi removed his glasses and looked at the screen.

'What is it?' asked Zhang.

'Peter Kennedy slipped through Beijing immigration just before the alert went out. He's on his way to Singapore.'

'When does he land?'

'In around six hours,' Liu Qi replied. 'What are you going to do?'

'Hunt him down.'

'In Singapore?'

'To the ends of the earth, if need be,' replied the general.

Zhang turned his attention back to the dead man; the blood from the scalp of the corpse had stained the carpet.

'What did you say he called himself? EMPEROR?' he asked.

Liu Qi nodded.

'Well, EMPEROR is done leaking secrets to anyone.'

The following day, Jack Ford walked down the narrow path that followed the contours of the artificial lake in the middle of the Singapore Botanic Gardens and wished desperately he was someplace else. One moment it was let sleeping dogs lie, the next, let slip the dogs of war. The lush tropical greenery put him in mind of the Garden of Eden. The Sunday school version of paradise, fruitful and divine – if you held with that sort of thing, which Jack didn't. He'd seen too much of what men could do to each other to believe they were made in God's image.

Jack heard the snap of a twig to his right and turned his head slowly in that direction. It paid to turn slowly, surveying everything in his field of vision. In his experience, sudden noises were often a decoy. The guy with the gun was someplace else.

It was Peter.

He spotted Jack, made to raise a hand in greeting, changed his mind and quickened his step to a trot. Jack watched him, noting the rounded shoulders, the gut hanging over his belt like a waiting avalanche, the thinning hair. Time changed a man. Even young spies with bright futures . . . *we have seen better days.*

As Peter approached, Jack noted he had a briefcase clutched in one hand. It was cuffed to his right wrist. He didn't want to know.

Peter stopped two feet away and didn't extend his hand.

'Jack.'

'Peter. How long has it been?'

'Thirty years.'

There was no forgetting for Peter either.

Jack looked at the man who had been his closest friend. Shaving rash. Bands of sweat marking his light blue shirt. And the eyes. Brown. Shadowed. This was hard for him too.

'You haven't changed a bit, Peter.'

The other man cracked a full smile and lost ten years.

'Neither have you, Jack. How've you been? I heard you joined up.'

Jack shrugged. 'You join up, you get around.'

'Delta Force?'

'It was a job.'

'That's not what I heard. Three Purple Hearts?'

Jack wondered how Peter knew and then shrugged off the speculation. What did it matter? Men like Peter Kennedy could keep track of an old friend, or an old enemy, if they so desired. Wasn't that why he'd contacted him in the first place to ask for his help?

'How about you?' asked Jack. He suddenly, desperately, didn't want to get to the point.

'I stayed with the foreign service.'

Foreign service – a euphemism for espionage more often than not.

'You always had a stronger stomach than me.'

Peter didn't respond. Instead, he glanced down at the brief-case cuffed to his wrist.

'I took a detour to see you. There'll be hell to pay if anyone finds out.'

'Did you discover anything?' Jack asked.

'Have I ever let you down?'

Peter's left hand slipped into his jacket and he retrieved an envelope. A4, brown. Sealed. Held it up but didn't hand it over.

'Jack, please, you don't have to do this.'

'I can handle it, Peter. I walked away once before and I can do it again.'

'I saw what it cost you.'

He thought about the photo of the girl, etched in his memory now. His daughter. *Maybe* his daughter. 'It's not just about me any more.'

'You can't trust her. You can't trust Xia. Not after everything. Not about *anything*.'

Jack closed his eyes and the tropical sun turned his vision blood red. He knew exactly what Peter could not bring himself to say. He couldn't bring himself to say it either.

'Don't you think I know that, Peter?'

He held out a hand and Peter handed over the envelope. It was reassuringly bulky. Peter had been thorough.

'I called in every favour I had,' Peter said, 'and that is everything I could get on Xia since . . . well, since then.'

'There's a kid?'

'Yes, a daughter – about the right age.'

The men clasped hands. A hello, thank you and goodbye all captured in the single gesture. Jack's grip tightened briefly. An acknowledgement perhaps that life was complicated, that choices were made in haste and regretted at leisure. So much of who he had been and what he had become was because of the man standing in front of him. And Xia. Always Xia.

Peter nodded a goodbye. 'Good to see you again, Jack.'

He was still a poor liar.

Jack watched him go. He sniffed the air and smelt the rotten vegetation, decay and death beneath the leaves. On second thoughts – this was paradise *after* the fall.

Peter had made twenty yards when Jack heard it. The distinct double tap of two bullets fired from a suppressed weapon.

FIVE

Jack hit the deck quicker than a drunk on his last legs. Instinct and training took over. He found the cover of bushes. On his stomach, face down. A brief silence after the shots. He risked a look. Only nanoseconds had passed but the layout had changed completely. His friend was lying supine. The sweat marks on his belly had turned red. Peter had stopped one of the bullets. Maybe both.

Jack scanned the horizon. The shooters weren't hard to spot. Three men. Advancing with intent. Chinese. Not out of place in Singapore except that these men had the purposeful gait of soldiers, not shoppers. He chanced another glance. The thick rough hair and high cheekbones – he'd have guessed Chinese from the mainland, north. All three wore dark suits – spot the guys that weren't tourists.

A friend in need. A friend indeed. It had been in a Hallmark birthday card that Peter had sent him once. He'd added the words 'of beer' after 'need'. Deadly serious now.

The men holstered their guns. This had been an ambush and Peter had been the target. The shooters reached his friend. A few picnickers noticed the man down as well and started to converge. Puzzled. Expecting an innocuous explanation. Heart attack. The heat was too much for a *gwailo*, a white man.

One called out, 'I will call nine-one-one!'

Someone else asked, 'Does anyone know first aid?'

'I know some.' A young woman hurried towards the prone man. People moved aside to make way for her.

A shooter squatted next to Peter and extracted something from his rucksack. The other two formed a loose cordon.

The first – short, thuggish, lines like a dry riverbed on his forehead – pulled a gun and waved it in a lazy arc in the direction of the onlookers and the woman approaching them.

'No call nine-one-one,' he said. 'Just run.'

The woman who knew first aid screamed; they all ran. The gun was holstered once more. No real heroes in that crowd. When they stopped running, they would call the police. But by then it would be too late for Peter. Maybe it was already too late.

Jack, still flat on his stomach in the long grass, turned his attention back to his friend. Was he still alive? He heard another sound and his blood ran colder than a Beijing winter. *No, please God, no.*

Chainsaw.

Whining. Churning. Cutting.

Memories fast-forwarded through his brain. Peter and him. In Beijing. In the villages. Memorizing Mandarin phrases. *What is your name? Where is the toilet?* Laughing and drinking tea from dainty cups. Following it up with American beer. And then the tanks and the soldiers. Caught in the crosshairs of a revolution.

A friend in need. What had George W. Bush called the second Gulf War campaign? Shock and awe. A sudden attack of overwhelming intensity, even if – as in this case – you didn't have overwhelming force. Hit them before they even understood that an attack had commenced. *A man can die but once.*

The Vice President of the United States, Elizabeth Harris, was five feet six inches tall. As the fecklessness of the Commander in Chief became more apparent, at least behind closed doors, she had taken over much of the day to day running of the White House. All the work, none of the credit. It reminded her of her marriage. Appointed from the Democratic Party after narrowly losing to the incumbent, as a sop to 'unity' after the previous VP keeled over, she was the most unpopular person in the administration precisely because she was becoming the power behind the throne.

The VP slipped her feet into her heels and gained a couple of inches. She was still dwarfed by the Secretary of Defence, Alberto Rodriguez, in her opinion a reasonable man for a warmonger. She waved him into a chair and chose one for herself. She felt better when he was seated and not looming over her like a mugger in a dark alley.

'Good morning, Madam Vice President,' said Rodriguez.

'Is it? That will make a first since I've sat behind that desk.' Her accent, the Southern drawl overlaid with an expensive education – Vassar, Harvard – was an asset on the campaign trail as long as she remembered to shed the layer that suggested Ivy League. It wasn't that hard. She'd had a lot of practice – there was only one slip-up, during the debates, when her opponent's attempt to sound like a man of the people – he of the golden spoon and East Coast pedigree – had annoyed her enough to provoke a put-down. She had delivered this in a plummy tone and the clip had replayed on Fox News endlessly. It had cost her victory and now she had to play second fiddle to a man who literally crapped in a gold toilet but was better at faking being a man of the people. Democracy. Definitely the worst system of government except for all the rest.

'Let me guess, POTUS asked you to brief me?'

'Yes, ma'am,' replied Rodriguez, face impassive.

'He's out playing golf.'

'Soon, ma'am.'

'So, why is it a good morning?' she demanded.

'Actually, it's no better than normal, Madam Vice President.'

'Spell it out.'

'We closed in on the Al-Qaeda leader in Yemen but he slipped through our hands again.'

'How come he isn't watching TV all day like Osama?'

Rodriguez rightly assumed this was a rhetorical question. 'We have to get a handle on these terrorists – they represent the greatest threat to the security of the United States.'

'The election is over, Rodriguez. Your guy won – so stow the speeches.'

'Yes, ma'am.'

'What did we use in Yemen?'

'Drones.'

She grimaced. 'Casualties?'

'Some collateral damage.'

'But not the guy we were gunning for . . .'

'No, ma'am.' Rodriguez sounded indifferent to the possibility of civilian deaths. She should be grateful, supposed the Vice President. He wouldn't be very effective in his job if he was some bleeding heart who wasn't willing to take risks. But a little bit of remorse wouldn't go amiss. Just to reassure her that he had a conscience. That he didn't like killing people. Unlike POTUS.

'Right – anything else I need to know?' she demanded.

'Kim Jong-Un has pulled out of the nuclear talks.'

'I saw that in a tweet from *our* Dear Leader,' she remarked.

'Corke at CIA says they won't have a viable ICBM to reach our mainland for a couple of years.'

'That's good news, I suppose. What was the President's approach?'

'He suggested assassination, ma'am?'

'Of whom?'

'Kim Jong-Un.'

The Vice President covered her eyes for a moment with a tired, if well-manicured, hand.

'You persuaded him otherwise?'

'For the time being, yes.'

She tucked a strand of iron grey hair behind her ear.

'So what's the plan?'

'POTUS is sending ships and defence tech to Taiwan as a show of force; a joint naval exercise. He thinks it will force the Chinese to rein in Kim.'

'He thinks or *Griffin* thinks?'

Rodriguez chose not to answer although the twisted mouth showed she had hit the mark.

'Poking a bear with a stick is my favourite diplomatic gambit,' complained the VP.

'Indeed, ma'am.'

'Do we have another plan?'

'As it happens, Madam Vice President, we do.'

'All right, spill it.'

'I have the CIA director outside, ma'am. He should join us.'

Vice President Elizabeth Harris, who had been Secretary of

State under the previous administration before running for president herself and losing, knew Corke well. He had been CIA director during her previous tenure as well.

'Very well, let's hear what he has to say.'

Two of the men were bunched close with their backs to Jack, attention on the downed man and their colleague on his knees beside him. They were speaking Mandarin, but he couldn't make out the words, wouldn't have understood much if he had. Jack calculated he had around two seconds. He left the blocks like a sprinter, quadriceps bunched, hamstring stretched. Accelerated smoothly. One assassin pitched forward as Jack's thrusting side kick found its mark. The other received a vicious elbow in the kidneys. Both hit the water. Both went under. This time, Jack calculated he had five seconds between splash and splutter. Again – more than enough. It only took a split second to land a blow on the last killer, the one crouched down next to Peter. Jack aimed a snapping low kick to the jaw of the kneeling man. But his unknown adversary, with that split second of warning, was good. Definitely trained. Chinese military. Jack didn't have time to wonder why they were after Peter.

The Chinese man ducked to avoid the blow. The kick missed the jaw, catching the man's shoulder. A glancing blow but enough to spin him round. He succeeded in getting a hand to his weapon. But the second time Jack made no mistake. The heavy toe of his leather boot caught the man on the chin. A crunching sound. Breaking bone. The man's head snapped back and he collapsed. Probably broken jaw, diagnosed Jack, as if he was an ER orderly seeking to fix the problem rather than a soldier who'd caused it.

Splutter. The first of the two he'd dumped in the lake had resurfaced. His five seconds were up. Jack lunged and retrieved the weapon from the fallen man. He rolled to his side. He was steady, in control. This was what he had trained to do almost his whole adult life.

Two bobbing heads in the water now.

Jack took the shots. An identical hole appeared in the middle of each forehead. A small mushroom cloud of blood. These two wouldn't be coming back up for air again. He turned around just as the third, despite his broken jaw, made a lunge for him, hoping to push him into the water.

Just as well there was a third bullet.

'What is this plan of yours to contain Kim Jong-Un?' demanded Vice President Harris after Corke had joined them.

'The North Korean situation cannot be solved without the cooperation of the Chinese.'

'I am aware of that. I am also aware that they've done bugger all to contain the threat so far.'

'The Chinese have elected their new Secretary General; he will be sworn in soon.'

'You feel that their attitudes might change? What do we know about the new guy?' she asked.

'He's the son of a Long March veteran, another engineer from Tsinghua University – you know, China's MIT . . . He's got good PR, orchestrated the Beijing Olympics, but he's also tough; his crackdown in the restive Muslim provinces was brutally efficient.'

'I know this already.'

'His wife is a popular actress.'

'How is that pertinent?' The Vice President was always on the lookout for any slights that smacked of sexism.

'It gives him a kind of modern, popular appeal with the population that's unusual in China.'

'The Chinese are becoming as celebrity-obsessed as we are? They've still managed to avoid electing a reality TV star to the top job. What are his *politics*?'

'According to our intel, Juntao's a chameleon, changes colour to suit his environment.'

'Intel? Usual sources?'

Corke nodded. It was evident that the VP, formerly a Secretary of State, knew about EMPEROR.

'Go on.'

'We think Juntao might be in the reformist camp.'

'Why?'

'Although he's a princeling, the son of a former Politburo member, his father was purged under Mao and he himself spent time farming in the provinces. Ate roots and lived in a cave, if his official biography is to be believed.'

'In other words, he's seen both sides? That's your theory?' asked the VP.

'Exactly, ma'am. He's been quoted as saying that he has drunk from the bitterest cup.'

'Which means what exactly?' Why did these people insist on speaking in metaphors?

'That he has suffered and therefore understands suffering.'

'A ploy,' said the Vice President dismissively. 'Trying to portray himself as a man of the people. It's been known to work.' Rodriguez ignored her provocative reference to their own POTUS.

'The Secretary General-elect's speeches might be indication of a genuine reformist and not just window-dressing.'

'Is that wishful thinking or do you have evidence?'

'There's a prominent school of thought in China – especially among some powerful guys in the military – that any liberalization will be a sign of weakness that the country can ill afford. We know that General Zhang – a member of the Standing Committee and the most senior military man in the civilian leadership – was *against* his appointment.'

'But the guy is still the Secretary General-elect. General Zhang hasn't been able to prevent that.'

'That's right,' agreed Rodriguez. 'Zhang has as many enemies as friends so although he is a powerful voice, he did not win the argument. It was a blow to the hardliners and their way of thinking.'

'Which is?'

'That China simply can't allow widespread internal dissent. In the current economic climate – exports falling off thanks to tariffs, workers being forcibly returned to the countryside, endemic corruption . . . they're sitting on a powder keg.'

'Isn't that an exaggeration?'

'One point three billion Chinese with a grievance . . . and no outlet for their anger?' asked Corke.

'I take your point. Only *half* this country is pissed off at me.'

'And our folk take comfort in the fact that they can vote out a sitting president within four years.'

'What are you trying to say, Dominic?'

'Nothing, ma'am. Just drawing a point of contrast with China, is all.'

'So how do we get this new guy, Juntao, to prevent North Korea developing an ICBM, attacking our allies or provoking our POTUS to do something rash?'

'We extend the olive branch, ma'am.'

Jack turned to his friend. The moist air was heavy with the smell of iron: fresh blood. Peter was on his back. The red stain from two bullet wounds had spread across his chest. Blood seeped from under his body and ran between the blades of grass like the first rains on a parched riverbed.

The briefcase was lying by Peter's side. Still manacled to his hand. Only now Peter's right hand was detached from his body. The chainsaw had done its work. Jack felt sick to the stomach. Tried not to think about what was in the briefcase that was worth a man's hand, worth his life. He quickly bound up the stump with a handkerchief from his pocket and then applied pressure to the bleeding chest wounds.

'Jack?' The merest whisper.

Peter was still alive. Jack bent over his friend and gripped his left hand, trying to provide comfort. Crimson bubbles formed on Peter's bottom lip. A punctured lung.

'I'm here, Peter?'

'Those men?'

'Dead.' Grim satisfaction.

Peter's eyes fluttered open at this information.

'Am I done for?'

Jack nodded, tried to speak, could not get the words out. It was impossible to know whether Peter would bleed out or choke and drown in his own blood as his lungs filled. Either way, he was done.

Concentrate on the mission, soldier. But what was the mission? If the mission was to save his friend, Jack was too late. If it was to take down the baddies, it was accomplished.

'Take it . . .'

'What?'

'You . . . have to take the briefcase. That's what they

came for. There will be others. It can't fall into the wrong hands.'

The words were low and soft but impossible to misunderstand. Jack didn't want the briefcase. He didn't want the mission; didn't want the responsibility. What do you say to a dying man when you don't plan on granting his last request? Jack could not meet the glazed eyes of his one-time friend.

Even in the state he was in, Peter sensed the reluctance. 'Jack – you owe me. Remember?'

He remembered.

The voice punched out a final command. 'Take it!'

Peter's eyes fluttered shut. The end would come soon, he had just minutes left. Jack heard sirens wail in the distance. Someone had called the police. The cavalry was on its way. He wiped the gun he'd used on his shirt and threw the weapon into the lake. By the time they found it, the prints would be long gone. It was time for him to go; to leave this place, to leave Peter. He had his own mission. To discover what he could about the woman that Xia claimed was his daughter. He felt in his pocket. The envelope Peter had given him was still there.

Jack stood up and looked down at his friend. What was so important to the Chinese that it had been worth murdering an American agent in a third country?

You owe me.

Peter was right.

Jack stooped, slipped the briefcase off the dismembered wrist and picked it up. He felt the warm blood on the handle. *To thine own self be true.*

He turned and walked away, case in hand. He sensed rather than saw his friend breathe his last. He didn't look back.

SIX

Jack flagged down a taxi close to the entrance of the Singapore Botanic Gardens. He would have liked to walk further, disguise his tracks more, but there was no time. He'd wrapped the briefcase in his windcheater and thus hidden the blood but he knew that he was pale, drenched in sweat and memorable enough for when the police started questioning taxi drivers.

'Balestier Road,' he said.

He ignored the chit chat of the driver and did not make eye contact in the mirror. He told the driver that he was staying at the Ramada although he was actually at Hotel 81 on the other side of the road. He alighted and waited until the car had turned a corner before he hurried across.

Five minutes later he was washing his hands of Peter's blood in the tiny porcelain sink. *Out, damned spot!* Jack watched the dark red swirl dilute under the running tap and then drain away. He dried his hands on a towel and took a deep breath, and then another – closing his eyes, seeking the quiet centre of the soldier where he could operate without the distraction of emotion.

He placed the case on the bed and examined it from the outside carefully but quickly. He estimated that he had an hour – no more than that – before there was a knock on his door. Strange men had already killed for this case, and so had he. It seemed a fair trade to spend one of his nine lives working out why. Knowing Peter and his bosses, he would not put it past them to have booby-trapped the bloody thing. Something out of a spy novel. A needle with a pinprick of poison. An explosive device that would cost him his eyes or his fingers. He persevered, opening the bag through the back hinges with his Swiss Army knife, counting on any booby traps being triggered from the front locks.

Jack didn't know what to expect from the contents. Whatever

it was, it wasn't a few shiny brochures for college education in the United States.

He ran the blade of his Swiss Army knife down the lining. It didn't take him long to find the hidden compartment. It wasn't intended to defeat an expert in espionage or ex-Delta operator who'd been trained to identify just this sort of secret space, only the curious onlooker who somehow got his hands on the case. He pulled out a slim document and stared at it but he was none the wiser. A memo of some sort, a few pages stapled together on the top left corner, written in Mandarin – Jack had only ever learned to speak a smattering of Mandarin, never to read the script – annotated in pidgin along the margins with a forceful red pen.

If this was it, why hadn't the Americans just scanned it and emailed it to their embassy? Jack would need to find someone to translate it before he knew exactly how much dynamite he was sitting on. He recognized a few words, including 'President', 'United States' and 'Taiwan', which didn't bode well.

Jack glanced at his watch. Twenty minutes. He shut the briefcase, packed his small rucksack and left the room. It was dark now although the streetlights and shop fronts were well lit. He sauntered down a side lane where slow-moving traffic tried to turn on to the main thoroughfare. The drivers were tired and impatient, their eyes glazed and red in the reflected glare of brake lights. He passed an open truck, stooped to tie a lace. As he stood up, he swung the case over the side and into the back of the vehicle. He kept walking until the end of the lane, stopped suddenly, shook his head and turned back. To all intents and purposes a man who had taken a wrong turn and was now heading back the way he came. Jack was just in time to see the truck turn the corner, case in the back. He didn't doubt there had been a signal beacon attached to it somewhere. He hadn't bothered to look for it. If he'd found it, he couldn't have been sure there wasn't another – a failsafe to ensure the document could be tracked. Well, whoever was behind this cloak and dagger exercise would have something to follow now that wasn't Jack Ford, ex-Delta Force, alcoholic, with one more daughter (maybe) and one less friend than at the beginning of the week. *The wheel is come full circle.*

Once he'd ditched the case and was confident that he couldn't be tracked, he caught a bus to Geylang where the evening flesh trade meant that rooms were available by the hour. He paid cash and ran up a flight of red, carpeted stairs that smelt of cigarettes and despair.

Only when he was behind locked doors again did he turn his attention to the envelope Peter had given him – the dossier of information compiled at his request on Xia and Fei Yen, the young woman who she alleged was his daughter.

General Zhang's phone rang and he stared at it as if it was a coiled snake. He picked up the receiver and held it pressed hard against his ear, as if he did not want the words spoken to escape into the room.

'The news is not good, sir. The briefcase is gone.'

Zhang's knuckles bleached as he greeted the information from the Chinese military attaché in Singapore, Major Dylan Choo.

'What do you mean?' he demanded. 'How can it be gone? It was a simple recovery mission!'

Zhang had planned the interception to recover the memo himself. Sent his best available men. Their mission had been straightforward – follow Peter Kennedy, recover the briefcase with the memo before he had a chance to hand it over to the Americans. Lethal force was acceptable. Casualties were acceptable. Collateral damage was acceptable. As long as the memo was recovered.

'There was an unanticipated development.'

'What the hell does that mean?' General Zhang strode up and down like a caged beast, the telephone wire pulled taut.

'Kennedy took a detour between the airport and the US Embassy. He went through the Singapore Botanic Gardens. My men went in after him. The mission was proceeding smoothly. Unfortunately, a . . . rogue element seized the case.'

'A *rogue* element? Dammit – what are you talking about?'

'Another man in the gardens at the time of the incident escaped with the briefcase.'

'Another man? A stranger just walked up and took the case? What were your men doing – sightseeing?'

'He engaged them, sir.'

'And?'

'Only one of our men survived – though he was shot as well.'

'We send our best men and they're defeated by a tourist? Is this what the PLA has become?'

'It would appear that the stranger was combat trained, sir.'

'How do you know?'

'We have questioned the survivor, Corporal Silas Fu. He's in hospital in Singapore custody.'

'We need him back here.'

To be debriefed and then court-martialled. A lifetime of solitary confinement or the firing squad. Preferably the latter, decided Zhang.

'We are leaning on the Singapore authorities. But this was a public incident – the whole thing went down in their Botanic Gardens – so they're dragging their heels about releasing him into our custody.'

'What did our man say about your rogue element?'

'White male, middle-aged. Effective against three of our men with the element of surprise in his favour.'

General Zhang tapped his fingers on the table. The nails were cut so deep that thin lines of dried blood ran along the tips. Was this just bad luck? How could it be? General Zhang was not a fan of coincidences. Not when his life and reputation were on the line, let alone the future of China.

'There's more . . .' added the major.

'What is it?'

'Our man doesn't think the interception was planned. He was unconscious for a while. As he came to, he heard a little of what was going on. He believes the man took the case reluctantly – had to be begged to do it by Kennedy. There was an appeal to friendship, to the past. It seems that the courier took a detour to meet this man in the first place.'

'Well, that's your starting point – look into Kennedy's past. Use our agents. Find this man! He has something that belongs to me.'

'Yessir.' Major Dylan Choo had just been shown the

haystack from which he was to extract the needle. He was not in a position to protest.

'Mistakes were made. Those who made them will answer to me. No one is immune. Do I make myself clear?'

There was a tremor in the major's voice. 'Yes, General Zhang.'

'I don't want any loose ends or loose lips.'

'I shall ensure that there are none, sir.'

General Zhang terminated the call and sat back in his chair. The briefcase was gone – seized by some unknown actor, but one with the capacity to take on three of his best men and succeed. Who was he and what was his agenda? There was a real possibility now that the memo, and thus their plans, would fall into the wrong hands. A journalist with a long nose, the Americans, MI5, his enemies within the Party. Zhang feared these last the most. Those who did not understand what was at stake were prone to make poor decisions. And he numbered many of his colleagues amongst them, especially those reformist weaklings in the Politburo. A lesser man might have panicked, but Zhang was not a lesser man. He drew in a long deep breath, considered his options dispassionately.

The election of Juntao as Secretary General was just over a week away. 'Coronation' would be a more appropriate term. The leader had been selected after prolonged negotiation – backroom deals and backroom brawls – and would then be subject to a so-called election for which everyone knew the results in advance. General Zhang knew the calculations. Whom did they fear? Who had influence? Who knew secrets? Who had secrets which could be traded for a desirable outcome or used for blackmail? The heir apparent – Juntao – was a man whose unique selling point was that he was so utterly nondescript as to have made few enemies. But Zhang knew that his instincts were liberal. He was the sort of leader – like Gorbachev – who ended up throwing the baby out with the bathwater in their attempts to carve out a place in history for themselves. Was this the leader China needed? Not if he, General Zhang, had anything to say about it. For Zhang, Juntao represented the nadir in a steady decline in leadership from Mao. And, as anticipated, the Americans had ordered two warships to sail up the Taiwan Strait for a joint exercise with the Taiwanese navy. POTUS was sticking his tongue out at China like a child believing he was safe behind a fence.

Zhang nodded to himself, decision made. The briefcase and memo were out there and would have to be recovered. In the meantime, there was only one option – to press ahead with his plans, to shave days, hours, minutes off the timeline so that the risk of failure was reduced.

'The mission has failed, sir.' Steward's tone was as crisp as when delivering the weekly financials.

Corke had excused himself from the meeting with the VP to take the call on his secure phone.

'What?'

'Our courier, Peter Kennedy, was intercepted and killed. The briefcase with the document sent by EMPEROR was seized.'

Dominic Corke felt a strong desire to pray even though he didn't believe in God.

'Do we know who it was?'

'The Chinese.'

It was worse than he could have imagined.

'EMPEROR is compromised?'

'We don't know, sir, but it seems likely.'

If they had lost EMPEROR, their entire China operation was up the proverbial creek. Corke felt as if he'd been punched in the gut.

EMPEROR had made overtures to the CIA years earlier – a novice in intelligence terms. Most intel sources, those that weren't compromised (usually another word for dead; maybe EMPEROR was dead now) had been around a long time. Masters of the art of deception, grown old in the role. Too lazy actually to spy and instead making up whatever they thought their masters wanted to hear. Demanding cash and rewards in kind. Whining about the risks. Not EMPEROR.

Corke pursed his lips, ticking off successes in his mind. His chief asset had managed to corroborate American suspicions that China had aided and abetted Pakistan's attempts to sell its nuclear technology to others; he'd warned when the expansion of facilities on the Spratly Islands began; he'd briefed them of the Chinese intention to invest in Africa in a big way. He'd informed them that China (or some Chinese companies with the tacit agreement of the authorities) was breaching the arms embargo to Libya.

No doubt about it, EMPEROR had given Corke – and the United States – a lot of wins over the years. And he asked nothing in return. Subtly undermining the power of China was sufficient reward. Dominic Corke was one of only three people on earth who knew the spy's backstory. But now, EMPEROR might be compromised. And if he was compromised, their insight into the multi-headed hydra that was the Chinese government was limited. And that, with this particular president in the White House and Griffin in his ear, could be catastrophic.

'The Chinese were following the courier, Peter Kennedy,' continued Steward, 'and took their chance in the Singapore Botanic Gardens.'

'What was he doing there?'

'No idea, sir. We are still trying to piece together the evidence. Two of the Chinese were killed and a third was injured.'

'By Kennedy? I thought you said he was a desk jockey.'

'He was, sir. Apparently, there was a third party involved.'

CCTV footage began at the gates of the park. Even in Singapore, they hadn't yet started attaching cameras to trees. That might change after this fiasco, thought Superintendent Mohammed Aqil of the Singapore police. The absence of CCTV meant that there was no record of the bloodbath of the previous day. Three dead men, two who turned out to work for the Chinese and the third – this one with a severed hand – from the US Embassy in China. Peter Kennedy was supposed to be a cultural attaché but Aqil didn't doubt that he was a spook. He'd been carrying a case that had been cuffed to his wrist. A case that was now missing, along with whoever had taken it.

Another Chinese national was still alive but with a broken jaw and a bullet wound. He was under guard at the Singapore General Hospital refusing to talk to anyone except his 'lawyer' from the Chinese Embassy.

The superintendent turned his mind back to the crime scene, going over every detail with a mental scalpel. A severed hand. Handcuffs. A puddle of blood. And, like the final touches in a slasher movie, two bodies floating face down in the water, their hair undulating like Medusa's head of serpents in the gentle breeze that had the surface rippling. When the bodies were retrieved, he'd seen the round holes in the foreheads, washed clean of blood by the water. Dead centre. Whoever had killed them was a man to be approached with extreme caution. Divers had retrieved the gun but there were no prints and the gun itself was untraceable; all identification marks had been filed. The only point of interest was that it was a Chinese-made military issue.

'Our killer didn't come to the party looking for a gunfight,' he said out loud but to no one in particular. 'The gun must have belonged to the dead guys or our live silent one.'

'There,' said his subordinate, freezing the tape as a man walked out of the iron gates, glancing quickly to the left and right. 'That's him. It must be. He's the only person matching the general description who left within half an hour of the shooting. And he's carrying a case.'

Superintendent Mohammed Aqil leaned in, tried to sharpen the grey images by squinting. 'Male, Caucasian, middle-aged, just under six foot. Who is he, how did he get involved? Why did he take the case?'

He turned to the other man in the room, who had remained silent while watching the tape. 'Any ideas, Major Choo?'

Major Dylan Choo of the PLA shook his head. Superintendent Aqil was not surprised. He'd been furious when told that he had to give this official from the Chinese Embassy access to the investigation. But the word had come directly from the top and the superintendent was not planning to risk his retirement package by protesting. The cooperation was clearly going to be a one-way street.

The sergeant printed a close-up of the man. He handed a copy to his boss and then, upon receiving a nod, one to Major Choo.

'Time for a manhunt,' said Superintendent Aqil.

More silence from the other man.

'I'll make sure Interpol has it as well,' continued Aqil, intimidated into talking too much. 'Don't worry – we'll find him.'

Without another word, Major Choo turned and walked out of the room. The superintendent was glad to see him go even if he'd taken a vital piece of evidence with him. He didn't doubt that the Chinese man was going to use his own channels to track down the man with the briefcase. The policeman – probably for the first time in his life – felt sorry for a fugitive if the Chinese found him first. He had killed two of their operatives and landed another in hospital. He stared at the frozen CCTV footage. An ordinary-looking man. A slightly worried expression on his face but no panic. A case held loosely in his hand, not clutched to his chest. Walking quickly but not running. Whatever had gone down at the Botanic Gardens, this man was too much of a pro to show signs of it to the uninformed. Superintendent Aqil's best guess was ex-military. Cops couldn't have taken down three men with their own weapons. And if they had, they couldn't have walked away looking no more worried than if they were a few minutes late to pick up a child from school.

A technician, Naufal Taib, in a white coat knocked on the open door.

'What is it?'

'The handkerchief,' he said.

'Yes?' Superintendent Aqil had seen the makeshift tourniquet around the dead man's stump where his hand had been.

'We might be able to raise prints,' continued the techie.

'From the cloth?' The superintendent was surprised.

'Using vacuum metal deposition,' Taib explained. 'It's cotton but the weave is tight.'

Superintendent Aqil was familiar with the method. The piece of fabric was inserted into a vacuum chamber. Heated and evaporated gold was spread over it, along with heated zinc. The end result was that fingerprints showed through the gold and zinc, almost like a photographic negative. He'd not heard that there had been much success getting a ridge count that allowed for a positive ID.

'There've been improvements in the technology,' said Naufal Taib, sensing the hesitation.

'We can do that here?' asked the superintendent.

'We have just brought in the equipment and some consultants from Scotland. Their research lab has been improving the technique and now we have the means to use it.'

Superintendent Aqil looked down at the fuzzy picture in his hand. It would be a struggle to find the guy from this image, that was for sure. He needed to try everything – even tech long shots. 'Do it,' he snapped.

His sergeant asked tentatively, 'Do you want me to inform Major Choo of this development?'

Superintendent Aqil paused, thought hard for a moment and then shook his head. 'Let's see whether we get a result first.' A small part of him really wanted to solve the murders and show these taciturn Chinese mainlanders that the Singapore police always got their man.

Jack locked the door, wedged a chair under it, drew the colourful geometric-patterned curtains shut and checked under the bed and in the tiny bathroom. He didn't imagine for a moment that anyone would have identified him that quickly from the altercation at the Botanic Gardens, especially now that he'd ditched the case. But he wasn't a man who took chances. Other lives had once depended on his ability to anticipate, evaluate and protect. Now it was just him. But he'd still work a room until he was as sure as possible that he was safe.

Finally, when he was satisfied he had covered the bases, he tipped the contents of the envelope out over the single bed; *there is nothing either good or bad, but thinking makes it so.*

The information provided by Peter had been meticulously organized but there wasn't a lot of it. Jack wasn't surprised. He didn't doubt that Peter had done his best but he hadn't given him much time and China was a notoriously secretive place. The file contained updated biodata on Xia. There was a series of photos clipped together – taken without Xia's knowledge, or perhaps she had agreed to them with the supreme indifference of someone who knew that it was her lot in life to be photographed.

The slim body, the shapely calves, the high cheekbones – remained the same. But there were fine lines around Xia's eyes, a fuller figure than he remembered. The other thing that had changed was the company she kept. Once upon a time, she had mixed with the student leaders of a nascent democratic movement. And with him, of course – a junior attaché at the American Embassy. In other words, a spy. Now – if the wide-angle lens was to be believed – Xia was surrounded by overweight men in heavy suits or overweight men in military uniforms.

It said in the file that she worked for an independent think tank on economic affairs in Beijing. Jack knew that was a lie. There was no such thing as an independent think tank on economic affairs in Beijing. She was divorced and had a daughter, a teacher at the University of Peking. There was only one photo of mother and daughter together and it was a few years old. But it was not difficult to see that it was the same girl as the one in the headshot Xia had sent him. The girl existed and was Xia's daughter. Was she his daughter too? Peter had not been able to answer the question definitively. It was possible, that was all.

Jack fingered the yellow Post-it note that had been stuck on the cover of the file. It was a note in Peter's handwriting. *I guess this means you opened the envelope. Not sure when I'll be back in China. I'm guessing you're going to head straight there since I could not answer your question. I truly don't know if she is yours. You might need a hand in Beijing. If you do, Confucius is the man – I'd trust him with my life.* An address was scribbled at the end. Trust Peter to be looking out for him from beyond the grave. A short postscript had been added – *Be careful!* Turned out it was Peter who had needed to be vigilant. Jack's thoughts turned to his last meeting with Peter: Peter walking towards him with the grin that hadn't changed. Peter handing over an envelope with the information. Peter dead. Killed by a trio of Chinese assassins. For a briefcase attached to his wrist. A briefcase that Jack had taken. A briefcase with a hidden compartment that held a memo written in Mandarin. Whichever way Jack looked at it, there was no bright side to that. God only knew why that memo he'd extricated was worth a man's hand, let alone his life.

Jack glanced at his watch. Four hours had passed since the incident. He didn't doubt that he'd have been captured on CCTV footage somewhere. Probably as he was leaving the Botanic Gardens. But he doubted that they'd be able to trace him from that, not quickly anyway. He'd kept his head down. He'd wiped the gun and chucked it in the lake, no fingerprints there. The only other thing he'd left behind had been the hankie he'd used to cauterize Peter's wound. And Jack Ford wasn't the sort of man to have monogrammed initials on his personal belongings. He was safe enough for now.

Secretary General-elect Juntao had played his cards close to his chest his whole life. Made friends, not enemies. Cultivated hardliners and liberals. Shown that he could be tough when it came to dissidents – wasn't he the one who had authorized the crackdown on separatists in Mongolia? Shown that he had the capacity for compassion – hadn't he insisted that the artist be released from house arrest when he was diagnosed with cancer? But now it was the endgame. He needed a decisive move that would sway public opinion towards him, make it impossible for General Zhang and his cronies to shout down the voice of a billion Chinese people, all demanding change at once.

Juntao wanted a moment that would be symbolic of his new China. The soon-to-be most powerful man in China smiled. The Secretary General-elect was pretty sure he knew exactly which match to light to ensure the old order went up in flames. There was only one slight problem, but steps had been taken to fix that. He was confident of a successful outcome. He was relying on good people, men who could be depended on to do right by him and by China. Men like Colonel Guo Feng, whom he had entrusted with the mission to find his hero, his symbol of the new China. And he would trust that man with his life.

The soldier languishing in hospital sat up to attention and saluted despite his wired jaw, bullet wound, bruises and prison pyjamas. Major Dylan Choo listened to his story once more, searching for clues. 'An unarmed stranger appeared from some bushes, killed two of our best men, left you for dead and made off with this briefcase that has the higher-ups passing bricks?'

'Yes, sir.' He added, 'He caught us by surprise.'

'You are a highly trained assassination team – you are supposed to eliminate the element of surprise.'

The soldier lowered his gaze and did not respond.

'Do you have anything to add?' demanded Choo.

'This man was military, sir – he was very quick, highly trained. He must have been sent as cover for the mark. From what I heard at the end, the men had a history together.'

Major Dylan Choo shook his head. There was something wrong with the analysis. His sources within the American establishment insisted that the briefcase hadn't reached them. If the briefcase had been stolen by anyone intervening in the fight in an official capacity, it would have reached the embassy by now. The contents would have been analysed. And the fallout would have begun. Major Choo did not know what was in the case. But he knew that the higher-ups – especially General Zhang – were in as close a state to panic as he'd seen. Whatever was in the briefcase, it wasn't good for them, for China or, by extension, for him.

The major produced the picture taken from the CCTV cameras. 'Is this him?'

The wounded soldier didn't hesitate. 'Yes, that's him.'

Major Choo thought back to the man in the CCTV footage – the way he had walked out, looked left and right and then turned to his left, away from the American Embassy, which was just a couple of hundred yards away. He was pretty sure he knew what he was dealing with. A loose cannon. Probably ex-military. Definitely some sort of special forces. Television always portrayed these guys as muscle-bound Rambo lookalikes carrying enough firepower to decimate small South American villages. Major Dylan Choo knew that the best men were the most ordinary, the ones who blended in, were easily forgotten. Those were the ones who did the most damage.

Which reminded him, no loose ends. He bent down and retrieved a capsule from a false heel in his boot and held it up to the other man.

'Must it come to this, sir? I have always been a loyal soldier to China.' When there was no response the corporal added in a desperate tone, 'I have a wife, a young family.'

'And if you do this, they will get a pension and be told you died a hero.' Major Choo didn't have to spell out the alternative.

The soldier held out a hand and took the capsule. He hesitated and then put it in his mouth and bit down. In moments, he clutched at his chest and stared with bulging eyes at his superior officer, his mouth opening and closing like a fish on land. He foamed at the lips and his eyes watered. The major stepped back. He waited until the soldier was still and reached down and felt for a pulse. There was none. He counted to ten slowly under his breath and then walked to the door and shouted for help. Hospital staff rushed in; he stood to one side and watched them desperately try to revive the dead man.

Finally, a doctor stood up, sweating with effort. 'We are sorry. We cannot save him.'

'You did your best,' said Major Dylan Choo. 'Nothing could have saved this man.'

SEVEN

'What's wrong?' asked Vice President Harris when Corke walked back into the office.

Did she have a woman's intuition? 'Agent down,' said Corke, not mincing words.

'Who? Where?' Her face was shocked.

'Peter Kennedy, shot and killed – most likely by Chinese special forces – in Singapore.'

'The Chinese attacked him? Why?' demanded General Rodriguez.

'He was bringing me a document from EMPEROR,' explained Corke.

'What sort of document?' asked the VP.

'I don't know – I just know it was important and the Chinese wanted it back very badly. They killed one of my men, for God's sake.'

'And they got it back,' the VP said flatly.

'No – this is where it gets complicated.' He slipped a picture across the desk and the Vice President and Rodriguez squinted at the blurred image. 'This is from CCTV outside the Botanic Gardens where the shooting took place. This man seems to have wandered off with the case containing the document.'

'Who is he?'

'We're trying to find out – about the only thing we can say right now is that he's not working for the Chinese.'

'A stranger took the document?'

'It seems so – it was in a case handcuffed to Kennedy.'

'So how did he get it off? I assume he didn't drag the body with him?'

'Someone – most likely one of the Chinese agents – brought a chainsaw.'

The Vice President winced. 'We have no idea who this guy is?'

'He seems to have had some priors with Kennedy.'

'One of ours?'

'Maybe – not in service any more or we would have found out who he was already. He's a dead man if the Chinese get hold of him. He must have had some sort of serious training, though. He took out three men – two killed with gunshots to the head – if the reports are to be believed.'

'What are we doing about it?' asked General Rodriguez.

'We are leaning on the Singaporeans to find him but I fear the Chinese are too.' Corke felt his adrenaline surge like a storm drain at high tide. It reminded him of the Cold War, this battle for influence over supposedly neutral countries. Next, he'd be trotting out the domino theory so beloved of Eisenhower – that if any one country in the region fell under Chinese influence, the rest were sure to follow. The CIA director shook his head. He personally thought the opposite was true. If one country in a region was under the yoke of a particular power, the others fled to a counterweight.

'Can we get *another* copy of this document?' asked Vice President Harris.

Dominic Corke ground his teeth. 'There's more bad news, I'm afraid. I'm not getting any response from EMPEROR.'

'Dead?' she asked.

'Dead or singing like a canary – it looks like this operation was compromised.'

'Maybe I should ask the Chinese directly, or get POTUS to do it?' She never shirked the direct approach. 'They killed an American on neutral ground.'

'Plausible deniability.'

'What are you talking about?'

'The Chinese guy who survived the intervention from our so-called passer-by just keeled over in a Singapore prison. Suicide, apparently.'

'No loose ends,' said Rodriguez.

'Let me get this straight,' interjected the Vice President. 'EMPEROR tried to send you a document. Our courier was attacked, presumably by the Chinese government trying to retrieve it. Some third party intervened and now he's got the document?'

'That's about the sum of it.'

'Why couldn't EMPEROR email us the damned thing? I thought with all our fancy encryption methods that was safe!'

'He said we'd need the original or we wouldn't believe a word of it. He is' – Corke paused and allowed the reality to dawn – 'he *was* an old-fashioned kind of guy. Never trusted modern communication systems.'

'Are you sure he's compromised?' The Vice President knew the value of EMPEROR.

'There's been no word from him since the memo handover failed,' replied Corke. 'We don't dare press for contact – he's always made it abundantly clear that he initiates any communication. If by some chance he's still in the clear – and he's very resourceful, we know that much – we don't want to raise any red flags.'

'No super spy, no document, no clue as to its contents, and a dead agent. Am I right in thinking we're worse off than when we started?' The Vice President's tone was sharply accusing.

'No, ma'am. It's not that bad. We just need to find this guy,' Corke tapped the photograph from the CCTV camera with an index finger, 'before the Chinese do.'

'Will you brief the President?' she asked.

The two men and the woman shared a look that spoke volumes.

'Let's . . . err . . . avoid interrupting the President until we know more,' said Corke.

'The Tank Man is the hero we need.' Juntao, Secretary General-elect, cleared his throat and spoke with conviction. 'And I have set in motion plans to identify and recover him.'

He sat at a small round table in a small room. Three of his Politburo colleagues – all members of the Standing Committee – were at the other points of the compass. A round table to signify equality, a nod to the egos of his colleagues. But Juntao knew that he was first among equals. One of the men was puffing on a vile-smelling cigar. Juntao wrinkled his nose and glanced over his left shoulder. The only other person in the room, his military adviser, Colonel Guo Feng, sat on a chair a little behind his left shoulder, privy to the deliberations, relied upon at the highest level, but not entitled to sit at the table with four of the most powerful men in the country.

Juntao's words were greeted with two grunts and a taciturn nod. These old men, resting like ancient toads in a mud hole, were not given to emotional outbursts. They were stalwarts from a previous era. Despite that, they were reformists, if not as a matter of principle, then as a matter of practicality.

'We are progressing smoothly towards implementing our reform plans,' continued Juntao.

'China cannot survive in its present form, so your news is reassuring,' said a senior member of the Politburo and closet reformist, Kai Pin.

'At most we can limp on for a few more years as the secret prisons overflow and the army and police become more brutal. Eventually, the rotten foundations will cause the collapse of the Party and then the state.' This was Bao En, a younger man and idealistic.

'This apocalyptic vision is the reason why we are here,' said Juntao.

'Are you sure you have identified the right man for the job – this Tank Man?' demanded Kai Pin. 'I remain a sceptic. At the end of the day, this so-called hero of yours, his fame is greater in the West than in China. *We* have spent years suppressing his memory and' – he smiled without humour – 'we have done an excellent job as always.'

Juntao was prepared to engage with the old man – he wouldn't see eighty again – to keep him on side.

'Comrade Bao En has arranged for opinion-shaping propaganda to be released when the man is found.'

'Yes, Comrade Kai Pin – our plan is to steer the country towards regarding him as a hero and a reformist. You know better than most' – Kai Pin had been head of the Propaganda Unit of the Party in earlier days – 'that we have the ability to turn a nobody into a hero of the people. This time – for once – we have a real hero. The Western press will back us up so the people will see independent corroboration of this man's heroics. At the Party Congress that will confirm Juntao as our next leader – we will reveal the Tank Man to the people.' Bao En spoke like the competent man that he was.

'And after that?' asked Kai Pin.

'After that, we announce far-reaching democratic reforms.'

A silence met this statement, as if the men felt that a failure to acknowledge their ambitious plans might put the genie back in the bottle. They were determined but they were also very, very afraid.

'You are certain of this path, comrade?' It was Li Keqiang, the fourth man at the table, with the question.

Juntao appreciated the fact that he was addressed as 'comrade'. It was Li Keqiang's way of showing that he was in for the long haul, whatever doubts he might have.

Juntao began ticking off his list on his fingers one by one. 'We will announce direct elections at provincial level; remove any military representation from the Politburo (after this, the military, including and especially General Zhang, will understand that they are subordinate to civilian rule); strengthen the court system; purge corrupt members of the Party; and . . .' he hesitated and looked around for reassurance, 'announce a five-year plan towards national representative democracy, including the right to form political parties.'

'Mao must be spinning in his grave.' The thought seemed to give Bao En pleasure.

'I am not worried about Mao, I am worried about General Zhang,' said Kai Pin. 'He will do everything in his power to stop us.'

'He poses the gravest threat to our plan,' agreed the Secretary General-elect. 'Which is why it's imperative to keep him in the dark until it is too late for him to cause trouble. He must know nothing about the Tank Man or our plans for reform.'

'Easier said than done,' said Bao En. 'General Zhang has eyes and ears everywhere.'

Behind him, Colonel Guo Feng broke into a fit of coughing.

The lights of Beijing city outnumbered the stars. The flight was in a holding pattern waiting for a landing slot. Thirty years earlier, Jack's relationship with Xia had been in a holding pattern too.

'I need to tell her,' he'd said to Peter over a beer.

'Tell me you're joking, Jack.'

He didn't answer. Just looked at his friend, sitting across from him on a rickety three-legged stool. He was perched on the end of the bed in his little apartment. He reached for a pillow, could smell the faintest traces of Xia's perfume. She had more or less moved in with him now. His handlers at the CIA had been delighted at his commitment to the cause of infiltrating the student movement.

'You cannot tell your girlfriend that you're CIA. What do you imagine she's going to say? "It's all right, Jack. I don't mind?"'

'I don't like lying to her,' he mumbled, feeling like a fool.

'Maybe you should have thought about that before you became a spy,' growled Peter.

Jack knew that his best friend liked his girl too – was probably in love with her, although he hadn't said so – and that he was putting him in an awkward situation by insisting on talking about Xia. But he had no choice. Nowhere else to turn.

'What do you hope to achieve?' demanded Peter.

Jack shook his head. 'I don't know. I just feel I'm living a lie.'

'You are,' said his friend. 'That's the whole point of being a spy.'

Jack wandered over to the window and stared moodily out on to the street below. It was the usual horde of bicycles, bells ringing furiously, the odd car with diplomatic plates and a few buses filled to capacity hurtling down the roads.

'I really care about her, Peter.'

'And she really cares about her revolution . . .'

Jack sighed and ran a hand over his eyes. 'You're right. I should wait – until this is over.'

There was a silence in the room punctuated by the familiar background sounds from the street below. It was impossible to know what 'over' meant, what it would entail. The revolution was now centred in Tiananmen Square. Every day, thousands of students joined the camp. The Chinese communist government had never been defied so blatantly before. The minor clashes with police in the early days had culminated in less politically active students joining the protest movement.

The students were organized and militant, their demands non-negotiable, their sphere the public spaces of Beijing and the other cities. The foreign press arrived in numbers. The Chinese newspapers changed their editorial stance every day depending on who was briefing them, the turmoil at leadership level thus visible to all observers. It was a truism of politics, thought Jack, that if you gave the people an inch, they wanted a yard. He looked at the calendar on his desk. It was hard to believe that it had been only a few weeks since protests began.

'What do you think is going to happen?' he asked.

'The Gorbachev visit was a disaster,' replied Peter.

'Why – a thawing of Sino-Soviet relations? Surely that was good?'

'Are you kidding me? A summit at the Great Hall with a lot of smelly students outside? Deng lost face, Li Peng lost face, and a price is going to have to be paid.'

Peter had always been better at understanding the bigger picture.

'Where is Xia anyway?' he asked now.

'Where do you think?' asked Jack. 'At the square, of course. Waiting for a chance to martyr herself in front of the Great Hall of the People.'

'The students are divided into a few factions. Hardliners who refuse to budge, those who want to clear the square and regroup; those for the hunger strike, those against.' Peter sounded twenty years older than the protesters, thought Jack. Able to analyse, not empathize.

'It's the PLA battalions – they're making people jumpy,' continued Peter.

'I don't believe the PLA will attack its own people.' Jack intended a statement but found a questioning tone.

'Apparently, that's why they've shipped in army divisions from the sticks,' explained Peter. 'The soldiers are less likely to feel any solidarity with these city kids.'

'How come you know so much?' asked Jack, forcing a smile.

'I'm a spy. How come you know so little?'

They both laughed because they both knew the answer. Xia.

The phone on the desk rang, the noise strident in the small space.

Peter reached for it, raised the receiver and held it to his ear, even though it was Jack's apartment. He had left the number in case the embassy needed him. He listened for a few more moments and then put down the receiver. His face was a whiter shade of pale.

'What is it?' said Jack. 'What's happened?'

'The army is moving into Tiananmen Square.'

Thirty years later, Jack's heart began to race as it had done that day when he realized that Xia was in danger. He clutched the seat dividers on the plane and gasped for breath, the panic attack almost crippling in intensity. *Present fears are less than horrible imaginings.*

'Flying is much safer than driving, you know? You really have nothing to worry about,' said the man next to him, misunderstanding the source of his fear, as they came in to land at Beijing Capital International Airport.

Griffin, National Security Adviser, and Bonneville, China expert, were back in the former's office. Griffin sat behind his big desk, leaning back in his expensive black leather chair. An American flag stood on a flagpole behind him. The crest of the office was on the wall, framing his head like a halo. Griffin liked people across from him to remember that in this building he was *numero uno*. The message was wasted on Bonneville – the guy was such a nerd, he thought with disgust, white-blond hair, wan skin, he looked as if he had been drained of every drop of blood. But Bonneville had a brain like a computer. You just had to point him in a particular direction and he'd chase information, gather data, collate it, analyse it and produce a conclusion or a plan of action that more often than not was a work of art. Griffin already had a plan, of course. And it was well on its way to being executed. But it was always worth investigating alternatives, challenging outcomes, determining options. And for that, he needed a guy like Bonneville, even if he looked like a human worm.

'Well, so what do you have?' demanded Griffin.

'A hypothetical plan of action, sir.'

'And what's the ob-jec-tive of this so-called hy-po-thetical plan?' He rolled the words around his mouth.

'To keep China's various factions at each other's throats. I believe that is in the best interests of the United States.'

'And how are we going to do that?' He hid a smile. It was always nice when the boffins came up with the same strategy as you.

'Divide and conquer, sir.'

Griffin nodded and scratched his unruly pepper and salt moustache. He liked that. And he liked that this fellow Bonneville was growing in confidence. There was every possibility that he could be very useful indeed.

'Spell it out for me.'

'Well, we know that the Politburo is divided between the Secretary General-elect Juntao and his supporters and the hard-liners led by General Zhang. Right now, I believe that the reformists have the upper hand. They have managed to secure the top job. The press is extolling the benefits of a more open society.'

'We need to give them a nudge backwards? Give the other guys a boost?'

'Exactly, sir.'

'What happens if the other side get too big for their boots?'

They were interrupted by a knock on the door. Griffin's deputy, a large African-American man with a gravelly voice by the name of Harrison Davies, walked in.

'That CIA agent killed in Singapore a couple of days ago,' he said.

Both of the men nodded. They'd heard the news on the grapevine, not through official channels.

'You asked me to find out what I could – well, I've been doing some digging. It's not been that easy. Corke's trying to keep a lid on this one.'

The CIA director would insist it was to minimize the risk of the information falling into the wrong hands, to avoid compromising ongoing operations. However, Griffin was sure that Corke just didn't want to admit to an almighty cock-up.

'I've heard it's something on China,' said Bonneville.

Davies nodded. 'A drop-off gone bad.'

'From EMPEROR?' Griffin didn't know the real identity of EMPEROR, although he'd been trying for years to get ahold of it. Corke had managed to keep the information to himself despite pressure about 'inter-agency cooperation' from high-level Senate Committee members. Griffin did know that anything useful that came out of China, EMPEROR was the source.

'That's what it sounds like. The whole thing was a rushed but very hush-hush operation. I've heard that there was a high-level document, a memo, that was on its way to the embassy in Singapore. It was intercepted by the Chinese. The agent handling it was killed.'

'Sounds like they made a real mess of it down at Langley.' Griffin sounded pleased and as if he didn't care who knew it.

'Yep. No one knows why the CIA courier decided to take a detour.'

'Their man decided to go sightseeing? Or maybe he was a double agent. He got cold feet and they killed him.'

'It gets better,' said Davies, always pleased, just like his boss, to throw some shade in the direction of the CIA. 'The Chinese didn't retrieve the document either. It was intercepted by a lone wolf.'

'Lone wolf?' asked Griffin. 'We suddenly switched to Nat Geo?'

'Some white guy – probably ex-military. His picture is out on all the wire services. Ordinary looking. But he packed a punch. Killed two of their guys. CIA are pulling out all the stops to find him. So are the Chinese and the Singaporeans.'

Griffin pulled the picture up on his wide screen monitor and swivelled it so that they were all staring at the grainy image of the man with the briefcase outside the Singapore Botanic Gardens.

'If we can find this guy before the CIA . . .' Griffin trailed off. He didn't have to spell it out. It would give them a lot of leverage.

Andrew Bonneville was staring at the screen. Now he bent closer so that his nose was almost brushing the monitor.

'What the hell are you doing?' demanded Griffin.

Bonneville straightened up slowly and turned to the others, a big grin forming. 'I know this guy!'

'We have a partial print,' shouted the junior lab rat enthusiastically. 'Enough points for a comparison.'

'Well, call Superintendent Aqil, then, why don't you?' said the technician, Naufal Taib, reclining in a chair, feet on the table, coffee mug held close between two clasped hands.

'It's past midnight!'

'He's desperate to find his man. I've been getting calls every hour on the hour.'

Naufal Taib yawned, put his cup down and stretched as his colleague went to the phone. He hated these jobs which had to be given the 'highest priority' – they got in the way of all the other work that was also always of the 'highest priority'. Sometimes, coming up with something new, or improving some old technique, like their newfound ability to get prints – some of the time – from fabric, was just a royal pain in the posterior. It was as if every murderer and thief on the planet had wiped his hands on a towel before leaving a crime scene. Not that towels were of any use from a forensic point of view. The fibres were usually too rough for fingerprints to adhere. But this guy from the Botanic Gardens mêlée had left prints on a bloodstained handkerchief. That had worked just fine.

Assuming that his prints were on some database somewhere, the police would soon have their man. And it seemed unlikely that the sort of man who killed two men in a public space and made off with a top-secret document wouldn't have his fingerprints on a database somewhere.

'They're sending someone to collect the print now,' said the lab rat, hanging up.

The boss and the lab rat shook hands. It felt good to help apprehend a killer. They would sleep like the righteous that night.

Jack Ford slipped out of the small, cheap but clean motel he had stumbled upon in Chaoyang district, Beijing. It lurked under the shadows of five-star hotels – none of which had been around when he'd been here last. He waved at a battered taxi that drew up with a screech. The driver made no attempt to understand his instructions in English and he had to dredge through his memory before he was able to persuade him – in rusty Mandarin – to take him to Peking University, which according to Google Maps on his VPN was still in the same sprawling location near the Summer Palace. He leaned back and tried to ignore the frantic weaving between lanes and traffic. The taxi driver looked like he hadn't slept in a year and had achieved that feat with caffeine and uppers. The lights turned red, the taxi screeched to a halt and the driver got out. He spat in a drain and then climbed back in. Definitely, China had changed, thought Jack. Thirty years ago, the cabbie would have spat in the vehicle.

An hour later, Jack found himself outside the law faculty of Peking University. The modern multi-storey building was ugly and functional. He glanced at the students and teachers streaming out of the big doors and realized that finding Xia's daughter – his daughter? – would be like discovering the proverbial needle in a haystack. He slipped the picture Xia had sent him out of his wallet and looked at it again. Long hair, a touch of auburn. Almond-shaped eyes, but light. A full bottom lip curved into a tentative smile. *Her name is Fei Yen*, Xia had written. She was beautiful, this girl in the photo, this Fei Yen. He looked around at the milling students breaking around him as if he was a rock in a stream. Jack dusted off a few more Mandarin phrases and approached a group of giggling female students.

'*Ni hao ma*,' he said, and then added 'Good morning,' as well. It had been a while since he'd resorted to any language of the Far East. Mostly, in recent years, he'd just needed his stock phrases of Pashtun. *Don't shoot. I am a friend. I have money.*

'I am looking for the daughter of an old friend,' he said carefully. 'Her name is Fei Yen and she is a teacher at the law faculty.'

'Fei Yen? You are looking for Fei Yen?' The response was in English and he smiled with relief.

'You speak English!'

'Yes, very much, thank you. My name is Connie.'

He held out a hand and shook hers. 'I'm Jack Ford. You know Fei Yen?' he continued.

There was a brief conversation in hurried Mandarin, too quick for him to follow, and he wondered if they were concerned about telling a stranger her whereabouts.

'My friend Chun here' – the first girl gestured at a short, plump red-cheeked teenager – 'has just had a class with Madam Fei Yen – she says that she has gone to the library to return a book.'

'Will she come out this way?'

There was more conferring with a few sideways smiles at him. Jack tugged his shirt sleeves so they covered his wrists. The puckered lines – knife wounds badly stitched up by friendlies in a small Iraqi town – peeked out if he wasn't careful.

Connie beamed at him. 'I will take you to the library so that you can find Madam Fei Yen.'

Jack followed Connie and allowed her to swipe him in and lead him to the escalator. His heart was beating faster, he noticed with clinical detachment. And his palms were sweaty.

They entered the library. It looked exactly like every other library he'd ever been in. Wooden shelves, stacks of books, computer terminals, po-faced guardians at the front desk. A closer look indicated differences – all the titles on spines were written in Mandarin. It reminded him that he needed to get the contents of the briefcase translated. Jack shook his head to clarify his thoughts. His first priority was finding Fei Yen. But he wasn't about to forget Peter – and his last request.

Connie walked with long strides down an aisle, nodding and smiling at various people but not stopping to chat. Jack kept pace, scanning the faces with a sharp eye. He wanted to spot Fei Yen before she saw him. He needed that small window of time to collect his thoughts.

'Madam Fei Yen!' said Connie in a loud whisper. He looked up and saw her. Head down, staring at a book, hair falling over one side of her face like a silk curtain. She turned when she heard her name and smiled at her student. Pearly white teeth, hair a lighter shade of brown that was traditional, a hint of a dimple in her chin. Unusual for a Chinese. Jack's hand went to his own cleft jaw. Genes or coincidence?

'Madam Fei Yen, this is an old friend of your family.'

Fei Yen looked at him with friendliness but puzzlement.

'My name is Jack Ford. I am a friend of your mother, Xia,' he explained. 'Just over from the US for a few days.'

'Oh! Jack Ford!' she said, and the smile grew wider and the puzzlement turned to curiosity. 'My mother has spoken of you!'

He nodded. 'Is there somewhere we could have coffee and catch up?' he asked. 'I'm terribly jetlagged.'

'Yes, certainly. There is a Starbucks not far away. You will feel right at home.'

Her English was flawless. He would not have expected anything else of Xia's daughter. She led the way. Connie watched them go with a sunny smile on her face. He had a flashback to the dour worried faces of the students of 1989 who had fought and laid down their lives in protest against the Chinese government. Times changed. There was no hint of that rebellious spirit on the faces of Fei Yen's students. The winter of discontent was no more.

A few minutes later they were sipping black coffee and Jack was trying to remember that he was in China. The peach blossoms on the trees that fell like pink snowflakes were a giveaway but otherwise this Starbucks could have been on any US main street. The kids were Chinese, but looked like any other group of trendy young things hanging out at the local mall.

'Have you seen my mother?' asked Fei Yen.

'No, not yet.'

'She is not in Beijing this week – she has gone to Nanjing.'

'She travels a lot?'

'Yes, always on the go but we speak almost every evening.' She laughed out loud, exposing pearly teeth. 'She says if I don't call or leave a message every evening without fail, she'll be on the next plane here. She's very protective and will not accept that I am a grown woman.'

Jack smiled. That sounded like Xia all right.

She stared at him openly for the first time. 'My mother only speaks of you when she is sad,' she said bluntly.

'A lot of water under that bridge.'

'And now you're in Beijing for business?'

He noted her take in the casual, off-the-rack clothes. Clean and neat – but not expensive. No discreet or not so discreet logo on his T-shirt to indicate wealth. Not quite the sharp-suited businessman looking for the pot of gold in the new China. Just an ordinary guy looking for some opportunities for a business that maybe wasn't going so well.

'Yes,' Jack agreed, 'Business.'

There was a nod and a surreptitious glance at her watch. Fei Yen probably felt she'd done enough to entertain an old friend of her mother.

'Xia says that you're doing a doctorate – hoping for a semester or more in Georgetown.' Actually, it was Peter who had provided that information.

'That's right,' she agreed.

'She thought I might be able to help – that's my neck of the woods.'

Fei Yen laughed. 'My mother is trying to arrange a babysitter in advance? Typical! She has always been overprotective of me – there's never been anyone else, you see.'

'Your father?' He watched her face.

There were no shadows when she said, 'He ran out on us before I was born.'

He reached into his pocket and retrieved a card with his telephone number scribbled on it. 'Call me when you get there,' he said.

'Thank you,' she said. She rose to her feet. 'I have to go now. Next class,' she explained. She must have suddenly felt sorry for him because she added, 'If you're feeling lost, I am happy to give you a tour of Beijing after classes?'

He nodded and cracked a genuine smile. 'That would be good. Everything has changed so much! Later this evening?'

'I'll see you here at four.' She smiled.

He waved her away when she tried to clear the mugs. 'I'll do that. You shouldn't be late for class. Your mom wouldn't thank me for that.'

He watched her walk out the door, same long-limbed stride as her mother, same hip sway. Once she was out of sight, when he was sure no one was watching, he slipped Fei Yen's empty mug into a plastic bag and into his rucksack.

His daughter?

Maybe. *Trust, but verify.*

'But where is this "hero of the people", this Tank Man who is going to symbolize this era of change? Do you have his likely whereabouts?' Kai Pin was still sceptical.

'Colonel Guo Feng will brief us.'

The colonel stood up and saluted smartly. He wore his uniform with pride and his broad face and matching broad shoulders inspired trust. Juntao relied on him when it came to the more delicate errands that the exercise of power required.

'Senior members of the Politburo, it is a privilege to be here in your august presence. As you know, the man in question disappeared after the incident in Tiananmen Square. Many believed that he was seized by the army and executed or kept under lock and key somewhere. The truth is' – he paused to ensure that he had their full attention – 'he was rescued by the Americans.'

'Why would they take such a risk?' muttered Bao En, pressing the tips of his fingers together like an irritable professor.

'This cannot be right. It would have been madness to interfere,' agreed Li Keqiang.

Juntao interrupted. 'Our working hypothesis is that they thought that if the 1989 rebellion succeeded in overthrowing the government, it would be useful to have lent aid to a potential future leader – at the very least a symbol of the resistance.'

'The other possibility, also recognized by the Party,' said the colonel, with a nod at Li Keqiang, 'is that a rogue element within the CIA smuggled him out without the involvement of the US government.'

'That seems more plausible!' exclaimed Kai Pin. 'Can you imagine if the Americans were found out, aiding and abetting an enemy of the state? The student movement would have been discredited – they would have looked like pawns of the Western powers.'

'But why would a rogue element assist him?' asked Bao En.

'Perhaps they were impressed with his courage?' suggested Juntao. 'After all, is that not why he has value to us?'

'We believe that the operation to smuggle the Tank Man out of China was conducted in the greatest secrecy and his new identity known only to a few,' continued Colonel Guo Feng.

'In which case, how will we ever find him? Your plan is in tatters before we have even begun, Comrade Juntao!' said Li Keqiang.

Juntao waved a hand at Guo Feng, indicating that he should continue with his narrative to answer the criticism of Li Keqiang.

'We have, through our agents, identified a man – a junior official at the embassy – who was involved in the operation to get him out of the country.'

'An American?' asked Kai Pin.

'Yes.'

'What is the use of that?' demanded Li Keqiang. 'He will not tell us where this man is. And we are not in a position to force him to talk.'

Colonel Guo Feng was too accomplished an operator to show any smugness but Juntao suspected that it was quite an effort to keep his face impassive. He was, after all, about to play his trump card.

'This American agent is retired and living in Washington, DC after many years in the military, where he served with distinction.'

'You imagine the CIA will let us get near him?' It was Bao En who interrupted this time. 'An American hero?'

'This man is presently *here*,' responded Colonel Guo Feng.

'He is here?'

'Yes, comrades. He is here in Beijing.'

Wide smiles broke out around the table.

'That is clever work, Comrade Juntao. It seems the reform agenda is in good hands.'

'This man, Jack Ford, will tell us every single thing he knows about the new identity of the Tank Man and his where-abouts,' continued Juntao.

Comrade Li Keqiang allowed himself a nod of approval.

'What if he refuses to talk?' asked Kai Pin.

'He will talk,' said Colonel Guo Feng with supreme confidence. 'We have the means to make it so.'

Secretary General-elect Juntao pressed his lips together and a thin line of moisture appeared along the top edge; should he feel guilty that Guo Feng's methods were likely to be harsh? No, he was working towards the greater good of China and its people. What was that expression he had heard once in the West?

'Unfortunately, comrades, there is no way to make an omelette without breaking eggs.'

EIGHT

'How can you possibly know him?' demanded Director Griffin, breaking the silence that had engulfed the other two men for a few moments after Bonneville claimed to have recognized the man in the photograph.

'I've seen his face – a file photo somewhere – I know it.'

'A mug shot?'

'No, he's one of us.'

'An agent?'

'Maybe.'

Bonneville was perched on the end of Griffin's desk. It was not a position he would have dared adopt if he wasn't lost in thought, brow furrowed like the cornfields of his home state Iowa, after the harvest.

'I've been looking through our China files – he must have been in one of them,' continued Bonneville.

'Which one?' asked Davies.

'I can't remember,' confessed Bonneville.

'Well, perhaps you should be lookin' rather than polishing my table with your butt?' said Griffin.

'On it, sir,' said Bonneville, and bolted from the room. He hurried down the long corridor, ignoring the doors at regular intervals, until he reached the conference room at the end. Bonneville had co-opted the room for his research and forged Griffin's signature on the request form. He needed space, not an open plan office with four other analysts discussing the football scores. He shuddered briefly. Sometimes he wondered whether Americans would sleep as soundly if they knew what some of these guys did during work time.

Bonneville dragged a box on to the table, opened it and started flicking through files methodically in reverse chrono-logical order. The stuff from the last twenty years was all computerized so the first physical file he looked at was 1998.

There were stacks of information from each year but Bonneville was confident of finding the needle.

An hour later he was beginning to feel discouraged. Had he really seen the guy somewhere? He only had the faintest memory of doing so and even that was rapidly fading. Why in the world had he sounded so certain to Griffin? He wasn't looking forward to having to tell him he'd been wrong.

Bonneville dusted another file, a slim folder on personnel in the embassy during the Tiananmen Square episode.

He hit pay dirt.

The man he wanted looked a lot younger in the black and white photograph in front of him but there was no mistaking the square jaw and the aquiline nose. Jack Ford. The man was listed as a junior official in the student liaison office. Code for agent? Probably. In those days, everyone had been a spy. He would have to crosscheck against the old CIA files. He dragged his chair around to the computer in the corner – a lot of the CIA archives had been digitized. It was just possible that this man might appear in their database without there being any further need to thumb through files, with the time and paper cuts that entailed.

Bonneville licked his finger, tasted blood, keyed in the name and waited. It only took ten seconds. Jack Ford had been young, handsome and fervent. The perfect agent to send into the field to befriend China's youth back in the day. No one, least of all the CIA, had predicted Tiananmen Square, either the activism or the crackdown. But they must have sensed rumblings of discontent. It would have seemed like a good idea to put a personable young man in the field. It was less obvious why he had returned to the States less than twelve months later and resigned with immediate effect.

The computer information was the bare bones, preserved by bureaucrats, not analysts. He needed flesh on the bones, which meant more digging in the subterranean filing laby-rinth. There was a story here, Bonneville was sure of it. But how had that story led Jack Ford to be caught on CCTV at a crime scene in Singapore? Coincidence? Not a word that made sense to Andrew Bonneville. There were always connections, fine lines between people and events, between the past and the present. He looked at the picture on the file and again at the one gleaned from the CCTV camera. What was the connection?

He had an idea. He hit a few quick keystrokes. Nothing. He turned to the ancient file again. Turned the pages slowly, scrutinizing the faces. Found him. Peter Kennedy. Attached to the embassy cultural division at the same time that Jack Ford had been there. Two young men in a foreign country, thirty years ago. Their paths had crossed again in Singapore. One was dead now and the other on the run. This was not coincidence. The two were linked by some shared and dangerous history.

He'd got his man. It was time to report to Griffin.

Jack ducked his head to get under the low, narrow doorway, past two stone lions wearing identical rictus grimaces which guarded the way. He found himself in a tiny, square courtyard with a few tables and bamboo chairs. Old men in black shorts and white vests played checkers with each other, stopping only to take long draws on hand-rolled cheroots and sip tea from fragile porcelain cups. An elderly man made a loud slurping noise as he drank soup from a bowl. There was steam rising from it and Jack realized he was hungry, hadn't had anything except that Starbucks coffee, black, no sugar, in the morning with Fei Yen.

Jack wondered for a moment if he was in the wrong place. The taxi driver had been adamant that this was the *hutong* – one of the narrow streets of Old Beijing – which he was looking for, although the man had been forced to drop him at the entrance to the street. It was too narrow, like a grey-walled corridor, for modern vehicles; only bicycles and handcarts traversed the lane and people bustled hither and thither.

As he stood there indecisively, the men within the square began to stare. Drawn by the sudden silence, an elderly man emerged from the small cottage fronting the yard. He was dressed in some sort of embroidered gown with wide sleeves and had a long white beard. Jack hurried to him, eager to get away from the curious eyes of the clientele.

'Are you Confucius?' he asked in Mandarin.

'Not the original,' responded the man in English and then chortled heartily at his own humour. 'However,' he added, 'I am sometimes called that. I fear it is shorthand for "pompous old windbag".'

Jack tried a smile but his heart wasn't in it. 'Peter . . . Peter Kennedy gave me your name. He said I should come to you if I needed anything. That you would lend a hand.'

'Peter is a good friend and *his* friends are always welcome here. Confucius says, "Never contract friendship with a man who is not better than thyself."'

Was the man nicknamed Confucius actually quoting Confucius? Did Chinese people do that? The Chinese man ushered Jack back into the house and the American blinked to adjust his vision to the gloom. 'Spartan' was the kindest word for the bare room with a small table and two chairs. A mat rolled up in the corner presumably functioned as a bed at night.

'Er . . . nice place,' muttered Jack.

'My ancestors have been here since the Ming dynasty,' responded the old man, 'when they were servants to emperors.' He continued, 'So how is Peter? I have not seen him for more than a week.'

'Peter *was* a good friend . . . I'm afraid he's dead.' Jack had a sudden flashback of the spreading bloodstain from the severed wrist.

'What happened?' asked Confucius. Even in the half light, Jack saw that he'd grown pale. The news had come as a shock.

'He was gunned down – in Singapore.'

'Why?'

'For a briefcase. He begged me to take it before he died, to stop it falling into the wrong hands.'

'What was in the briefcase that was so important?'

'That is why I have come to you. I need your input to translate the documents – they're in Mandarin. I never did learn to read the language.' Jack slung his rucksack on to a rickety table and undid the clasps. He took out the three-page document, handwritten notes in the margins. 'It looks like a memo from some sort of meeting,' he explained.

'How do I know that you did not kill Peter for this yourself?'

'In a way, it was my fault,' admitted Jack. 'He took a detour to see me . . . about . . . a personal matter. It gave the men a chance to ambush him. He was only five hundred yards from the American Embassy when they got him.'

'Who were they?'

'Chinese, from their methodology – I'd say military.'

'What happened to them?'

'Two are dead,' said Jack bluntly. 'The third caught a bullet and has a broken jaw at the very least.'

Confucius drew a curtain over the open doorway. 'Some deeds are too dark to be discussed in sunshine,' he said. 'Why have you come to the Forbidden City? Surely it would have been safer to get the document translated elsewhere? In Singapore?'

'I had to come to Beijing on some . . . personal business,' said Jack.

Eyebrows were raised, but Jack had no intention of mentioning Fei Yen. He continued, 'This briefcase is a side-show for me. But I owe it to Peter to figure out why someone killed him to get it. I want to get rid of it – but right now I don't know who the good guys are.'

'Your embassy in Singapore? Isn't that where you thought Peter was going? Why didn't you just take it there?'

'There must have been a leak,' said Jack. 'Someone knew Peter was on his way and told the Chinese. I couldn't just hand it over to the doorman. The bad guys may well have plans for getting their hands on this. Besides, they would have arrested me after the mêlée at the Botanic Gardens, and I needed to come here to Beijing.'

'You are a tactician,' said Confucius.

'Just a soldier,' retorted Jack.

'I don't want Peter to have died in vain,' said Confucius. 'We were friends, Peter and I.'

'Did you know he was a spook?'

'He told me he was the cultural attaché at the embassy. It was never a very likely story. So, in answer to your question, yes – I guessed that he was a spy.'

'He trusted you,' said Jack. He made it sound like an accusation. He remembered the note urging him to seek out

Confucius. But that had been about Fei Yen, not a secret memo that men had died to obtain. Did that change anything? He looked at the other guy. Ridiculous clothes, ridiculous beard obscuring his face. Thin face. A mole with hair sprouting from it like an epiphyte.

Jack made up his mind. He held out the memo and Confucius took it with a reluctant hand. Jack understood his hesitation. The men who had attacked Peter for the case weren't going to be keen to allow anyone to live who knew its contents.

'They don't know who I am so they can't find out who you are,' he said. 'Once you tell me what's in it, I'll walk away. All you have to do is tell me what it says. What was so important it was worth killing Peter over?'

Dominic Corke was briefing the Vice President. Once again, he had decided to avoid the man in the Oval Office in favour of the number two. There would be hell to pay if it became public knowledge that he was bypassing the Commander in Chief. But Corke was a patriot, not a lackey. Harris sat behind a big desk. He stood on the other side of it and tried not to shuffle his feet. Vice President Harris had her mind on other things. 'The Singaporeans got his fingerprint off a handkerchief? I didn't even know that was possible,' she exclaimed.

'Some sort of new technology. The key thing is that we know who this guy is now. His name is Jack Ford.'

'From that long face of yours, I'd guess he's one of ours. CIA?'

Corke nodded reluctantly. The Vice President was famous for her ability to read people and her sudden and accurate insights. Corke had assumed she was just lucky. Now he wasn't so sure. 'He got out a long time ago. His first and only CIA posting was to China during the Tiananmen Square massacre. After that, he just walked away.'

He added, knowing it was going to be a red rag to a bull, 'From the file we know he served in China at the same time as Peter Kennedy.'

'Your dead guy?'

'My dead guy.'

'What else do we know?'

'Jack Ford was Delta Force.' Corke explained what he knew. 'Decorated. A patriot.'

'If he was such a patriot, how come he didn't take the case to the US Embassy?'

Corke remained silent. Even if the Vice President had been expecting an answer, he didn't have one. He turned his head away from the penetrating gaze and found himself looking at a bust of Obama. It was rare for a sitting vice president to acknowledge a president other than her immediate boss – but exceptions had to be made, he supposed.

'He knew Peter Kennedy. That's very interesting – but not at all reassuring,' she said.

'It could have been personal. The meeting between them could have been personal.'

'They met for a chat in Singapore while your spook was supposed to be rushing an important document to you from your precious EMPEROR?'

'It sounds unlikely, I know. The alternatives are not great either.'

'That this Jack Ford is working for someone else?'

'We have to consider the possibility.' Corke frowned. 'If that is the case there is every possibility that EMPEROR has been compromised and is now dead – or wishing he was dead.'

'Well, looks like you need to find Jack Ford. Any leads?'

'Yes, ma'am. Once we found out who he was, there was no problem tracking his immediate movements.'

'And?'

'He caught a flight to Beijing.'

'China?' she exclaimed. 'You're saying that this document of yours that you were working so hard to get *out* of China has gone back to China?'

'That seems to be the size of it.' If Jack Ford had cost him EMPEROR, decided Corke, he would personally find a spot for him in some outsourced prison run by mad mullahs on the CIA payroll. Helmand Province, maybe. He didn't care how many medals the guy had. He was toast.

'Well, do you have a plan?' demanded the Vice President.

'I plan to track down Jack Ford and recover the briefcase, ma'am.'

'That's your goal, not your plan,' said Vice President Harris, voice like cold steel. 'And until such time as you have a plan, it's also just wishful thinking.'

'Jack Ford?' Director Griffin had never heard the name before.

'Yes. Ex-CIA. Posted to China before Tiananmen. Apparently, he was quite useful – became friendly with student leaders.' Bonneville was briefing Griffin on his discoveries. 'He quit and left China. No explanation given.'

Bonneville handed over the thin file of information he'd found on Jack Ford. 'He signed up with the military instead,' he continued. 'Joined Delta Force. Served with distinction in the first Gulf War. Three Bronze Stars and a Purple Heart are on file.'

'A real American hero,' said Griffin.

'He resigned his commission about two years ago.'

Griffin eased the folder open and looked at the headshot of Jack Ford as a young man. 'Thirty years we hear nothing from this guy and then he pops up in Singapore, kills two Chinese agents and steals a briefcase?'

'Well, from the file, I'd guess he knew Peter Kennedy. They served in China at the same time. It must have been a pre-arranged rendezvous.' Bonneville put forward his theories in a diffident tone. He could tell the boss was on a short fuse.

'Just catching up with old friends?' Griffin was sceptical. 'Seems an odd time for Kennedy to do it – while carrying a top-secret something-or-other from EMPEROR to the embassy.'

'We need to take into account the possibility that Ford is working against our interests, sir.'

'Whaddaya mean? Whose interests? The NSA?'

'The United States,' responded Bonneville.

Griffin ignored the implied criticism. 'You think he's a traitor? That's a leap.'

'The stuff in his file just doesn't add up,' said Bonneville, refusing to commit himself.

'If he's working for the Chinese, why did he kill two of their men?'

'I didn't say he was definitely working for the Chinese, sir. The only thing we know for sure is that he isn't working for us.'

'Have we put out a BOLO?' asked Griffin, referring to the alert to 'be on the lookout' used for urgent or dangerous criminals.

'Waiting for your go-ahead, sir.'

Griffin paused. He understood the implications. If they put out a BOLO, the other agencies would get wind of Jack Ford. Right now, his department had an advantage. On the other hand, they still needed to find the guy.

'Put one out,' he barked. 'Don't tie it to this matter. Obfuscate – he's a person of interest, no more . . . make something up.'

'Yes, sir.' Bonneville typed rapidly into the terminal, watching the information come up on the big screens in their operations room. His face glowed green, reflecting the screen. The computer let out a series of beeps.

'They found something already?' asked Griffin.

'No, sir, that's not it.' Bonneville sighed. 'I'm afraid there's already a BOLO out on this guy.'

'Who's looking for him?'

'CIA, sir.'

Griffin slammed his hand down on the table. 'Dammit – how'd they find his identity so quick?'

'He's in China,' said Bonneville. 'Jack Ford's in China.'

'What?'

'He caught a flight to Beijing after stealing the briefcase.'

'Out of the frying pan into the fire? It's amazing Jack Ford has lived so long.'

'I am not afraid of the consequences.' Confucius added with a sigh, 'Just of the contents of this memo.'

He sat down on a plastic stool, slipped a pair of reading glasses on to his nose and peered at the first page. 'I will try and give you the gist of it as I go along. I will write up a version for you as accurately as possible if you give me time later.'

Jack nodded and shifted his weight from foot to foot. The

kick from that guy by the lake had caught him square on the kneecap and it still hurt.

'Would you like some tea?' asked Confucius, noticing his fidgets.

'No, no,' said Jack, but it was too late. Confucius bustled around with a kettle, set it on the flame of a small gas cooker and set out a small glass teapot and a couple of cups. He tipped some closed buds into the pot, poured the water. 'Not quite boiling,' he murmured, 'or it singes the petals.'

Jack was handed a cup of tea which he gulped down, ignoring the pained expression on the other man's face. 'Maybe we should get started?' he asked, tapping on his watch. 'I need to be someplace else pretty soon.'

'Ah, Americans! Always so impatient.' But he did focus on the document in his hand.

'There does not seem to be anything of interest here,' he said at last. 'Just a memo about some internal housekeeping issues within a government department – health and safety regulations in Chinese factories. A warning that corruption must be stamped out. Nothing you can't read in the papers or on Chinese blogs.'

'Really?' Jack was gobsmacked. What had the whole thing in Singapore been about, then? Had there been a mistake? His head and heart shied away from the idea that Peter had died for some bureaucratic document on health and safety in Chinese factories.

'What about the handwritten notes along the side?' he demanded.

'Just comments on underperforming regions.'

'You're quite sure?'

'Yes.' Confucius looked up at Jack with an expression of mild surprise. 'It would seem that there has been some mistake. I would leave this document with me – it is completely unimportant – but I will still translate it for you. You may return to the personal business that brought you to this country.'

Jack slammed his fist on the table, unable to contain his rage. 'You're lying to me! I know enough Mandarin to have recognized a few words at least. And they weren't about health and safety.'

Confucius stood up slowly, as if his joints were seized with arthritis. 'It is better if you go,' he said.

'I'm not going without some answers. Do you hear me?'

'You should go. Now!' The Chinese man's tone was urgent, panicked.

It was too late.

'Perhaps *I* can help you with the answers you seek, Jack Ford.'

Jack whirled around to see two men step out of an ante-chamber. Both were in civilian clothes. Both were armed. Military-issue semi-automatic pistols. He recognized the Chinese QSZ-92, smaller and lighter than the standard Western makes but just as deadly. Both men had their guns trained on him.

NINE

Jack put his hands in the air, elbows bent, palms forward. There was nothing else he could do. He was unarmed and the two men in civilian clothes – both carrying army-issue guns and handling them like elite forces – had their weapons trained on him. He noted the steady hands. They didn't look like they'd hesitate to shoot him. But Jack had a lifetime of looking down the barrels of weapons. He knew that – if this wasn't going to be the last time he was at the wrong end of a gun – he'd have to wait for his moment. He looked the men over quickly but carefully, noted the military haircuts. These weren't spooks, just army guys in temporary disguise. Not to fool him, he realized. To fool anyone who might have seen them wander into this particular *hutong*.

'I am sorry,' whispered Confucius. 'They arrived fifteen minutes before you. There was no way I could warn you without endangering your life.'

One of the soldiers – the one Jack had identified for convenience as 'the ugly one', sticking-out front teeth and a drooping left eye – took time out from aiming a gun at Jack to smack Confucius hard across the mouth with the back of his left hand. His bottom lip split and blood dripped down the front of his white gown. 'Shut up, old man.'

Jack kept his gaze away from the open rucksack and the documents lying nearby, trying not to draw attention to them. The mysterious memo had caused him quite enough difficulty. But his training still determined his actions. Don't give anything away. Don't show the enemy what you value. Keep your eyes on them – that way you won't miss an opening. An opening to escape. An opening to kill before being killed. That would have to be one hell of an opening. Big enough to drive a truck through.

'We know why you are here,' said the first man in heavily accented English.

'I'm here to see the Great Wall of China,' replied Jack. 'It is the only man-made structure you can see from the moon, you know?'

He was met with a torrent of abuse accompanied by a reddening face and some spittle. Jack didn't mind. He'd learned something already. Number one guy – the not so ugly guy – had a temper he struggled to keep in check. In the absence of a gun or knife, information was the next best weapon.

Number two guy took a step forward. 'Tell us where he is.'

'Where who is?' Jack was genuinely puzzled.

'You *know* who I mean.' The voice of the other soldier was even, the English better. Ugly had a rein on his emotions, assuming he felt any. Which made him the more dangerous of the two. Whatever Jack decided to do, this guy was going down first.

Jack sensed rather than saw Confucius looking at the documents in puzzlement. Like him, the elderly man had assumed the men were there for the memo. A memo on safety standards, according to Confucius. Which didn't explain why Peter had been killed for it. Had Peter's assassins been in cahoots with this lot? Jack would have assumed so except for the questions about some mystery man. Why were there multiple Chinese factions after different things?

'Where is he?' demanded Ugly.

'Seriously, I have no idea what you're talking about.'

The gun swung around to Confucius. 'Tell us what we want to know, Jack Ford, or I kill him.'

'Hey, I just met the guy. As far as I'm concerned, he could be one of you,' said Jack.

Confucius looked pained but did not protest.

'Then I shoot your knees and you never walk again.'

Jack winced. The men hadn't even looked at the documents. They must have listened in on the conversation earlier. Confucius said they arrived fifteen minutes before him. He tried to remember the details. He'd asked for a translation of the memo. The old man had fobbed him off. It was only when Jack had threatened to leave that the men had barged in.

'Do you mean Peter?' he asked. 'He's dead. Killed in Singapore. I thought your lot killed him.'

'One, two . . .'

Did the Chinese count to three as well? Jack wasn't about to wait to find out.

'All right, I'll tell you. Put the gun away, for God's sake.'

The barrel was lowered slightly, or maybe it was just an optical illusion.

'You talk now.'

'He's not here,' said Jack.

'You think we don't know that? China is not big enough for such a man to hide.'

'They want the Tank Man? That's their plan? To rehabilitate a traitor?' General Zhang was flabbergasted, Guo Feng could tell from the breathy, almost asthmatic tone coming down the secure line.

'It would seem so,' he replied, red phone in a tight grip. He was sufficiently senior to have one on his desk; Juntao had insisted upon it. Nothing was too good for his blue-eyed boy. It was just as well, thought Guo Feng. There was no way he could be seen with General Zhang. Politburo members and their staff gossiped like chicken sellers at the market. Word that he had been seen with the general, when everyone knew that there was no love lost between Zhang and Juntao, would spread like wildfire. The red phone – symbol of power and influence – was a direct line to the other people within the Chinese hierarchy who were entitled to have one. These included not only power brokers like military leaders and members of senior Party cadres but also, in the new China of Deng Xiaoping's creation, the corporate titans who flexed China's domestic and international corporate muscles. The phone line, regularly swept for bugs – the men who had the most access also had the most secrets – was the most reliable communication device in the whole of China. Guo Feng, conscious of the irony, was using it to betray his leader.

General Zhang was still contemplating the revelation about the Tank Man. 'I would not have guessed at this bizarre plan if I'd had all the time in the world,' he mused. 'And yet, there is a certain cunning in it. I can see that the Tank Man would be a formidable propaganda tool in the wrong hands.'

Guo Feng didn't answer. Zhang had no interest in his views on the matter.

'So where is the Tank Man?' asked the general.

'We have not been able to ascertain that.'

'But? I assume there is a "but" and you have some way to find this skulking coward?'

'We have a lead. My men are on their way to apprehend him. We will be able to extricate information about the whereabouts of the Tank Man fairly quickly after that.'

Zhang didn't contradict him on this point. He too had complete faith that Guo Feng, who was not averse to using all the necessary methods, would have this man singing like a canary.

'Who is it – who is your lead?'

'An American.'

'An American – are you sure? What do they have to do with anything?'

'Our information is that the Americans were responsible for smuggling this man out of China.'

'That is very interesting indeed. You are sure of this?'

'My sources are reliable,' said the colonel, keeping any irritation at being doubted out of his voice. 'It was either a lone wolf operation or done with the sanction of the embassy. In any event, my men are on the way to apprehend him.'

'This American of yours is in China? That's very convenient!'

'There is no such thing as a coincidence, sir.'

General Zhang guffawed into the receiver and Guo Feng moved his own away from his ear with a fastidious expression on his face. Really – it was unfortunate that he found himself betraying Juntao, a man he genuinely respected, to this crude gangster in a uniform. But that was just the way the fortune cookie crumbled. A man with secrets sometimes had to pay a heavy price to maintain them.

'What do you plan to do with your American?'

'Find out the location of the Tank Man. Seize him. Prepare him for his rehabilitation and star turn at the next People's Congress.'

'Excellent – we will let the matter proceed for the time

being. It will lull Juntao and his motley band of traitors into a false sense of security. And when you have the Tank Man, I will strike.'

Guo Feng could not resist needling the general, although he knew it was foolish. 'How do you know this Tank Man will agree to work with the Secretary General-elect, sir?'

'Are you kidding me? The man stared down a row of army tanks. Would such a *hero* refuse an opportunity to help his country?'

He didn't have to spell out for Guo Feng what would happen to the Tank Man when the hardliner got his hands on him. He would disappear into one of the network of prisons maintained by the PLA for dissidents. Or he would be found face down in some pig trough in the countryside. And no one would be any the wiser. Another pawn in the chess game between the competing kings and kingmakers within the Politburo.

'This is just one element of Juntao's plans to prepare China for a reformist agenda,' warned Colonel Guo Feng. 'A careful man has more than one string to his bow.'

Again there was the chuckle but this time Guo Feng heard the menace. 'You have a great admiration for your boss, although it does not prevent you from betraying him,' remarked Zhang. 'Perhaps you should bear in mind that I too have as many options as there are dishes on a Chinese menu.'

Guo Feng suspected that General Zhang was speaking no more than the literal truth. A man like him was unlikely to rely just upon a thwarting of Juntao's plans. He would also have options to turn defence into attack. It was an essential element of the art of war and Zhang fancied himself a master.

'What else does Juntao have in mind?'

'The wish list of the reformist movement,' warned Guo Feng. 'Direct elections, a free press . . . the usual.'

'Anything new?'

'He plans to reduce the PLA's authority,' said Guo Feng. 'The PLA chief will no longer be a member of the Politburo.'

'What? He dares take me on directly? Does he not know that I have a million men under arms?'

'That is precisely what he knows . . . and fears,' replied Guo Feng. 'Which is why he plans to use the goodwill of the

people at the time of his elevation and the symbolic power of
the man who stared down the tanks to rein you – and the army
– in.'

'It seems that I might have underestimated Juntao's recklessness,' said General Zhang. 'Never mind, forewarned is
forearmed – and I have you to thank for that, Guo Feng.'

'I betray the Secretary General-elect reluctantly,' said the
colonel.

'Of course you do,' said Zhang. 'But if you choose to lie
with other men, you must understand that there is a price to
be paid.'

Guo Feng did not respond. General Zhang had pictures, that
was all there was to it.

'The key is the Tank Man,' said Zhang. 'I look forward to
hearing from you when you have him in custody.'

'Very well, General,' agreed Guo Feng before ringing off
and staring at his orderly desk. He did not expect that Zhang
would have long to wait. He had sent two of his best men to
seize the American. He realized he had not told Zhang the
identity of the American. It did not matter. It would mean
nothing to the general. Guo Feng stared at his phone expectantly. He anticipated a "mission accomplished" report within
the hour.

'He hasn't made contact with any of our people in Beijing.'
Dominic Corke was at the airport briefing the Vice President.
She would shortly board Air Force Two to Tokyo for the annual
APEC meeting. NSA Griffin was on the flight too. He was
there at the insistence of POTUS, probably to keep an eye on
the VP.

Corke was on the next commercial flight to Beijing. The
VP had been adamant. 'You need to go to China. Boots on
the ground. That's what we need. And you're it.'

Corke could have said that the director of the CIA did not
sully his hands with operational work. On the other hand,
EMPEROR was his baby. And he'd been an operative once.
All in all, it wasn't such a bad idea to go to Beijing. Check
out the lie of the land for himself. Maybe even get a lead on
this renegade, Jack Ford.

Right now, all Corke had to offer the VP were more dead ends. Jack Ford had disappeared without a trace into the fog and fumes of Beijing. A couple of decades back, a *guizi* in China would have stood out like a sore thumb, leaving a trail of the curious and bewildered behind him. Easy to follow. Easy to find. But now, every second hippie, student, businessman and tourist was from the West, determined to get something out of China whether it was enlightenment, knowledge, commercial opportunities or cheap jade.

'I still don't understand why he decided to go to China,' said VP Harris.

'According to our records, it is his first trip back since he walked away from the CIA in 1989.'

The Vice President was puzzled but interested. The enigma that was Jack Ford had caught her attention. She stared at his picture again. There were two now. The grainy recent CCTV image and the hard-faced glare of a Delta operator from his file. The earlier shot had been taken over ten years ago. The hair was the same length – Delta types didn't go in for the short back and sides of the rest of the military – and the expressions were identical: grim and single-minded. The CCTV version still looked pretty trim although he must have lost some combat readiness. On the other hand, he'd been up for a fight at the Botanic Gardens.

She turned to look at Corke, brown eyes muddy with irritation. 'Have you found out anything more about this guy?'

'I've talked to a few of his superiors. Glowing reports about his abilities, less than glowing reports about his attitude. It sounds like they dropped him behind enemy lines in almost every country we've gone to war with in the last fifteen years.'

'A hundred war zones to visit before you die?'

Corke ignored this facetious interruption. 'Sometimes Ford did not understand the chain of command.'

'Give me an example.'

'He was one of those who cornered bin Laden in Tora Bora.'

'And?'

'And he wasn't pleased about the fact that we didn't do a whole lot about it.'

'We invaded Iraq,' responded Harris wryly. Her vote, as a

senator, to go to war had contributed to losing the presidency to a television star.

'He explained his views to General Tommy Franks.' Corke was referring to the man who'd been in charge of the Tora Bora operation when bin Laden had escaped.

'I guess Franks didn't appreciate that. But that's still no reason to turf him out.'

'It's not in his file but I spoke to one of the general's aides who was present during their altercation. It turns out he explained his views with his fists.'

'Oh, I see.'

'He could have been court-martialled. As it was, his senior officers stood up for him. Said he'd cracked under the pressure. Needed a break, not prison.' Corke smiled. 'They couldn't save Ford's job. Sounds like the man himself was ready to call it a day. Apparently – and this is a quote – he "didn't know who the bad guys were any more".'

The Vice President of the United States returned her gaze to the hard-eyed soldier who had fought for his country and then become disillusioned. Was that rebel streak apparent in his face? She couldn't see it – unless it was in the thin, mobile mouth.

'None of this explains why he's gone to China with EMPEROR's document,' she said.

'No – but it explains why he didn't feel the need to come in from the cold. He doesn't really trust authority.'

'He doesn't fit the profile of a traitor,' she said at last. 'Doesn't seem like the kind of man who can be bought.'

'No,' agreed Corke. 'Doesn't seem to be the kind of man who would exchange one boss for another, either.'

'Does he have family?'

'No – never got married. Except to the army. He's pretty much alone in the world.'

China is not big enough for such a man to hide. Suddenly, Jack knew exactly who the soldiers in plain clothes were talking about. He'd been obtuse, stuck in the present. Thinking about Peter, the memo, coffee with Fei Yen at Starbucks. Not thinking back, not looking back. He felt his mind go blank.

It was thirty years ago and he was a smart young thing on his first overseas posting. The blue-eyed boy of the CIA. Peter had been his colleague then. A couple of years senior. A plodder. A friend. A man with a conscience. And of course, there had been Xia. She of the ideas, the ideals, the protests. Xia, whose letter – safely back at the motel – had brought him to China. Into this mess.

Memories dragged him down as if he was drowning in a deep well. It had been late night when Peter and Jack set out. The call from the embassy was meant as a warning to stay off the streets, stay out of trouble, now that the PLA was moving in to Tiananmen Square. Neither Peter nor Jack saw it that way. Their thoughts turned immediately to Xia – somewhere out there in the eye of the storm. Their plan, such as it was, to get to her and haul her out of trouble's way.

It was impossible to go to the square directly. Beijing residents, on hearing that the army was moving in, had taken matters into their own hands. There were roadblocks everywhere, pitched battles, blood. Jack and Peter were both sure that Xia would make her last stand at Tiananmen Square. She was not one of those who had advocated for diplomacy or withdrawal in those last frenetic days.

'Confrontation will make certain that the authorities – including Li Peng – understand we are serious,' she had insisted.

'I think they know you're serious,' Peter responded. 'That's why there are tanks all round Beijing.'

'Would you have us blink first? This is the first chance we have to ensure lasting reform in our country. I for one will not back down. They play for keeps. But I do too.' She waved an arm in a circle to indicate the rest of the student leaders. 'And so do we all.'

Jack had looked around at the others. Some of them were standing a little straighter after Xia's mini-speech. She was their backbone, she gave them strength, belief that theirs was a cause that could be won. At the very least, a cause worth dying for.

And if they didn't get to Xia in time, she might be one of those dying for the cause.

'What are we going to do?' asked Jack, his face covered in soot and dirt. The two young men were crouched in an alley a few blocks from Tiananmen. They'd seen it all on their slow trek through the city. Burning tanks, makeshift barriers, bodies lying in no-man's land. It was not just the civilians dying either – Jack had seen burned-out armoured cars with the corpses of young soldiers lying half in and half out, as if they had been trying to escape the death trap.

It was past midnight. In the distance, they could make out the glow of fires burning.

'I don't know.' Peter looked tired, worried, afraid.

Jack peeped around a corner. Yet another barricade. This one manned by men and women of various ages. Mothers, fathers, brothers, sisters. Holding sticks and staffs. No real weapons. Huddled behind burning tyres and overturned cars. Facing off against armoured personnel carriers and tanks. Brave. Some would call it suicidal.

A tank commander shouted something from the open hatch of his vehicle.

'He's telling them to clear the way,' whispered Peter.

Jack didn't bother to tell him that he'd understood too. His Mandarin was improving; immersion – wasn't that what always did it? Especially when coupled with a desire to understand the girl you loved in her mother tongue.

'You will not pass here.' An elderly man took a few steps forward so that he was in no man's land.

'Why are you doing this?' asked the tank commander.

'Our sons and daughters are at Tiananmen Square – we will not let you do to them what you have done to the rest of Beijing.'

'We mean them no harm . . .'

'Then why do you arrive in tanks and with guns? A peaceful man comes bearing gifts.'

This caused the tank commander to pause for thought. 'They are troublemakers who must be dispersed,' he said.

Reverting to the party line, thought Jack. That didn't bode well. He looked at the stern faces of the young soldiers. The same age as most of the students at Tiananmen Square. But these kids were peasants from the villages who'd joined the army to escape from perpetual graft and perpetual hunger. They didn't care whether the Party's campaign against bourgeois liberalization was misguided. They were trained to follow orders, trained to fight, trained to die.

'This is your last chance to move,' said the vehicle commander.

The rebels were so still it could have been a waxwork display of the French Revolution. Only the acrid smell of burning rubber and the sound of distant gunfire spoke of an ugly reality.

'If it is your desire to join your children in martyrdom, so be it,' continued the soldier. He barked a command and Jack's futile shout of 'No!' was drowned out by the sounds of gunfire. Even in his stunned state, he could see that they were using PLA-issue Type 56 rifles. Against the defenceless citizens, they might as well have been bazookas. As he watched the massacre, he could feel Peter's hand grip his arm as if fearing that his friend would intervene. Jack felt the bitter taste of helplessness in his mouth but he didn't plan to stop a bullet with his body to buy a resident of Beijing an extra thirty seconds of life. Not today. Not when Xia was out there somewhere with the might of the People's Liberation Army rolling towards her.

The first man killed was the old guy who had been brave enough to walk around the barrier to talk to the troops. The rest did not last much longer. The barriers they had set up were not capable of withstanding heavy machine gun fire. Their use had been symbolic, an attempt to dissuade the soldiers, not to deny them. As Jack watched, soldiers obeyed an inaudible command and ran forward, clearing the barricades. In ten minutes, they had forced a passage wide enough for the convoy. They did not stop for the dead and wounded. Neither did Jack and Peter as they followed in the wake of the vehicles rumbling down the road towards Tiananmen Square.

'Where is he?' The curt bark from the armed man dragged him back from 1989 to the present and Confucius's little room in the Old Beijing *hutong*.

'I don't know where he is – if I did, I'd tell you. That's history to me – I'm not dying for it. I swear – I don't know.'

Jack couldn't keep the note of panic out of his voice. For a moment, just a moment, he wasn't the man who had fought innumerable foreign wars on behalf of his country. He was just a kid on his first mission – one that had gone wrong on his watch.

The men conferred briefly. He hoped they believed him. The PLA were well indoctrinated. For them, all Americans were cowards. He guessed they slept easier at night thinking Uncle Sam's false teeth were in a jar next to his bed.

Jack's ears pricked up. He could hear voices coming in their direction. Perhaps one of the chess players was looking for Confucius. Either way, this was about to get messy. He gritted his teeth, slowed his breathing. He didn't want any collateral damage on his conscience.

The men heard it as well. 'You will come with us,' said the first one, making his mind up quickly and waving his pistol in the direction of the door. The second guy pulled a silencer from his belt, screwed it on with an expression of concentration, turned to Confucius and – just as Jack feared the worst – clubbed the man across the side of the head so that he collapsed in a heap on the ground.

'You might have killed him,' said Jack. 'He's an old man.'

'He needs to keep his long nose out of other people's business.' He waved the pistol towards the door. An instruction to get moving.

'Where are we going?' Jack was still trying to buy time but he was running out of credit. He knew that once these guys got him back to their HQ, escape would no longer be a possibility. And they would have the ways and means to make him talk. Jack caught a slight movement out of the corner of his eye, turned slightly, as if he was following instructions, and saw that Confucius was conscious. Not just that: one eyelid drooped slowly and deliberately. Had the old man just winked at him? He was tougher than a marine if that was the case. It seemed that Confucius had a plan, though – and that meant he had to concentrate and wait for his opening.

It came even sooner than he expected.

The old man emitted a theatrical groan. Both soldiers turned to look at him. Number one guy took a step forward, gun raised. Planning to club him again, or shoot him this time. Anything to keep him quiet until they'd made their escape. In a move that would have looked slick even in the movies, Confucius lashed out in a full semi-circle with an extended leg. Jack didn't stop to admire the kung fu. Instead, he saw his moment and went for it. As number one guy came crashing to the ground, Jack aimed a roundhouse kick at number two. He aimed for his head; the man ducked away just in time, but he was off balance now. Jack led with his fist. He felt the man's nose flatten and give beneath his knuckles. Blood spurted like a fountain. Number two bent over double, clutching his face, moaning under his breath but still trying to raise his gun hand. Jack caught the gun arm and twisted it to point the gun away. He brought his knee up hard, caught the man on the chest. Number two would have fallen except for the lock Jack had on his arm. As he rebounded towards the American, Jack bunched a fist and the guy came looking for it with his chin. This time Jack let him go. He fell over backwards like a ton of bricks. The gun fell from his hand and skittered across the floor. He estimated that it had taken six seconds to put the guy down.

Jack dived for the weapon, quickly noting as he did so that Confucius was locked in a clinch with the other guy, trying to keep him from taking a shot. He was strong for an old man – but he was losing. Jack reached the weapon on the floor just as number one managed to shove Confucius away from him. The soldier trained the gun on the old man, finger tightening on the trigger. It was a mistake.

It only takes one mistake to lose a fight.

The Chinese man had misread the main threat. He should have turned on Jack, used the gun to silence the greater danger. Instead, he'd opted to put Confucius out of commission. Anger had impeded his judgement. Maybe he hadn't noticed that Jack was going for the other gun. Maybe he was a fool. Whatever the reason, it was about to cost him. Jack raised the gun, took aim and fired. The silenced gun spat twice, a double tap to the chest. Man down.

Jack relaxed a moment too soon. Despite the mess where his face had been, number two was still game. It only takes one mistake to lose a fight. Maybe – but not when Jack had the gun. As number two launched himself across the room, all raging fury and flying fists, Jack whirled around, didn't hesitate although he was bringing down an unarmed man at ten paces. Another double tap. Just as well he'd picked the gun with the silencer. Otherwise, the gunshots would have brought in the town. Jack glanced across at the door and then at Confucius, who was slowly clambering back to his feet. He looked shaken but unhurt in any significant way. Jack loosened his grip on the gun, twirled it round once and tucked it into the pocket of his windcheater. The way this trip was going he needed to get himself a shoulder holster.

TEN

Confucius appeared to be a man of many talents. 'I have friends who will be able to help me.'

'You have friends who will help you get rid of two bodies of PLA soldiers?' Jack was sceptical. That was the quickest way to a firing squad that he knew. He'd been away almost thirty years but he doubted that China had changed that much.

'A friend in need is a friend indeed.'

Was he quoting the original Confucius or a Hallmark card now? Had Peter taught him the expression too?

'What about the memo?'

'Leave it with me – I will translate it for you. It will take a couple of hours, I think.'

Jack glanced at his watch. It was almost time to set out for his evening sightseeing date with Fei Yen. He didn't want to be late.

On the other hand, did he trust Confucius? He remembered the attempted obfuscation about the contents of the memo and the sliding scissor kick that had taken the legs from under one of the bad guys. Confucius had definitely saved him from a very unpleasant encounter in a cell somewhere as they tried to extricate information from him.

Would he have talked? Probably. Eventually.

Jack was pretty sure that the Chinese would never have released him. Kidnapped and tortured American citizens were never good for diplomatic relations. Instead, his body would have been found in some back alley frequented by lowlifes pickled in drugs and alcohol. An unfortunate end for a tourist who had gone on one bender too many. For every soldier killed in a war zone, twenty-five American ex-servicemen committed suicide. Death by binge drinking and looking for trouble in a foreign land were just complicated ways of slashing one's wrists.

'Can you give me the gist of the memo?'

'It is safer to be accurate. It appears to have something to do with Taiwan.'

Jack scowled. That inevitably meant conflict.

'I will photocopy the memo for you,' said Confucius.

The old Chinese man drew back another curtain to reveal an alcove that clearly functioned as an office space. In contrast to the outer room with its Spartan air, this one was comfortable and, more importantly, filled with the latest in technology. Confucius was a man of many parts.

As Jack watched, Confucius ran the memo through a printer scanner. He held out the copy and the American waved it away with his hand and nodded at the original. 'Better for both of us if I keep hold of that one.'

Confucius handed it over with equanimity but for some reason, Jack's radar for trouble – the hairs on the back of his neck – suddenly stood to attention. Jack shrugged it off. There wasn't time for doubt. Not if he was going to see Fei Yen.

As he reached the door, Confucius asked, 'Those men – I assumed they were here for the memo. But they wanted a man. What man? Someone you knew? What was that about?'

'Believe me,' said Jack, 'you really don't want to know.'

'The American got away.'

'What do you mean?' The response from Secretary General-elect Juntao was high-pitched with shock.

'The American who knows the location of the Tank Man got away. The two men I sent to apprehend him have disappeared. I fear the worst.' Colonel Guo Feng was cringing inside. This was not the news he'd expected to bring to Juntao. And in a short while he would have to report the same information to General Zhang. It was rare that he managed to screw up so badly that he infuriated both his bosses. Usually, since they had diametrically opposing interests, information that annoyed one pleased the other. Jack Ford's disappearance was different. Without him, they didn't know where the Tank Man was hiding out. That was bad news whether you were a reformist or a hardliner. And it was especially bad news when you were the army colonel charged with delivering his man who really couldn't afford to offend either leader.

'How is this possible? You told me you sent your best men!'

'I'm looking into it, sir.'

'I want answers, Guo Feng.'

'You will have them as soon as I do, sir.'

'What do we do now?'

Guo Feng could not see him but he did not doubt the Secretary General-elect was pacing up and down his plush, red-carpeted, red-curtained room with the gold carp sculptures in a glass case and revolutionary posters on the wall. Pacing was Juntao's default activity when he was under pressure. He used to run his hands through his hair. But now he prized his appearance and had managed to cure himself of that nervous tic.

'Well?' demanded Juntao. 'What next?'

'I have other options, sir. I did not anticipate this hurdle but I do have contingency plans.'

'What are they?'

'I think you would prefer not to know.'

Battles were not fought or wars won by those who were afraid to use the available weapons. At that thought, Guo Feng sighed. He never enjoyed it when he found his thoughts running on a parallel track to those of General Zhang. He despised the crude army man and his lust for power. Unfortunately, he often agreed with him.

'Will your plan lead to the American?'

'I believe so, Secretary General-elect.'

'Then you have my permission to proceed.'

'Thank you, sir.'

'Be aware, Colonel Guo Feng, that I will not tolerate further failure. We must get our hands on the American, Jack Ford. Otherwise, my blueprint for a new and better China will have failed to clear the first hurdle.'

'Surely you can proceed without the Tank Man, sir?'

'Of course – but bringing democratic change to China requires powerful symbolism.'

'Yes, sir.'

Juntao hung up and Colonel Guo Feng took a deep breath

and dialled General Zhang's number. However unpleasant that confession of failure was, this second round was going to be exponentially worse. A house divided against itself cannot stand. A man divided between two masters is a man on the rack.

Jack had agreed to meet Fei Yen at the Starbucks near the university. Beijing's complexity and crowdedness was such that if two people were familiar with or had previously been to a single location, it was best to use it again. It eliminated the need to have long mobile phone conversations about precisely which street corner or side lane the other had meant when the meeting was set up.

The taxi driver was rattling down the asphalt, swerving down side lanes whenever a light turned red ahead of him. It was a wild ride but Jack didn't care. Too many people had tried to kill him in the last few days – he somehow didn't believe the fates had a car wreck lined up for him. Not when there were so many men with guns about. Besides, the roads were in good shape. He pondered the worst urban trails he'd raced down, horns blaring, guns blazing, and decided on Baghdad, with Beirut a close second.

The memo was folded and tucked into his jacket pocket. The copy was with Confucius, awaiting his translation efforts. Jack tried again to figure out what had gone down at his place. Two men after him. He'd assumed they were there for the memo. After all, lives had already been lost in pursuit of it. Instead, they'd been asking him about something quite different. A moment in the past when a nation's history had crossed paths with his own life. The acrid stink of memory filled his nostrils.

Thirty years ago, almost to the day, Jack had been out looking for Fei Yen's mother.

The fourth of June, 1989.

It wasn't a date that he and many other people were likely to forget. Jack remembered again the clarity of that June day; the uneasy quiet, the smoking vehicles, the bodies.

He and Peter had finally found their way to Tiananmen Square, focal point of the rebellion, in the early hours of the morning as dawn broke over the horizon. The place was almost deserted except for a heavy military presence. A few onlookers stared in curiosity, their movements skittish, ready to take to their heels if the guards took an interest. Despite all the violence and death Peter and Jack had witnessed on their way to the square, there was no evidence that there had been much blood-letting at Tiananmen. Barricades had been torn down, there was rubbish everywhere; a few young men, clothes torn and spectacles cracked, were still being escorted away under guard – but they saw no bodies and hardly any blood. A few reporters from the Western press were milling about.

Jack suspected that the army guys watching him and Peter probably thought that they were press too. Their expressions were hostile, a warning not to get too close, but they had not tried to chase them away. Waiting for instructions. That was what one did in China as an underling: waited for instructions. He didn't doubt the soldiers would just as soon arrest him, beat him or shoot him as look at him. But their options hadn't been narrowed down for them yet so for now they just watched.

'There's no sign of her,' said Peter, grabbing his friend's arm and trying to drag him away. 'She must have got away.'

'Or she's in a cell somewhere with the rest of the student leaders. I doubt she'd just have abandoned the square. I mean – where is everybody?'

Jack's voice was hoarse from a night of fires, fear and soot.

'We will find someone at the embassy with connections – find out where she's been taken.' Peter tried to sound reassuring but his efforts were unconvincing. Jack could read the fear in his eyes, mirroring his own. 'But there's no point hanging around here.'

'I have a better idea,' said Jack, pulling away from Peter. 'We're at the square, she was at the square. I'm going to ask one of those uniformed comedians what they've done with the students.'

Jack heard Peter's whispered protest even as he marched over to a group of soldiers.

He rehearsed his sketchy spoken Mandarin in his head as he approached. 'I need to see a senior officer,' he demanded.

'No press, no photos, nothing here for you to see. Please leave at once.'

'I'm not press, I'm government. US Government,' he said baldly, blowing his cover completely, as if anyone was listening or cared. 'I have important information.'

The less you know, the more confident you need to sound. Well, Jack sounded very confident indeed. A young man with a big attitude. The sort whose daddy was somebody important. The grunt looked worried, although he was the man with the gun.

'It's urgent,' insisted Jack. 'I suggest that you act immediately.'

There was a short, heated conversation between two soldiers and then he was ushered forward. One of them said, 'You will come with me. I will take you to the senior officer.'

Jack followed immediately, wishing that Peter was with him. It was so much easier to make one troublemaker disappear than two. On the other hand, if he disappeared, Peter knew where he'd been last – which might help them recover his body. Despite the nerves, he walked with a swing in his step and a wide stride. A man with nothing to fear from a couple of soldiers or their bosses.

A group of senior officers was standing in the distance. The huge grey buildings loomed behind them, making them look like toy soldiers. As he looked around while maintaining the quick even pace, Jack noted the evidence of quick flight. Upturned boxes, handmade signs trampled, bundles of flyers scattered. The early morning breeze would lift one into the air like a kite and then it would flap back down to rest. A metaphor for the revolution. A pair of black plastic-rimmed spectacles had been ground underfoot, the lenses glittering like diamonds on the hard ground. The students had been overrun, he guessed. Those who had the opportunity would have fled, back to the safety and anonymity of family. They'd have had to run the gauntlet of the troops moving inwards from the outer ring of the city but maybe some of them had successfully melted away. He hoped so. But the PLA had most likely picked up the ringleaders and whoever else looked like trouble. Xia ticked both boxes.

The soldier reached the officers, stopped a few feet away

and saluted smartly. He said something that Jack didn't catch.

'What is it you want? How dare the Americans come here and poke their noses into internal Chinese affairs?' The colonel's face – Jack guessed his rank from the uniform – was suffused with red from the neck to the tips of his ears. 'I will have you charged with espionage and it will be a lesson to your government not to interfere.'

Jack decided to come clean. The colonel looked young. Maybe he'd been in love once.

'I am sorry. I'm afraid I misled your soldier. The American government does not know anything about my trip here. I have come on my own.'

'What is it you want, then? Do you think this is a tourist spot?'

Jack could have said that, on most days, when the PLA was not attacking its own people, Tiananmen Square *was* a tourist spot, but he bit his tongue and refrained.

'There was a girl here. A friend of mine.'

'You are here looking for a girl? Are you insane?'

'No,' replied Jack. 'But I am worried.'

'Was she one of these misguided youths who was camped here?'

'Err . . . no,' said Jack, realizing even as he did so that he might be about to get Xia into even more trouble. 'She was just passing this way when the disturbance broke out.' It sounded lame even to his own ears.

The colonel decided he was harmless, just stupid. It was probably a fair assessment in the circumstances. 'There is no one here,' he said, waving an arm in the air. 'The young people have realized the error of their ways and been allowed to return to their families. The People's Liberation Army serves the people of China. As you can see, the square is empty.'

They both looked around as if to confirm the emptiness and spotted a small convoy of vehicles headed in their direction. The lead vehicle drew up next to them. It was an open truck of some sort and the driver saluted and barked out, 'We have captured more enemies of the people, sir. They were hiding in an alley not far from here. What do you want me to do with them?'

Perhaps mindful of Jack's presence the soldier did not answer at once, so Jack had time to look at the captives, a row of young men with their heads bowed and their eyes glazed, faces streaked with dirt and the tracks of tears. One of them held his arm at a crooked angle and was pale with shock. He whimpered, 'My arm is broken. The soldiers hit me with a gun.'

The colonel did not give any impression that he had heard, or that he cared.

A girl in the truck with her back to them turned around and Jack was almost too startled to speak for a moment.

'Xia?'

'Jack? What are you doing here?'

Jack was almost at his destination, the Starbucks around the corner from the University of Peking where he had agreed to meet Fei Yen. This was not the time to be thinking about Fei Yen's mother or that terrible day. Not if he wanted to stay in control. The spindly trees that lined the road looked grey and defeated. Much like the workers he'd seen on the construction sites dotted around Beijing, building high-rises on every avail-able piece of land. The Chinese economic miracle was not an automated leap forward. The poorest – the desperate who had come in from the villages to find work and now huddled in shanty towns within the city – were bearing the physical brunt of China's new skyline. He'd seen the workers in their dirty grey Mao-style pyjamas breaking rocks with hammers and carrying broken stones in wicker baskets on their backs. The pyramids of Egypt had been built the same way. No wonder the government was terrified of rebellion. They had crushed the students at Tiananmen while he had watched. Now, in the present era, they were cleverer – turning student ire on the West, playing up the propaganda about Chinese greatness, drawing a direct line from the empires of old to China's economic might in the present.

Jack's own experience of the Chinese capital hadn't changed much. Back then, he'd been dodging men with guns. He was doing exactly the same thing this time round. Jack gestured to his taxi driver to stop. His instruction was executed with the (in his opinion) unnecessary squealing of tyres. He handed over a fistful of yuan and clambered out. He had barely shut the door before the man was off in a cloud of exhaust and imprecations – maybe he had expected a bigger tip.

Jack spotted Fei Yen. His heart leapt and he was transported into the past. For a moment he was certain that it was Xia, not her daughter. The slim figure, the way she held her head, the tapping of one foot in an unconscious gesture of impatience. She was her mother's daughter all right, but was the resemblance just skin deep, or did it go further than that? He started walking towards her, not calling out, wanting the privacy of an observer for a few moments.

A young man in a dark suit sauntered up to her. Jack wasn't surprised that Fei Yen was propositioned on street corners. She was a beautiful woman. The man tried to take her by the elbow but she took a step away and shook him off. There appeared to be a heated exchange between them. Jack quickened his step. Maybe this was a boyfriend and the break-up hadn't been amicable. A Delta Force operator, albeit retired, might be considered overkill for the mission but Jack was grimly determined to see the presumptuous young man on his way. No one bothered his maybe-daughter and got away with it.

Jack saw a dark van out of the corner of his eye. It turned on to the main road from a hidden alley. He wasn't sure why it had caught his attention – the street was crawling with cars, vans and bicycles. Perhaps it was the moderate, almost methodical pace at which it was moving; different from the stop, start, accelerate, brake, horn, swerve, weave pattern of the rest of the traffic. Jack knew to trust his instincts. The van was moving down the lane towards Fei Yen and her persistent suitor. Jack had a second look at him, noting the smart dark suit, out of place on that street, the broad shoulders and the sudden fear in Fei Yen's stance.

Without quite knowing why, Jack started to run. He called Fei Yen's name, once and then again. The second time she heard him. She looked down and across the road, spotted him and raised a hand in greeting. He could see the tension go out of her body. Jack quickened his pace. He was closing fast. The black van was drawing closer. Jack looked for a lull so as to cross the highway. Was there such a thing in Beijing?

The man spotted Jack and grabbed Fei Yen by her upper arm. He began to drag her away. She screamed and struggled. The people around made no move to intervene. Jack was desperately weaving through vehicles now, the horns and yells of irate drivers almost drowning out the screams of Fei Yen. The black van drew level, the back doors were flung open. Even as Jack closed to within thirty yards, running as if his life depended on it, the man in the suit bundled Fei Yen into the vehicle. He slammed the door shut, but not before Jack caught a glimpse of more men within.

The man stopped, turned to look at Jack for one long second. Out of the blue, an old stooped woman stepped forward and started to hit him with a folded umbrella. The man turned, shoved her away and leapt in the passenger side. The old woman collapsed to the ground. With a squeal of burning rubber, the vehicle took off just as Jack reached the spot. In a second, it had turned a corner and disappeared. Jack ran on to the road, waving at cars and taxis, trying to get one to stop so that he could give chase. It was no use. No one was prepared to stop for the *guizi* screaming manically at them. They averted their eyes, pretended not to see him.

He turned to the people who had been standing around, who had witnessed the whole incident but done nothing. They stood in a semi-circle, gaping at him.

'Why didn't you stop them?' he yelled. 'Didn't you see what just happened? The girl has been kidnapped.'

There were mutters and murmurs. The passers-by drifted away, ducking into shops and alleys or hurrying away down the street. The old woman who had tried to intervene was sitting on the ground, leaning against a telephone pole. Her face was as wrinkled as old parchment. She was breathing heavily, and her blue veined eyelids were closed. He knelt down next to her, took one of her hands in his. It was fragile and fine-boned, like a small bird trapped in his calloused hands.

'He said he was her husband – that she was refusing to come home,' she whispered, opening her eyes a crack.

'And no one did anything?'

'In China, it is always better to walk away from trouble.'

'You tried to stop him . . .'

'I am a fool,' she said.

She tried to get to her feet and Jack helped her up, his mind racing, trying to decide what to do. Who had taken Fei Yen, and why? Did it have anything to do with the dilemma he was in or was it just a coincidence? Jack felt panic overwhelm coherent thought. That wasn't good. Panic was only useful if it was the other side that was panicking. Usually, that was the situation he tried to induce. He remembered the thoughtful expression of the man in the dark suit just before he'd driven off. The other side was still in control. Jack took a deep breath, slowed his breathing, controlled his heart rate, reminded himself that this was what he was trained for – the ability to function under immense pressure, to win out against the odds.

'Who is she, that girl? What is she to you?' asked the woman, one small hand on his forearm for balance, the other gingerly feeling the back of her head where she had smacked it against the pavement, looking for the lump, feeling for blood.

'Fei Yen,' he answered. 'She is my daughter, Fei Yen.'

ELEVEN

Dominic Corke, CIA director, landed at Beijing Capital International Airport. He hurried through immigration and customs with the world-weary air of someone who had spent a lifetime chasing the next deal in far flung corners of the globe. A fifty-something businessman, already successful, who wanted to make one last killing in China. He glanced around and saw he was not alone in fitting that stereotype. The Middle Kingdom's rapacious growth had drawn them all in like moths to a flame. Many were singed by the experience but there were sufficient success stories to keep them coming back. He noted the Indians, the Japanese, the South Americans; his countrymen were only a fraction of those trying to grab a slice of the pie.

But what was going to happen now that the Chinese juggernaut was slowing down, the provinces were getting restive and the leadership was at loggerheads? Dominic Corke had a fear that some of the answers to the questions spinning in his head like a carousel had been in the missing memo.

His driver waited outside, Corke's name typed and pasted to a small board. The driver was built like a steamroller and had military written all over him, from the blond crew cut to the lantern jaw. Army, but at the cannon fodder end, unlike special forces.

'Where to, sir?'

'Take me to the embassy.'

It was already late afternoon but there was no time to waste. He needed to get in and put out some feelers for EMPEROR. He hoped the summit on economic matters that he planned to attend might provide a few leads. It was the sort of thing that EMPEROR might be expected to appear at if he wasn't in a dark cell somewhere having water pumped into his stomach through a hose. On the other hand, even if he *was* there, there was no guarantee all was well. Chinese power politics played out in different ways. EMPEROR might have been urged to continue to play a public role to avoid any appearance of instability. Anyone he was close to (his wife, probably; there had been a son but he'd been killed during an uprising in Tibet) would have been arrested and shipped out to some detention camp to ensure his good behaviour. Corke would have to gauge which was the most likely scenario without approaching EMPEROR or speaking to him.

At the same time, he needed – somehow – to track down Jack Ford. The man who had taken his precious memo *back* to China. He didn't even know where to start. He glanced out of the window. It was one of those unexpected crystal-clear days with shiny, bright blue skies that only served to highlight the filthy air the citizens breathed the rest of the time.

The new embassy, a massive green block on a ten-acre site (it looked like a single-tone Rubik's Cube to Corke, but he'd never been much for architecture) loomed large in the distance. When he reached the embassy Garett Lim, the ambassador, was waiting for him. It wasn't often that the CIA director visited. It apparently merited a personal meet and greet. The two men walked through the grounds and past the giant tulip sculpture by artist Jeff Koons, sitting in a square shallow pool of water.

'Hope you had that thing swept for bombs and bugs,' muttered Corke. He never liked these massive construction projects in foreign countries and he didn't care if the US wanted a token structure to symbolize the importance of the relationship between the two countries. As far as he was concerned, every worker on site was a potential spy or terrorist and there was probably a bug in every petal.

'We sweep the compound for listening devices more often than we sweep for dust,' said Lim.

They reached the ambassador's plush office where the CIA station chief, Ian Woodroofe, was waiting. After perfunctory pleasantries Garett Lim asked, 'You're attending the economic summit?'

'Yup, if Ian can get me in!'

'The Chinese will smell a rat – why would the CIA director be at something like that?' The station chief didn't sound impressed. He probably didn't like the CIA director stomping all over his territory. In Corke's experience, these station chiefs would piss on trees if they thought it would keep people out of their fiefdoms.

'A cover identity?' he asked.

'You're not exactly unknown, are you?'

Corke grimaced. The Chinese were so distrusting they'd smell a rat even when the nearest rodent was a thousand miles away.

'Put it out that I asked to come? Suggest I'm about to retire and have been offered a good job as CEO of some multinational in China. I'm here to check out my future on Uncle Sam's dollar.'

'All right,' said Woodroofe. 'That might even be credible – half the folks that used to work in the previous administration have landed cushy jobs here.'

'What about my other problem – Jack Ford?'

'I've made some discreet enquiries. You told me that he and Peter Kennedy were posted here together during the Tiananmen incident in 1989?'

Woodroofe had a reputation for being a methodical man who preferred to get his facts accurate before he put forward any suggestions. But the CIA director was on a short fuse. The Vice President had sent him in person to clear up the mess and he needed to get it done before the President got wind of his predicament. 'Yes. So?'

'They had a chance to exchange information before Peter was killed?'

'He got his hands on the damned memo, didn't he?'

'There are two possible leads,' said Woodroofe.

'That's two more than I have right now,' was the terse response.

'In the last couple of years, Peter became friendly with a Chinese dissident – known around here as Confucius.'

'Why wasn't I told about that?'

The other man shrugged bulky shoulders and Corke remembered that he'd been a football player once. One of a rare few who'd had a brain to go with all that brawn. He was also a soldier, a scholar and a spy. The perfect man for the most challenging posting in the entire espionage service, station chief in Beijing.

'It wasn't viewed as a problem. The initial contact appears to have been a coincidence – the subsequent friendship genuine.'

'You let it be because you thought the relationship might come in useful some day.' Dominic Corke's tone was matter-of-fact. 'And you didn't want anything on record in case it leaked.'

'Exactly,' said Woodroofe. 'My thinking is, if Ford was coming to Beijing and needed assistance that was off the grid, Peter would have suggested Confucius as his go-to guy.'

'OK – that works for me.' He continued, 'You said that there were two possibilities? What's the other?'

'A woman . . . Jack used to know her when he was posted here. According to the personnel files, they had a relationship.'

'I suppose we should have guessed,' said Corke. 'It's always a woman, isn't it?'

The other man nodded once. 'Her name was . . . her name is Xia.'

Jack wasted the rest of the day trying to make a police report. The Beijing cops were sceptical that he had a daughter, that she had been kidnapped or that he had witnessed it. He left when it seemed likely they would lock him up as a troublemaker. He spent the evening trawling through the internet and pounding the streets looking for leads, his mind jumping between worst-case scenarios. Had Fei Yen been kidnapped for the illicit organ trade in China? Had she been sold into sexual slavery? Or did it have something to do with the memo, or the attack by those two men? How could anyone *else* know about Fei Yen when he had not known about her until a couple of weeks earlier?

Jack kept going over the kidnapping in his mind. Was there anything he could have done? Why hadn't he spotted the danger earlier? Surely he should have started running the minute that man grabbed Fei Yen by the arm. Why had he decided that he was a persistent suitor and not a real threat? Had he hung back like a concerned parent to see if she could take care of herself – a necessary skill in a world where fathers were not always around, or in time to save the day?

The next morning, Jack went back to Confucius. He didn't know where else to go. Didn't know what else to do. Confucius was the only person he knew in Beijing. Peter's friend. A man who had already saved his life, with whose complicity he'd killed two men. It formed a bond in his experience, the conspiracy to kill. It was a bond he now shared with crack Delta troops and an elderly Chinese man with a ridiculous nickname. *May you live in interesting times.*

'They took my daughter,' he said by way of an opening, when he had hurried past the chess-playing elders in the courtyard and into the sparsely furnished living room. He absently noted that the bodies were gone, and ticked off efficiency as another of Confucius's attributes. Jack didn't even bother to wonder what he'd done with them. Weighted down in a canal was his best guess.

Confucius met his quick return with equanimity but now looked at him sharply. 'Daughter?'

'That's why I'm here. In China. I recently discovered that I might have a daughter. I was on my way to see her. Just as I reached our meeting point, she was snatched.' Jack had difficulty keeping his voice, or his hands, steady. Anxiety was pushing stomach acids into his throat.

'By whom?' Confucius asked, pouring out a cup of steaming fragrant tea and handing it to Jack. Jack wrapped his hands around the warm cup and had a sip, noting wryly that he'd hit the bottle before with much less excuse than he had today.

He answered the question carefully, thinking, reliving, trying to avoid the black hole of panic. 'Don't know – men in suits, black van. Professional job.'

'Related to what happened here earlier?'

'Or what happened in Singapore – or just a coincidence. I don't know. I don't see how it can be?' He took a deep breath. 'All I know is that someone has my daughter.'

'By happy coincidence . . .' muttered Confucius under his breath.

'What?'

'In Chinese folk tales,' he explained, 'it is said that without coincidence there is no story.'

'You think the events are unrelated?'

'No – that is the stuff of folk tales.'

Jack scowled. Why did the man have to talk in riddles? 'What do I do? How do I get her back? I don't have a clue how to find them! The van had no plates.'

Confucius sat down on a stool and stroked his beard. Jack was unable to sit; he marched up and down the small room, cracking his knuckles, feeling fear give way to despair. He had no idea what he was going to do, how he was going to save his daughter. *His daughter.* The two words he had feared to use, even in his own mind, even after meeting Fei Yen. His daughter, whom he'd only met once. He'd looked at her hair, at her eyes, trying to find some resemblance so that he could believe Xia's letter. *You have a daughter,* it had read. *Her name is Fei Yen. She does not know about you.* Did he believe it? Did it even *matter* now that the girl had been taken?

'How did you find out about her?'

'Her mother, Xia, wrote to me. She is Chinese. We met in Beijing thirty years ago. For a short while, we were in love. But I never knew about Fei Yen.'

'Why? If she had kept a secret so many years, why would she suddenly tell you?'

Jack had wondered the same thing. Now, under cross-questioning from Confucius, he felt defensive. 'I don't know – maybe she thought I had a right to know?'

'After all this time?'

'She suggested that Fei Yen might be in danger but there was no explanation.'

Jack had spent fruitless hours worrying about Xia's motives. Decided in the end that he had no option but to act on the information. Whether true or false. Whatever Xia's motive was for telling him, he had no choice. He had come to Beijing. But only after doing the prudent thing – asking an old friend based in China to find out what he could. About Fei Yen. About Xia. Peter had agreed. After a week of silence, he had called. 'I'm on my way to Singapore,' he'd said. 'Not sure when I'll get back to China. Meet me there and I'll pass you everything I've found.'

Jack had flown to Singapore. Arranged to meet Peter at the Botanic Gardens. Been in time to watch him die.

'You believed this Xia whom you once knew?' continued Confucius. 'You believed that this girl was your daughter?'

'I wasn't sure,' admitted Jack.

'And yet you came to see the girl.'

'I had to find out for myself.'

'You were going to look at her and see – what is it you say? Whether she was a chip off the old block?'

Jack rummaged around his bag and produced the mug from Starbucks. 'No, I went to get a DNA sample.'

Despite the seriousness of the situation, Confucius smiled. 'You are a careful man, Jack Ford.'

'Let's just say that Fei Yen's mother has not always been honest with me in the past.'

'Why did you go back to see her again?' asked Confucius. 'Before testing the DNA?'

Jack wondered how to explain that he'd felt such a longing to get to know this girl, such hope that she was indeed his daughter. That after all the years of being alone, being a loner, he had family. He met Confucius's eyes and knew that the other man understood loneliness.

'And if she turns out *not* to be your daughter?' he asked.

'Either way – she's my responsibility now.'

'Why do you say that?'

'Why?' Jack was angry. 'Because they took her when I was just a hundred yards away! Because she called my name as they threw her in the van!'

Confucius resumed stroking his beard as if it were a pet rabbit. 'They are trying to flush you out,' he said at last.

'What do you mean?'

'We can assume that people are looking for you because they know you have the memo. That you took the case from Peter.'

'No one saw me.'

Confucius looked pained. 'You are being naive, Jack. By now, they will have identified you – from CCTV cameras, from fingerprints.'

Jack opened his mouth to protest and then decided against it. It *was* naive to rule it out, even though he had covered his tracks. He'd been at the receiving end of all the technological know-how a soldier could have – wiretaps, satellite imagery, drone weaponry. This was no time to underestimate what governments could do – his or any other – when they really wanted something.

'And,' continued Confucius pedantically, 'soldiers came here – also wanting something you had or someone you knew.' He smiled. 'You're a popular man, Jack Ford.'

'They haven't got me yet.' The self-confidence was that of a trained operative who had fought and won two pitched battles in the course of a few days.

'Yes, and so they've decided to use leverage – to flush you out. Either the men who were here – and you haven't told me yet *who* they wanted – or someone else has found your trail leading from Singapore to Beijing. They are using Fei Yen to get at you.'

'That can't be right.'

'Why not?'

'Because no one knows Fei Yen is my daughter!'

'That's not entirely accurate. One other person knows.'

'Xia? You mean Xia?'

'Yes, that is exactly who I mean.'

An APEC meeting was a ridiculous parade of dictators in fancy dress. It was not Griffin's idea of a good day to be a small part of the entourage of the Vice President attending such an event. But the President had insisted he come along to keep an eye on things. He didn't trust his VP.

At present, Vice President Harris was dressed in a gaudy kimono for the group photo. In his opinion Harris looked like a cheap geisha, not a representative of the leader of the free world. Griffin's own father had died in the Battle of Midway, less than eighty years ago. Was human and national memory that short? What next? A Western leader wearing an Arab headdress and sitting cross-legged in a tent in the desert, kowtowing to a bunch of terrorists? No, wait – that had already been done. Tony Blair kowtowing to Gaddafi in the desert on behalf of the West.

Griffin's reverie was interrupted when a thin, cadaverous man with hair that stood up like a wire brush sidled up to him. He stood at Griffin's elbow, appearing to take in the spectacle of the leaders of Asia-Pacific nations jostling to get closer to the Vice President for the photo op. Griffin knew that most of the leaders – from Singapore to the Maldives – were at the summit hoping to get a picture they could splash all over the front pages of their controlled presses back home. Nothing boosted the credibility of an authoritarian figure more than the ability to show that they had access to power.

The thin man took out a large white handkerchief and blew his nose vigorously. Griffin looked at him in disgust. This, however, was the opening the man had been waiting for. Speaking into his hankie in a muffled tone, he said, 'Mr Griffin, I have been asked to invite you to a meeting.'

'With whom?'

'It is better that this remain confidential for the time being.'

The NSA gave the man a searching look, trying to remember if he'd seen him before. What was he? Chinese? Korean? He didn't have the dapper smoothness of the Japanese or the wide-eyed impassivity of a Korean. If he had to guess, he'd say Chinese. He took in the man's physique – lanky and underfed, but with a knowing look in his eyes. Griffin knew it wasn't the politically correct thing to say but goddammit, he couldn't tell these Asians apart.

'All right,' he said.

'It is always a pleasure to have dialogue with the Americans,' the Chinese man said, and handed over a business card with a theatrical flourish. He reached out for Griffin's hand and shook it vigorously. Griffin nodded, smiled thinly – a good impersonation of a man cornered against his will – and then palmed the small note that had been slipped into his hand, putting it into his pocket with the card. The man bustled off to corner other stray delegates. He was good, admitted Griffin. Anyone watching their exchange would not have seen anything different from the pattern of behaviour exhibited by the skeletal man in his other dealings. There were always ghastly creatures at every summit, determined to rub shoulders with – and add their cards to the Rolodex of – the powerful, so that they could convince their bosses of their worth.

Griffin made a beeline for the toilet. He slammed himself

shut in a stall and took out the note. A small scrap of paper with the words, *Room 712, 4 p.m.* He looked at his watch. He had twenty minutes. He tore the note into tiny pieces and flushed it down the toilet.

Confucius shrugged as Jack struggled to come to terms with what he had suggested: that it was through Xia that his enemies had found out about Fei Yen.

'She would never do anything that might endanger Fei Yen.' He was absolutely certain of that.

'I'm not suggesting that she would have done so intentionally. But a wise man does not ignore the facts.'

Jack buried his face in his hands, his heart rejecting what his mind told him was an intelligent hypothesis. Xia might easily have told someone – a friend, a lover, her family. It might not even have been a recent revelation. But someone somewhere had known – and Fei Yen had been taken. To get at him.

'If we are right,' said Confucius, 'you don't have to find her – they'll come to you.'

'Or to Xia. My tracks have grown cold since yesterday. They might assume I am in contact with her and use her to get to me.'

'That is possible,' agreed Confucius.

'I must find her, find Xia . . . so that they – whoever they are – can contact me.'

'To trade for what you have or who you know?'

Jack pondered the thought from all angles. What he knew was the secret the two men had tried to get the previous day; what he had was the memo he had taken in Singapore. He had no idea who would contact him or what they wanted. But they had Fei Yen. Somehow, they knew about her. Maybe it was Xia; maybe there was a thread in the tapestry that he had not yet identified. Either way, he was ready to see this through.

'They took Fei Yen to flush me out?' he said coldly. 'Well, that's just fine with me.'

TWELVE

'Our Secretary General-elect does not understand the dangers of a rush to democracy.'

'None of us have any interest in an unstable China,' agreed Griffin.

The identity of the man waiting in room 712 was no surprise. Now they sat across from each other on two small chairs, a carved wooden table between them, drinking water from tall glasses. The hotel room was opulent but smelt of old cigarette smoke. The heavy curtains were drawn but the chandelier was as brilliant as glittering diamonds. Griffin wondered if the room was bugged. He doubted it. General Zhang had even more to lose than he did if the meeting became public. He took a small sip from the glass of water in front of him, trying to decide how to play his hand.

'As we have discussed previously, I am taking steps to ensure that the liberal faction of the Party does not undermine the security of China,' continued Zhang.

'What will be the outcome of your efforts?' A blunt question, but Zhang had a reputation as someone who disdained Chinese parlour games and doublespeak. His mere presence in that hotel room spoke of a man who was willing to gamble big. They had been working together on common interests but this was their first face-to-face off-the-record meeting. Griffin doubted that even General Zhang would be able to talk himself out of trouble if it became known that he'd had a clandestine meeting with the National Security Adviser of the United States. Neither, for that matter, would he.

'Juntao will not be the next Secretary General.'

'And *you* will be?'

'It will be as the Chinese people desire.' Perhaps, recognizing the irony, he added, 'I will be willing to serve in whatever capacity the nation requires.'

'You are a patriot, General Zhang.'

'That has always been my foremost motivation,' agreed the Chinese general.

'And mine,' insisted the NSA, not to be outdone. 'What do you want from us?' Time to cut to the chase. This wasn't a social call. Zhang had effectively told him that he planned a coup. That was information of almost unparalleled value. It wasn't being handed over for free.

'Not from "us"; from you.'

'What do you mean?'

'I will speak frankly,' said Zhang. 'I do not believe that the current administration in your country understands the dangers inherent in the Chinese situation. Your president destabilizes the Chinese economy with his tariffs and undermines the global world order with his "America First" nonsense. That is not *convenient*.'

Griffin's glance was almost admiring. The man was a master of understatement. 'There are some in my country,' he said, 'who support the progress of democracy and human rights as propounded by your Secretary General-elect.'

Zhang snorted out loud. 'You mean your vice president, who thinks she is running a separate government? She is one of those who do not see the dangers in front of her face.'

When Griffin was pragmatically quiet, Zhang continued, 'The US turns its gaze away from these democratic principles when it is expedient. You think anyone has forgotten Putin or Duterte or that Saudi Arabian prince, Mohammed bin Salman? You support hardliners and turn a blind eye to their so-called crimes when it suits American interests.'

'At present the American government does not speak with one voice, whether it be one of principle or pragmatism.' This was not news, but it was true. This president's ship had many captains and would-be captains. Griffin was one.

'And you?' asked Zhang.

'I always put my country first.'

'Good – it seems we are both patriots. In which case, there *is* something you can do for me.'

'Before you do anything reckless, I think you need to see this.'

Jack tried to concentrate on what Confucius was saying but

his head was still spinning. Xia. Xia must have told someone about Fei Yen. But whom? Whom would she trust? There were not many people in China you could safely tell that your illegitimate child had been fathered by a CIA operative in the middle of a student revolution. China had changed a lot since Jack had been here last but he doubted it had changed that much.

The older man was holding up a piece of paper between two fingers, as if to touch it was anathema. 'This is just a quick summary.'

Jack stared at him blankly.

'A quick summary of the *memo*,' snapped Confucius. 'Or have you forgotten it already?'

'I've had other things on my mind,' Jack retorted. 'The memo is not at the top of my list of priorities right now.'

Confucius walked over to him until they were toe to toe. 'Are you a patriot, Jack Ford?'

'What?'

'Are you a patriot? Do you love your country? Do you sing the national anthem with your hand over your heart?'

'Well, I don't sing very much but I was a soldier for twenty years. That changes a man.'

'A soldier . . .' mused Confucius. 'Marines?'

'Rangers . . .'

'Rangers lead the way?'

'. . . and then Delta.'

'I should have guessed. I thought you were a spy.'

'Spy first, soldier later, drunkard last.' The last was said with a slight twist of the lips. Confucius would read the truth in his words despite the flippant delivery but Jack didn't care. The old man was full of surprises. How did he know the motto of the Rangers? Surely it wasn't general knowledge amongst elderly Chinese gentlemen who ran tea shops in Beijing *hutong*s? If his head wasn't already full to bursting, he'd be curious – and suspicious – about the Chinese man's antecedents. As it stood, Jack was going to rely on his instincts – that he could trust the man. Two dead PLA men seemed proof enough, he hoped, that they were on the same side. And he needed someone on his side if he was to recover Fei Yen. Besides, Peter had trusted him.

'Once a soldier, always a soldier?' demanded Confucius, still up close and personal.

'Don't believe everything you see on TV. Most American soldiers have a great second career protecting Qatari princes and Mexican drug lords.'

'I don't think that you're ready to forsake your country, Jack Ford. I believe that you are a patriot.'

'What is a *patriot* called upon to do?' asked NSA Griffin.

'In order to arrange the defeat of the liberal wing and the humiliation of Juntao, a situation will have to be engineered,' explained Zhang. 'One in which his weak leadership is exposed.'

Griffin felt a trickle of sweat down his back despite the coolness of the room. General Zhang's sheer implacability was disconcerting. 'What are you planning?' he asked abruptly.

'A number of different scenarios are being looked at. All of them are capable of achieving the desired outcome.'

'Why are you telling me this?'

'In order to ensure the long-term stability of China which is in the interests of both our countries, American actions and responses . . . will need to be calibrated.'

Griffin stood up and walked to the curtains. He opened them a crack. It was dark now and all he could see were the glistening streetlights and well-lit buildings with their flashing neon signs. Tokyo Tower gleamed in the distance. Tokyo at night was a vision of a dystopian future.

Griffin wondered whether the Vice President had completed her geisha routine. Already she was the toast of the Japanese newspapers, most of which were gushing in their praise for her easy manner and general respect for international process – a contrast foreigners were quick to make with the actual POTUS. The Vice President's positions on issues – no wars of choice, no pre-emptive strikes, mutual defence – suited the international order. The general consensus, except in Israel and Russia, was that Americans had elected the wrong person for the top job.

The VP might be looking for him, he supposed, but he doubted it. He was at the APEC summit because Corke had gone to China to rescue his failed mission and find EMPEROR. The President didn't trust Vice President Harris so Griffin was along for the ride. And now it seemed there was going to be payback.

He turned to look at Zhang, who was watching him, his head like a block of granite, his expression carved from stone. 'I think you and I are well positioned to act in the best interests of both our great nations,' he said.

General Zhang smiled. Griffin could see that he was not surprised that he was cooperating. A good reader of men? Or someone with a file on him thick enough to ensure that he could successfully predict his thinking?

'What did you have in mind?' asked Griffin.

'At the time that Juntao appears before the Party to be elected the next Secretary General, there must be a disturbance . . .'

'What sort of disturbance?'

'The sort that will require some sort of response from my government.'

'Taiwan?'

'Yes.'

Griffin looked Zhang straight in the eye and decided that the unblinking gaze was almost reptilian. 'I still don't know what you want from me.'

'For the disturbance to be effective,' continued Zhang, 'it would be best if, first, there was *genuine* cause for Chinese outrage and, second, America was to take a hard line thereafter.' The general counted out his two points on stubby fingers. 'We know that you have the President's ear and will be able to . . . persuade him to take strong action.'

'And why would you want that? How does it benefit either country if China and the US are at loggerheads?'

'Juntao will look weak before his people – I will see to that. He will back down and it will be a matter of national shame. The Chinese people will clamour for his removal.'

'Surely there must be an easier way to get rid of your rival?'

'Yes,' agreed the general prosaically. 'I could have him killed. But I want to destroy more than the man – I want to destroy his *ideas* as well. There will be no more talk of liberalizing China or aping Western democracy in my lifetime once I am done.'

This was the sort of ruthlessness that had been missing from the United States government since Reagan had approved Iran–Contra. 'I see,' said Griffin. And he did see. General Zhang wanted his leader pushed into a corner. It made sense. 'I will need to know more details, of course. But I think I will be able to steer the President. His instincts are aggressive.'

'We know that,' grunted Zhang.

'Others in my government have connections in the Chinese government. There cannot be a leak of information. The President does not like being played or made to look like a fool.'

Zhang laughed suddenly. 'If it is your spy, EMPEROR, that you are thinking about, then I'm afraid I have some bad news for you.'

'EMPEROR is compromised?'

'Dead.'

Confucius's assertion that he was a patriot triggered a sudden flashback that caused the sweat to break out on Jack's forehead.

Tora Bora. Afghanistan.

Unfiltered sun. Scorched, cracked earth. Crouching behind red rocks against the red dirt. Skin burned, legs aching, shoulders sore from lugging around enough weaponry to take out a village. Definitely enough weaponry to take out a man. And they had their man. *Hell is empty and all the devils are here.*

They'd cornered Osama bin Laden like the rat he was in a warren of caves. Dark shadows, cave openings, covered the rocky face like open mouths. The cave where bin Laden was hiding out was no more than five hundred yards away. Jack itched to be the one who brought him down. He had been airlifted into Afghanistan with a Delta unit from Squadron C to do just that. And now, finally, after weeks in the mountains following leads as insubstantial as pipe smoke, he'd found his man. He was sure of it. And he didn't care how many mujahidin he had to go through to get him.

'Call in an airstrike, sir?' His second in command asked the question.

Jack shook his head, squinting into the distance. 'No one is going to believe we killed him unless we bring back his head on a platter.'

'DNA samples?'

'You want to blow up that rock and then crawl around with a teaspoon hoping to find the right piece of brain or splash of blood?'

'No, sir!'

'The American people have a right to see and know that he paid with his life for what he did.' He smiled. 'I want a body. I don't much mind if it has been shot up a bit but I am not having him vaporized.'

'We're going in?'

'We're going in.'

'Sir, brass on the line.' The radio operator crawled over without once exposing the top of his head over the shelter of the rocks. Smart man. The mujahidin were like ghosts, drifting in and out of the horizon. But the bullets were real and had already resulted in a couple of team members being medivacked out.

Jack took the radiophone reluctantly and settled behind a rock, gesturing to his men – index and forefinger pointed to eyes and then over the horizon – to keep watch. Not that they needed telling. But Jack was determined that their man wasn't going to sneak away while he wasted time in social chit chat with the higher-ups holed up safely in Pakistan.

'Jack, how is it going over there?'

He recognized the precise, old-maidish enunciation, a one-star general, Mike Connelly. Not a bad guy for a desk jockey. He'd been a real soldier once too. 'I think we have HVT number one, sir.'

'Again?'

Jack bit the inside of his cheek to stop a sharp retort. He'd been wrong a couple of times before about high-value target number one – Osama bin Laden. What did they expect? This was Afghanistan, plaything of the superpowers for decades. The informers were often working both sides, and a couple more for good measure. Was he supposed to ignore leads until someone had given him a signed form in triplicate from the man himself assuring him that he was holed up in cave number seven from the left and would stay there till they came calling? 'It's rough country, sir – easy to make mistakes. But this time I'm sure.'

'Afraid you've run out of time, Jack.'

'What do you mean, *sir*?' The honorific was used as a term of abuse this time and he didn't doubt that the general had picked up on it.

'This is the third time this month you've been sure that you've found our man.'

'This time I'm one *hundred* per cent.'

'We can't wait. I'm sending in a chopper to get you and your men the hell out of there. There's a new mission. It takes priority. Delta Squadrons A and B have already been deployed.'

'What sort of mission could possibly take priority over getting our hands on bin Laden, sir?'

'One word, Jack. Iraq.'

Griffin managed not to bat an eyelid but inside he was exultant. Corke's precious spy had gone belly up. 'Who was he?' asked Griffin. 'I was never told who he was.'

'A senior aide to Liu Qi, Standing Committee member. That old fool shared one too many secrets with his man.'

'In which case, I think I can help you with the provocation you suggest. What did you have in mind?'

'You have warships headed to the Gulf of Taiwan?'

'Yes.' Griffin was not surprised the other man knew. The Chinese tracked US ships assiduously. Besides, what was the point of a show of strength to intimidate an ally if they did not see it?

General Zhang leaned forward and whispered what he wanted. Griffin straightened up and could not prevent his eyes from betraying his surprise.

'It is a bold idea,' he said.

'It is a masterstroke,' retorted Zhang.

'There is a memo,' warned Griffin. 'I have heard there is a

memo out there. This remains a problem even if EMPEROR is done.'

'Yes, we are taking steps to recover it. Do not let it concern you.'

'What's in it?'

For the first time that evening, Zhang seemed less sure of his footing. 'Some of the possible scenarios to create the disturbance we have been discussing.'

'My name?'

'No – at present I am the only person who knows of our long-term arrangement to act for the mutual benefit of our two great nations.'

Griffin did not believe him for a second. 'You need to get the memo back,' said Griffin. The memo wasn't so much a smoking gun as a smoking bazooka. If it mentioned him and found its way into American hands, he would be lucky to avoid a charge of treason. Griffin made up his mind that it was time to take out some insurance.

'Recovery of the memo is my responsibility. The question is – can you do your part?'

Zhang was impatient now. His stubby fingers were locked together in a two-handed fist and the firm expression became a glare.

'Yes,' said Griffin. 'I can do it. What happens after that?'

'I rescue the Chinese people from losing face by presenting the Americans with an ultimatum. In an about-turn, your president will accept this when confronted with a stronger character than the Secretary General-elect – myself, for example.'

'And what do we get in return for this "about-turn"? My guy doesn't like to look weak.'

General Zhang leaned forward. Griffin caught a whiff of sweet tea and garlic on his breath. Zhang whispered his trade in an undertone although the room was empty.

'You would do that?' asked Griffin.

'Yes, I would.'

'Then you have a deal.'

'I'm not ready to forsake my country,' said Jack, memories fading until he was once again in a dark room on a narrow *hutong* with an old man for company. 'But I'm not ready to sacrifice Fei Yen either.'

'Look at the memo, Jack.' The piece of paper was thrust in his face. Jack took it reluctantly and glanced down, noting that the handwriting was as elegant as that of a master brush-stroke painter, even though here the prose was in English. As he read the contents, his hands began to shake and beads of sweat condensed on his brow.

'As you can see,' said Confucius, 'the situation is quite serious. However, the first thing to remember is that the memo is a proposal – not a plan of action.'

Jack was still holding the sheet of paper in his hand, which had steadied. But his heart was still racing and, for once, not even his training seemed sufficient to slow it down. He needed to pull himself together. He gave himself a mental kick; panic was a weapon in the enemy's hands.

'Are you quite sure of the translation?' he asked.

Confucius looked pained. 'I think we can exclude translation error as a reason to dismiss this incendiary document. I am considered quite a scholar of Mandarin.'

'Can't blame a man for hoping,' answered Jack. 'This was a memo for a meeting? But it doesn't say who attended.'

'Although the names of the attendees are not listed – not surprising when you think of the contents – I have been able to deduce two of them.'

'How?'

'Reference is made to different roles to be undertaken by the . . . participants. And there are red pen annotations along the sides which also provide clues.'

'Well, tell me, then!' barked Jack, and then quickly lowered his voice. He didn't want any curious tea drinkers or chess players to stick their heads around the door. He was so on edge he might shoot one of them by mistake.

'One of the men involved is General Zhang.'

'Who is that?' demanded Jack.

'The head of the PLA, member of the Politburo and Standing Committee and a man who had designs on the leadership before Juntao was designated Secretary General-elect.'

Jack buried his face in his hands and spoke through his fingers. 'Let me guess – the other is the pope?'

'Why would the pope be party to this?' asked Confucius.

'It was a joke.'

'This is no joking matter, Jack. The other man I have identified is Liu Qi – also a senior figure in the Party, also a hardliner. I think it is his copy of the memo that we have.'

'Why is that?'

'He appears to have doodled his name down the sides.' Confucius indicated a string of identical Chinese characters scribbled down the margin of the second page of the document. 'He seems to have been quite bored at the meeting.'

'Who can blame him?' asked Jack. 'This must be everyday stuff – collaborating with the NSA to ship nukes to Taiwan or providing North Korea with ICBM technology.'

'What are the implications of such a technology transfer to North Korea?' asked Confucius.

'Kim Jong-Un will be able to reach the mainland of the United States with his nukes.'

'And Taiwan will be able to reach the Chinese mainland with *their* nukes if such weapons are shipped to them in secret by the Americans,' responded Confucius. 'It seems there are actors within our two governments who wish to bring the world to the brink of a nuclear holocaust for their own tactical gain.'

THIRTEEN

East Gate. The Temple of Heaven. Once upon a time Jack had thought it was the perfect place to meet Xia. A heavenly place to meet a heavenly creature. Now he waited there impatiently for the modern incarnation of the woman he had once loved with all his heart. Confucius had tracked Xia down on the internet. It had not been difficult. She was famous and successful. Easy to find. Difficult to get access to, though. In the end, Confucius had been forced to leave a cryptic message with someone describing herself as 'Madam Xia's personal assistant'. A meeting of old friends was desired, at their favourite spot of yesteryear. The friend had news of Fei Yen. The matter was urgent.

'Will she come?' he'd asked as Jack left for the rendezvous.

'I don't know. I think so, if she got the message.' It was a big 'if'. In any event, if she didn't show, Jack had every intention of discovering her schedule and waylaying her in public. This way was quicker, though. And there wasn't time to waste. His daughter was somewhere out there in the hands of a group of trained thugs and he still had no idea what they wanted.

'She might not even know that your daughter has been kidnapped.'

Jack considered that possibility, then shook his head. 'She will know that Fei Yen is missing. Fei Yen said Xia was like a mother hen.' He cracked his knuckles, as if wishing there was someone he could punch. 'I assumed Xia was just over-protective. Now I'm wondering if she knew about some threat.'

'Of course, this Xia of yours might also have heard from the kidnappers,' pointed out Confucius.

'Yes, she might.'

'What about the memo?' asked Confucius, changing the subject to the one that was uppermost in his mind.

'What about it?'

'You are not going to do something?'

'What would you have me do?'

'Go to the embassy, find a contact in your own country. This must not be allowed to continue! Surely you can see that?'

'I'm not sure the two things aren't linked,' Jack confessed. 'The memo and the kidnapping, I'm not sure there isn't some connection.'

Confucius stroked his long beard with a bony hand. 'You yourself said that you ended up with the memo purely by accident.'

'Yes, and *you* said someone might have figured out that I was the person who retrieved it from Peter.'

The two men glared at each other, reduced to adopting each other's positions.

'How? How could they have found out about you?'

'How do I know? But you've been to the movies! There are no secrets left, no privacy, no laws. Just very effective electronic surveillance of every single one of us.'

'Actually, I prefer not to attend the cinema,' said Confucius primly.

Jack acted as if he hadn't heard the interruption. 'We have to assume someone – the Chinese, the Americans, who knows – has figured out who I am.'

'And that you have a daughter.'

'And that I have a daughter.'

'What about the men who came here? They wanted something else?'

'It is better if you don't know anything about that.' Jack closed his eyes for a moment, desperate to shut out the past. 'And all things considered, I would leave this place once I am gone. This is the time to hide, not serve tea.'

'I agree. I will go into hiding once you have left.' He picked up a scrap of paper and scribbled a number. 'This number will reach me.'

Jack took it and slipped it into his pocket.

'The memo is quite bad enough,' said Confucius. 'I don't want to know what else you know that the Chinese government wants, Jack Ford. That way lies a lot of trouble.'

'If Fei Yen's kidnapping is about the memo, it might be my

only leverage – the only thing I have to negotiate with.' The tension in the room was thicker than an early morning winter fog.

'You would turn the memo over to save your daughter?'

'What would you have me do?'

'Your duty,' said Confucius. 'Your duty as a patriot!'

The economic summit was as boring as these things always were. An overheated conference hall at the Bvlgari hotel in Beijing, the stench of a hundred varieties of musky eau de Cologne *pour homme* and an interminable array of speakers. The wealthy and influential rubbed shoulders and predicted the course of the Chinese currency, the American deficit and tariffs; Corke did his best to stay awake. There was no sign of EMPEROR. Chinese bureaucrats seemed to come in only two types – dapper and dark-haired in well-tailored suits or scruffy and overweight in ill-fitting ones. He knew his man fell into the latter category but hadn't been able to spot him.

Finally, they had reached the end of the day and champagne in crystal glasses and canapés that looked like mini-pieces of installation art were being served to the bigwigs. Small groups had formed in the lobby under the elegant low pendant lights and beside the overwrought white floral displays. Corke wandered back and forth, holding his glass loosely by the stem and avoiding conversation.

'Is he here?' The ambassador asked the question *sotto voce*.

Corke scowled at the other man. 'If I told you I'd have to kill you.'

Garett Lim sauntered away trying to keep the irritation off his face. Corke wasn't bothered. The man knew full well that he was not cleared for the identity of EMPEROR. Narrowing the possibilities by revealing whether he was in a room that held fewer than a hundred people was almost as good as telling.

The big doors at the far end of the room were thrown open and another collection of elderly men wandered in, forming a loose group around the man in the centre – the Secretary General-elect, Juntao. Corke watched as Ambassador Lim hurried over, wreathed in smiles, the American Treasury Secretary with him. The CIA director was very glad indeed that he hadn't gone into the diplomatic service. He couldn't have stood the glad-handing. He just wanted EMPEROR.

Suddenly Corke saw him, standing towards the back of the new group. EMPEROR was holding a small cup of tea and sipping it slowly. He'd aged since the CIA director had last set eyes on him. But he was alive. What was more, he was with Juntao. Even if the people in power had decided against any sudden move, they would never have allowed EMPEROR so close to the centres of power if he'd been compromised.

Corke allowed himself a small smile of relief and a big gulp of champagne.

EMPEROR was not a happy man. He'd risked everything to get the memo out of China and now it was back, in the hands of some rogue American operator. The CIA, it appeared, could not be relied upon to execute a simple document drop. They'd allowed their man, Peter Kennedy, to take the scenic route and it had cost him his life. Unfortunately, he would not put it past his Chinese compatriots – especially that bastard Zhang – to track down both the thief and the memo successfully. After all, the memo thief had come to Beijing. The fellow was either mad, bad or entirely ignorant of the document's significance.

EMPEROR cracked his knuckles together and then straightened his fingers. The joints were swollen with arthritis. He wasn't a fighting man – he was a thinker, a planner, a strategist. Despite that, he'd taken bold and dangerous steps to maintain his cover. It had cost him dearly. Only the knowledge that he was thwarting his enemies and gaining his revenge kept him interested. Otherwise, he would have been tempted to tell the Americans to forget about him, that he was abandoning his role as a traitor. That the prodigal son was returning to the fold.

He paused to wonder what they would do if he walked away. Dominic Corke was a good guy – but soft. Too interested in doing the right thing instead of the expedient thing. He doubted that he would threaten EMPEROR with exposure. He'd probably just thank him and offer him a gold watch to mark his retirement. Wasn't that what they did in the United States? It wasn't an issue anyway; he wasn't planning on retiring – not yet. Not until he'd fatally undermined the Beijing Party elite and destroyed their grip on power. In the long term, nothing else mattered to EMPEROR except to avenge his son and save other sons of China from being pawns in a political war.

However, his immediate concern was getting word to Corke that his cover had not been blown. That was why he was appearing in public at this idiotic summit: so that the Americans could set eyes on him. By now, knowing that the drop had gone awry and wondering at his silence, they would be assuming that he'd been compromised or killed.

He glanced around the room and was genuinely surprised to see the man himself, Dominic Corke, CIA director and his handler, gulping from a glass of champagne. EMPEROR allowed himself a small smile. The Americans must have been really worried. And from the way Corke was chugging the bubbly, he'd already set eyes on EMPEROR and drawn the appropriate conclusions.

So now his priority was to recover the memo – or get his hands on another one of the original set. Neither option was straightforward. The former required finding Jack Ford before General Zhang and his minions. The latter was well-nigh impossible since there were only three memos in existence, one for each of the plotters. But without the smoking gun, EMPEROR would be hard pressed to convince anyone that the Chinese hardliners had a plan to destabilize the entire world just to get an edge over their bitter rivals. Without the rustle of paper in his hand, EMPEROR himself wondered whether the whole thing wasn't a construct of his fevered imagination.

EMPEROR felt his gut turn over with the familiar pain of his inflamed ulcers. He reached over to steady himself against a table, groaned at another stab of pure agony, grabbed a handful of pills from a pocket and swallowed them. He needed to last long enough to see his mission through. Revenge, honour, conscience – these were all just words. And words were cheap, meaningless and without the power to hurt a man like General Zhang. Only the thwarting of his ambition would achieve that goal and avenge the death of his son.

* * *

Jack turned a full circle again, hoping to spot Xia. The vast acreage of the temple gardens was almost empty. In the distance, he could see a group of elderly Chinese practising t'ai chi. An old man in a blue beret was stooping over his pavement calligraphy. A woman crumbled bread for pigeons. It was as if time had stood still in this part of Beijing. Jack remembered a similar master calligrapher thirty years ago, also hoping to please the gods with his words. He turned to look into the vaulted entrance of the Hall of Prayer for Good Harvests. The entire edifice had been built without the use of nails, or so Xia had told him many years ago.

'For want of a nail the shoe was lost?' he'd asked.

He remembered Xia looking at him with that half smiling, half quizzical expression she adopted when he brought up subjects outside her sphere of knowledge. When he'd explained the meaning of the phrase, she'd smiled mischievously and said, 'Not in China.'

She'd also explained that the blue tiles embedded in the roof represented heaven. Jack muttered a brief prayer to whichever gods resided in that heaven to keep Fei Yen safe and remembered doing the same thing for Xia the last time he'd seen her, that fateful day in Tiananmen Square.

'Jack? What are you doing here?' she had asked when she had spotted him from the back of the truck three decades earlier.

'Xia!' Relief ran through his body, as cool as a waterfall. She was alive. She was unharmed. He could have wept. Instead, he stepped forward, hand outstretched, wanting to reach for her, to convince himself that this was indeed the woman he loved and not the product of a tired and fevered imagination. The barrel of a gun across his chest stopped him in his tracks. The guard wasn't allowing any familiarity between him and the prisoners. He looked at the others, sullen and bruised, eyes wide and pupils distended. He was pleased that Xia didn't look the worse for wear. In comparison with the others – he had a flashback to the bodies in the streets – she'd come through the night in good shape, despite being at the epicentre of the rebellion in Tiananmen Square. It was more than he had allowed himself to hope through that long, dark night.

'Have they hurt you?'

'I'm OK,' she said, but her tone was leaden.

'You know this man?' The officer asked the question sharply. He nodded at his men, who moved in closer to Jack. To stop him running. To shoot him in the back if he did. Jack ignored the threat. He was fixated on Xia.

'This is the girl I was looking for – let her go, please. I will take her away from this place, I promise. She will not cause you any trouble. Please, let her go.'

Jack knew he was talking too much, begging too much, showing weakness. He was terrified of the man's response. He was sure in his heart that there was no way that they would let Xia go. She had been too high profile. She had found a spot front and centre of the revolution and faced the TV cameras defiantly.

The colonel seemed to stare at Xia for a long moment as if assessing his choices. Was it possible that they did not know who they had in custody?

'She is no one,' insisted Jack. 'Small fry. You don't need her.'

Jack turned to Xia. She was standing alongside the prisoners, but was not in shackles as they were, probably because she was a woman and they didn't expect a struggle. She was standing straight and tall, unbowed by events. The morning sky was crisp blue behind her and the sun highlighted her hair. She had never been more beautiful to him. Or in greater danger. Once the beast of the PLA swallowed his girl whole, she would be impossible to find, trucked out to a remote spot; a life breaking rocks if she was lucky, a firing squad at dawn if she was not.

'Xia? Tell them that you're sorry. You didn't mean any trouble.' She remained silent.

'There is no reason to keep her,' Jack said to the colonel. 'Many students have been allowed back to their families. You said so yourself. You have my guarantee that you will have the gratitude of the American government if you let her go.'

Xia suddenly trotted out a few rapid sentences in Mandarin to the soldiers, too quick for Jack to follow. Adding her pleas to his.

'What is your name?' asked the colonel.

'Jack Ford,' he breathed. 'I'm with the US Embassy. Let her go – I won't make a scene.'

The officer raised a single shoulder as if indifferent to his or Xia's fate.

'Otherwise, you'll have to arrest me too and that will cause a diplomatic incident,' he urged. 'Your government won't look kindly on that.'

The other man made up his mind. 'Get out of here, both of you.' His tone was brusque. Decision made, he turned his back on Jack. Xia leapt out of the truck, ignoring the puzzled glances of the other exhausted prisoners. She grabbed Jack's hand and hurried him away from the small group towards the perimeter of the square. Again, Jack noted the debris of failed protest – leaflets, headbands, blood, posters. Xia walked with purpose, her stride longer than his, although his desire to leave that place equalled hers.

'I can't believe we did it!' He was exultant.

'Keep quiet and keep walking. They might change their minds.'

'About letting you go?'

'About letting *you* go.'

They reached the perimeter in silence but she didn't stop. Jack spotted a lone figure in the distance.

'Peter is waiting for us,' he said.

'You're both here?' There was anger in her question. 'You don't think I can look after myself?'

'We were so worried. When we heard that the army was coming in, we knew you were in trouble. What happened?'

She threw a sideways glance at him but shook her head. 'Not now.'

Peter saw them approach and hurried over, a broad grin on his dirt-streaked face. He grabbed Xia and gave her a bear hug. 'I was so worried,' he said. 'I thought you were a goner.'

'You two look like you've been through the wars.'

'We have been,' said Jack.

By common but unspoken consent, they put more distance between themselves and Tiananmen Square.

'It's been rough on the streets,' explained Peter. 'How was it at the square? We feared the worst.'

'I didn't see any violence,' she said. 'Except when one or two students tried to fight. It was futile. We were outnumbered. They were beaten. But I didn't see any deaths.'

They had retreated into a dark doorway to catch a breath. The street was empty in both directions. In the distance, a burned-out bus was still smouldering. Above, the sky was as bright and clear – without the hint of a cloud – as Jack had ever seen it over Beijing. Maybe the factories had been shut to keep people off the streets. The thoroughfares were empty of traffic; the population of Beijing was in hiding.

'The rest of the city is burning,' said Peter. 'I assumed that Tiananmen was the focal point.'

'They rounded up the leaders and anyone who offered them resistance; the rest dispersed. The army let them go.'

'And they let you go too?' Peter's grimy face was wreathed in smiles.

Xia grinned back, pushed a strand of hair behind her ear. 'Jack was very persuasive.'

Sitting on a bench thirty years later, waiting in the cold, Jack heard the same voice call out to him again.

'Jack, is that you?'

It was as if all the time that had elapsed since he'd last seen Xia, those three long decades, disappeared in a twinkling and they were once more two young people falling in love during a revolution.

It had begun innocuously enough, as these things usually did. A small group of monks outside the Ramoche monastery in Lhasa banged gongs and chanted in protest at the Chinese presence in Tibet. The local Chinese police chief, originally from a small village in Szechuan, was eager to curry favour with his Party bosses far away. He spotted the first opportunity to be noticed in a lifetime of mediocrity and cracked down hard. The beatings were public and energetic.

One of the monks, a teenager with a baby face and cherubic round cheeks, set himself alight. It took him quite a few minutes to die, orange flames overwhelming orange robes, the crowds keening with despair. A few rushed to help him; others held back, knowing it was too late. The police chief's face was rutted with disgust. These Tibetans could never resist a theatrical display. He let the spectacle continue – it might be beneficial, he reasoned, for the other monks to see that this was not an end to be sought, whatever the temptation to martyrdom.

He misjudged the mood. The monk's sacrifice was widely discussed. The violence was quick to spread. Ordinary Tibetans sensed a chance to strike a blow. Han Chinese – moved into Tibet ostensibly to bring economic nous to the backward country but in reality to dilute the indigenous bloodlines of Tibet and reduce the local people's economic independence – were attacked. Small Chinese businesses were razed to the ground by roving gangs of Tibetan youths. Cars were burned. Their metal funeral pyres dotted hilly tracks at regular intervals. Individuals from China were set upon and beaten, sometimes to death. Chinese immigrants found themselves barricaded indoors and running out of food and water. Monks, emboldened by the support of the people, led protest marches down the streets. Many Tibetans, and not a few Chinese, believed the riots were orchestrated by the Dalai Lama and had his blessing. The Chinese media quoted the Chinese Premier as saying, 'This incident was organized, premeditated, masterminded and incited by the Dalai clique.' The Tibetan people redoubled their efforts.

Later, when EMPEROR was investigating events, he discovered that two weeks into the Tibetan uprising, his son became involved. He himself had been busy dealing with the diplomatic fallout from the downed American fighter jet on Hainan Island. It never crossed his mind that Yongkang could be in any real danger. He was an intelligent, well-armed young man – more than a match for reactionary thugs. The Chinese being killed by rioting Tibetans were shopkeepers and taxi drivers. He did not fear for his son. He hoped that Yongkang would have a chance to distinguish himself in the uprising. After all, the strongest metal was tempered by the hottest flames.

The Party decided there was propaganda value in airing the riots on Chinese television and so the screens in Beijing and the rest of the country were filled with pictures of burning shops, houses and cars. The watching public were assured in solemn voices that these belonged to innocent Chinese. Their ungrateful Tibetan hosts, provoked by that master criminal the Dalai Lama, who called himself a man of God, had turned on them. EMPEROR called Yongkang then – to warn him to be careful, not to take any unnecessary risks. The boy was not worried, proudly telling his father that he had put down a riot with tear gas and cattle prods without a single casualty on his side.

Reassured but not yet confident, EMPEROR called General Zhang to ensure the situation was under control.

'Of course,' said the other man with a chuckle. 'We could snuff it out in an instant.'

'Why don't you? My son tells me the whole city is in flames.'

'It is good that the Chinese people see what we have to deal with in Tibet. And it gives us an excuse to marginalize their puppet leader, the Dalai Lama. We will let it run on for a few more days.'

'I hope you know what you're doing,' he said. 'Remember that it only takes a match to start a forest fire.'

He sensed the other man's irritation as he resorted to aphorisms.

General Zhang rallied. 'In fact, I should thank you. You are the reason that Tibet has turned into such a valuable propaganda exercise.'

'Why is that?' asked EMPEROR.

'The foreign journalists would normally be reporting on the story in Tibet.'

'But they are not doing so?'

'No, the media is preoccupied with your downed American plane on Hainan Island. For once we have a free hand in Tibet and I intend to use it to teach those backward hill dwellers a lesson.'

'Always a pleasure to be of service to the People's Liberation Army,' said EMPEROR, not caring whether the sarcasm was audible to Zhang across the crackling line.

And then the attacks on the Tibetan police stations began.

FOURTEEN

For a man of EMPEROR's experience, it wasn't hard to imagine what had happened next – to picture in his mind's eye the fate of his son. The vivid mental pictures were later confirmed as accurate by his own investigations and formed the substance of his nightmares.

Yongkang was sitting at his desk in the small wooden police building in Lhasa, nursing a bad cold. The station was almost deserted – there were just two of them on duty – because the rest of the squad had been sent to break up a disturbance in another part of town. Yongkang had stayed back. And to think they said a cold wouldn't kill you.

The prison cells at the back were filled to the brim with unruly monks, their saffron robes stained and dirty, some bearing the signs of a hasty beating. The route leading up to the station was narrow and steep with a sharp bend a few hundred yards away from the summit and the station. The lower reaches of the route were out of sight. When he visited the site after his son's death, EMPEROR shook his head at the foolishness of the location. As he turned to look down the steep road, disappearing around a bend, he imagined his son doing the same thing.

Yongkang would have heard the mob before he saw them. The chants, the singing, the shouting. He would not have been worried at first. Those were common sounds in those days. It did not mean that danger was imminent or targeted. However, his father guessed, as a good policeman, he would have decided to investigate.

Yongkang sent his sergeant down the road – warned him to be careful – just to peek around the bend, get a sense of the size and mood of the crowd.

His subordinate came back a few minutes later as a prisoner at the front of the mob. At first, Yongkang held his fire. In retrospect, this was a mistake. A hail of bullets might have been just enough to turn them back. But Yongkang hadn't wanted to risk the life of his man.

'Release my man or we will open fire,' he shouted.

The leader, the man at the front of the mob, said, 'You are alone. We know your men have left – we watched them go.'

'Do you think we are so foolish as to leave a station with inadequate protection?' demanded Yongkang, bluffing because he had no choice.

'Yes, I do.'

'If you release my man and back away, I will see that you are treated leniently.'

'I've got a better idea. Why don't you release the monks?'

'They have been arrested for crimes against the state – I will not let them go.'

'Surrender now or we will roast you like a goat on a spit in the flames of your police station.'

The mob edged forward. The torches were held higher. Yongkang could feel the blood lust radiating from the crowd like sound waves, as if it were a tangible thing.

'Let my sergeant go!' he shouted.

The leader, with a deliberation that was at odds with the rage in his voice, held a lit torch against the prisoner's cheek. In a second, hair oil turned the policeman into a human candle. The sergeant screamed like a pig at the slaughterhouse.

Yongkang howled his rage and charged out of the station. He fired and fired again. His pistol had six bullets. He used four, firing wildly at the crowd. He saw men go down. With the fifth, he shot his colleague through the head – saving him a few last seconds of agony. He looked at the leader, still unmarked. He held the gun to his own head. He would not give them the pleasure of torturing him, of making him watch while they defiled his station and released the prisoners.

'The coward's way out?' laughed the leader, ruddy cheeks red with triumph.

Yongkang cocked his weapon, turned it away from his temple and shot the other man between the eyes.

Then he was overwhelmed by the mob.

*   *   *

'Where is she?'

Jack whirled around and for a moment was transported back in time, felt his heart do a triple somersault. And then he noticed the fine lines on her face and the wisps of grey escaping above her ears. Xia. Grown older, still beautiful – and not his love any more.

'Where is she? Where is Fei Yen?'

This time he noticed the bloodshot eyes. She was worried sick.

'I don't know. She was snatched. Outside the Starbucks near the university. A group of men in a black van. Professional.'

'Why didn't you stop them?' She grabbed the front of his shirt and pounded on his chest with bunched fists. 'Why did you let that happen?'

He gripped her shoulders, held her at arm's length until she calmed down. 'I was on my way to see her. I wasn't close enough. I tried.' He paused, the bitter taste of failure in his mouth.

'I thought you were a *soldier.*'

She still knew how to hurt him. Had she kept tabs on him all these years or only after she decided to tell him about Fei Yen? She had always been thorough, with an attention to detail. He wouldn't put it past her to have kept an eye on him for three decades. Just in case.

'Did you get any plates? Any description we can use? I have contacts in the police and PLA.'

'I bet you do,' was Jack's response, out of his mouth before he was able to prevent himself ratcheting up the antagonism.

'What is that supposed to mean?'

Jack was angry. Angry that Xia thought he'd stood by while someone snatched their daughter. Angry about what had happened all those years ago. Xia always took charge, determined the conversation, determined the direction, determined everything. Not any more. He wasn't going to play the game by her rules any more. He looked up at the sky; a storm was on the horizon, black clouds an over-the-top metaphor for the future. Jack took a deep breath and put the past away, back where it belonged. He needed to concentrate on the present-day mission. Recover Fei Yen. For that he needed Xia.

'Who were they?' he demanded. 'Those men – who were they?'

'I don't know.'

The years rolled away. Once again, he knew she was lying to him.

'You know something. What is it?'

Xia hesitated and then nodded, just once. Economical with everything, including movement. She looked around as if fearful of prying eyes and then said, 'Let us walk.'

He fell into step beside her, noticing that she was as slim as she'd always been, but dressed much more expensively than he remembered in a blue brocade silk *cheongsam* that ended just below the knee. She was distraught but putting on a brave face. For now. While there was still hope.

'I received a call,' said Xia.

'And?'

'They said they had Fei Yen.'

'Who did?'

'The voice was muffled, disguised. There was no way to tell. The man spoke Mandarin. He was not a common thug anyway.'

'Were you quite sure it was legit? It wasn't a hoax?'

'They put her on the line. She said she was all right . . . and then she screamed.'

Xia grew pale at the memory of her daughter's fear and pain until her skin looked like rice paper, her eyes just black ink calligraphy. 'The man said . . . that they'd broken her finger. To get my attention. Then he said there were nine more fingers to go. He would be happy to break them all, one at a time, if I did not cooperate.'

Jack felt sick to the stomach. He knew the type. Had met them in Lebanon and Iraq and Afghanistan. Men who enjoyed inflicting pain. 'What did they want – a ransom?' he asked.

She stopped so suddenly that he was two steps ahead before he realized he was on his own. He turned around and faced her, trying not to be distracted by memories. Trying to stay in the present. The first drop of rain fell against his cheek and doubled for a tear.

She bit her lip. A habit from long ago. 'No, they didn't want money.'

'What do you mean? What did they want?' He guessed her answer before she opened her mouth to speak.

'They want you.'

Dominic Corke was alone except for a Chinese guide from the embassy. No back-up, no nothing. Not exactly appropriate behaviour for the head of the CIA, but what choice did he have? If he set out with an entourage he would be followed, his destination would become known and EMPEROR might be endangered. From his presence at the economic summit and his proximity to Juntao, it seemed to Corke that EMPEROR was still a valuable asset and all precautions for his safety were merited.

He made his way down the narrow lane of the *hutong*. Corke was on Jack Ford's trail, following up the Beijing bureau chief's lead on this man who called himself Confucius; this friend of Peter Kennedy's who in turn had been a friend of Jack's. Two degrees of separation. What was it they said – everyone on the planet had a maximum six degrees of separation from the Queen? He didn't know if it was true but on the other hand, he wasn't interested in the Queen. Only Jack Ford. Ex-spy. Ex-soldier. Who, for reasons that were about as clear as mud, had absconded from a crime scene with the most secret of documents.

Corke had read the file on Confucius. A man of mystery. Well connected through his father, who had been one of Mao's confidants, he was eventually sent to a re-education camp when his father was purged for having an opinion of his own. Unlike many of the others who had been sent to the villages, Confucius turned deprivation into a philosophical lifestyle and remained there long after it was safe to come back, turning down offers of rehabilitation and reintegration. He became an artist and developed a reputation for being an independent thinker who wrote a thoughtful blog which was sometimes blocked but had never been closed down. Confucius generally flew below the radar and had not got himself into significant trouble with the authorities.

Dominic Corke reached the *hutong* in question and his guide pointed at a narrow entrance flanked by grey stone lions. He nodded, indicated palm up that he wanted the guy to wait. The CIA director took a deep breath, ducked his head so as not to hit it on the painted stone archway and walked in. The place was deserted. There were a few cups of tea on the wooden tables. He felt one and it was cold. He walked to the big doors at the back of the space and knocked. When there was no answer, he thumped on it with a closed fist. The doors were heavy and the sound muffled.

Corke looked at the door, paused to consider what he was about to do and whether it was appropriate, and then picked the lock. There was no difficulty doing so – his money clip, straightened out, was sufficient to the task. The interior was gloomy and sparsely furnished; he smelt rusty iron and knew it was blood. He took a torch out of his pocket and shone it around the room. He spotted a streak of dark red against the wall, pooling on the floor. He knelt down and reluctantly – he'd been behind a desk for many years – tested the blood with a fingertip. Coagulated. He used the torch again, following the arc of light with his eyes. Nothing else to see – the place felt deserted and it was as silent as a tomb. He looked at the blood again. Someone had been hurt here. Maybe someone had died here. Whoever it was, they'd moved or been moved.

Confucius?

Corke drew back the curtain that separated the living room from the rest of the space and drew a quick, shocked breath. The place had been trashed. Expensive computer equipment lay in smithereens on the floor. Shards of glass from monitors reflected the light of his torch against the uneven, sloping ceiling and the walls. The CIA man concentrated on what he was seeing. There was method in the madness, he decided. This was not the act of a few men with cudgels and a grudge. Every single piece of machinery had been systematically destroyed. His best guess was that the vandals had been looking for something – no way of knowing whether they found it. He poked through the rubble with a shoe. No disks, no thumb drives, no floppies. The storage devices had been taken. Come to think of it, not a single piece of paper remained – except for some old newspapers. Nothing that could have been the memo, certainly. Maybe Confucius had destroyed the place to hide his tracks.

Of Confucius himself, there was no sign.

Corke reached for his mobile and then changed his mind. At some point, the local cops would turn up. If they found the CIA going over the place with a fine-tooth comb, there would be hell to pay. A diplomatic incident. Ruffled feathers. POTUS would get mad. No, he'd have to leave the place as he found it. Corke stepped back into the other room and his eyes were drawn to the bloodstain again. He'd assumed the blood belonged to Confucius. But what if it was Jack Ford's? The CIA director took out a credit card, scraped blood off the floor and then sandwiched the sample between that card and another. He'd send it for DNA testing – find out whether it was Ford's. He walked out of the open door, shut it carefully behind him and went out to find the guide. He made a mental note to call Amex and ask for a replacement credit card.

'Why do they want me? What am I to them?' demanded Jack.

'That's what I want you to tell me! You have put Fei Yen in danger.'

Jack scanned the horizon again. He pondered Xia's words. He had put Fei Yen in danger. Had he? It was hard to understand how and why. On the other hand, she'd been just another academic teaching at a university and dreaming of a big future until he turned up the previous day on a quixotic quest for family.

'What is it you have? What is it you know?'

Xia hadn't changed that much. It was still about leverage. What did he have to trade?

He looked up, met her eyes. 'This is about the past. The ghosts that weren't laid to rest.'

'What are you talking about?' When he didn't respond, she grew even paler until her skin was almost translucent. 'Jack, tell me. What's going on?'

He'd had time to think about it in the taxi. The Chinese might have figured out who he was – maybe from the CCTV footage at the gardens. Even Delta operators, secretive as they were, had their mug shots on file. But the way Jack saw it, even if the authorities had figured out who he was from the incident at the Botanic Gardens in Singapore, they hadn't had time to chase down his work in China decades earlier. They hadn't had time to figure out that he knew Peter and then to track down Peter's friends and acquaintances – and Jack's ex-lovers – and work out that there was a child who could be used as leverage. The men after Jack were good – but not that good. He knew that because he was good, had once been the best, and *he* wasn't that good. Whoever had Fei Yen was playing a longer game; had started earlier. They'd had time to find out about Peter, about Jack's relationship with Xia; time to entice him to China using Fei Yen as bait and then to get to Confucius ahead of him. When that hadn't worked, they'd snatched Fei Yen for leverage.

'Jack? What do you mean? What do they want?'

'*Who* do they want,' he said; a statement, not a question. 'The question is, *who do they want.*'

Her pupils grew big until her brown eyes had turned completely black in the muted stormy light. 'They want you, that's what they said, they want you.'

'They want me to get to someone else,' explained Jack.

'That can't be right,' she said.

'It is right.'

'After all these years . . .?'

'Yes, after all these years. They want the Tank Man. And they want me to give him to them.'

FIFTEEN

Jack could see that Xia remembered that day as clearly as he did. The day that they had come across the Tank Man and the world as he knew it had disintegrated around him. The day after the Tiananmen Square massacre. The fifth of June, 1989.

They were all three crouched in a dank stairwell, arguing in whispers about what to do, where to go, now they had rescued Xia from the clutches of the military in Tiananmen Square. The familiar smells of Beijing, food being cooked and fresh laundry, seeped down to them from the upper floors. Life was going on as normal just a few storeys up. The sun was shining but the air was still as crisp as fresh milk in the early morning. Jack was about to stand up, to step out on to the open road, to walk like a tourist instead of a fugitive, when Peter grabbed his collar and yanked him back.

Peter put a finger to his lips and then cupped an ear. He'd heard something. He wanted Jack to listen too. Jack squatted back into a crouch and listened hard. Sure enough, he could hear the distant rumble of vehicles. But this was not Beijing motorists taking back their streets. From the even rumble and the low growl of the engines – 'Tanks,' he whispered.

Xia was silent. She was annoyed that they'd come to rescue her. Jack privately thought she was being ridiculous. Being the damsel in distress might hurt her feminist sensibilities but the alternative was being in the tender hands of the PLA.

The sound of the tanks drew closer. They were definitely coming down this boulevard. None of the three was able to decide what to do – to try and get away before the army arrived or to stay put and wait for them to pass, assuming it was just a convoy on its way to somewhere else. As was often the case, a failure to make a decision was a decision in itself. They stayed where they were, peering around the corner with morbid curiosity.

The tanks rolled into view. They trundled down the street as if it were a national day parade and not an active military exercise. Jack half expected cheering crowds waving government-issued red flags and chanting patriotic slogans, despite the memory of bloodstained pavements, crushed barricades and the screams of the injured and dying from the previous long night.

The lead tank was almost level with their position. Jack noted that the hatches were firmly locked down. No smiling soldier waved from the cupola. This was not a drill or a parade. This was war.

A man suddenly walked with a firm step on to the street. It was as if he'd materialized out of thin air. Jack only spotted him when he took up a position right in the path of the first tank.

'What the hell is he doing?' whispered Peter.

All three of them had their eyes fixed on the thin Chinese man in the smart white long-sleeved shirt, shopping bags in hand. He had his back to them so they couldn't see his features, guess his age. But he looked quite young to Jack, there was a youthful quality to his stiff-backed slimness.

'Is he mad? They're going to kill him!' Peter's voice was hoarse with soot and shock.

The entire convoy came to a slow halt, just a few feet away from the pedestrian. The first tank (Jack could see the red star glowing on its camouflage) turned slowly as if it intended to manoeuvre around the man.

'He is very lucky that they're not running him over,' whispered Xia.

'Or just blowing him away,' agreed Peter in an undertone.

To their horror, expressed in a collective sharp intake of breath, the man, instead of letting the tanks go around him, quickly skipped in front of the lead tank again.

'Is he insane?' demanded Jack *sotto voce* as the stand-off was repeated a few more times: the tanks tried to go around, the man jumped in the way.

The lead tank came to a halt, the hatch was flung back and an officer poked his head through. He shouted at the man.

'What did he say?' whispered Peter.

'I cannot hear,' answered Xia.

Jack added sarcastically, 'Maybe he's asking for directions.'

The pedestrian and the tank commander had a few brief words. The man listened carefully to what was said but then resumed his position in front of the lead tank. Jack was struck by the fact that he was completely non-threatening in his demeanour. He stood slightly stooped, the natural posture of a tall man. He didn't shout, didn't gesticulate, didn't do anything except stand there, shopping bags in hand, holding up an entire convoy of tanks. Tanks that only a few hours earlier had probably participated in the battle for Beijing. Had the pedestrian been there? Had he seen loved ones die? Was he missing friends and family?

'Why in God's name is he playing chicken with a bunch of tanks?' asked Peter, his eyes half shut as if he feared to watch the denouement. It was like a horror film, thought Jack. One of those where the suspense is building up and the viewer knows it's going to end badly. The only question was how. And when.

'He is going to be killed,' said Xia. 'What is he trying to prove? What can he achieve from this foolishness?'

Jack, more than the others, understood the bravery and beauty of this lonely protest, but he wasn't in a position to explain it. The tank engines roared to life once more. The man ducked in front of the first tank. For whatever reason, this stranger dressed for the office had decided that he'd seen enough, been hurt enough, had those around him damaged enough – he was drawing a line. He was standing his ground in the face of the might of the People's Liberation Army armoured division.

'I'm going to get him,' said Jack, rising to his feet slowly, keeping in the shadows of the doorway.

'Are you mad?' hissed Peter, grabbing his arm to restrain his friend physically.

'You can't save him,' said Xia.

'I can try,' said Jack.

'April twelfth – that's our D-Day,' said Griffin.

'What do you mean?' The President wore his white golf

spats and stared longingly out of the window at the sunshine.
He did not look well. His deep tan seemed to ebb about his
eyes and there was a pale moat around the red-rimmed lids.
His skin was blotchy and his hair like parched grass. It made
his appointment of Harris as vice president all the more
dangerous, thought Griffin with disgust. She was just one
overfed, fast-food loving, unexercised elderly heart away from
the presidency.

The President's term had been won narrowly with a minority
of the popular vote and aggressive voter suppression tactics.
The appointment of Harris as vice president, when the previous
VP collapsed suddenly under the weight of his own morality,
had been hailed by the liberal media as a sign that he was
growing into the presidency, finally. He was becoming the
elder statesman who was prepared to cross party lines in the
country's best interests.

'A way to heal the wounds,' the President had said when
he announced his choice for vice president. 'A house divided
against itself cannot stand,' he'd added. Very convenient.
Shades of Lincoln being dredged up – but it appeared to work.

Director Griffin still thought it was the most dangerous act
of a reckless presidency.

Left-wing commentators pointed out that the Left had their
chosen woman just one heartbeat away from the presidency.
The right-wing commentators had been irate, accusing them
of encouraging an assassination attempt. Finally, the new Veep
herself had been called in to pour oil on troubled waters.
She'd smiled pleasantly and spoken in her cultivated accent.
'There is only one job in the world that I want,' she'd said,
'and that is to be *Vice* President of the United States of
America, serving at the pleasure of the Commander in Chief.'
Harris liked to use military language – to remind people the
President had dodged the draft in Vietnam. 'And don't you
worry about POTUS,' she continued. 'The secret service has
got his back.'

Griffin had almost admired her in that instant. She was a
really fine liar. Not want to be President of the United States?
Griffin knew for a fact that it was the ambition that drove her
every waking moment and kept her up at nights.

Still, her nemesis, not she, was president. And Griffin had POTUS on a very short leash.

'What's the deal on April twelfth?' asked POTUS.

'That's the date the new Secretary General – Juntao – takes over, makes nice with the rest of the world – and China becomes a nation we have to fear.'

'Why is that?'

'Mr President, Chinese citizens kick our butt in pretty much everything, *even* when they're under the heel of their communist masters. Can you imagine what it will be like with a billion of them at liberty to exercise the freedoms we hold so dear?'

'We'd be a Third World country full of immigrants from shithole countries while they'd dominate us in trade and the military?'

'Yes.'

'How do I stop it? More trade sanctions?'

'No, sir – I can assure you that Mr Juntao and his beautiful wife will be discredited. The hardliners in China will soon be back in charge and keep the Chinese under tight control.'

'Discredited? How?'

'They intend to make him look weak. That will destroy him.'

'I have already made China weak with my America First trade policies.'

'Yes, sir – none of this would be possible without your vision.'

The President puffed out his chest and rubbed his small hands together. 'What do we have to do?'

'We need to trigger an incident. It's going to have to be big – but I know you, sir. Big is your style. This isn't the time for complaining about currency manipulation or intellectual property protection.'

'It's going to have to be big? Great.' POTUS was excited about the chance to wield the power of his office.

Griffin wondered yet again how it was possible for a man with so little strategic knowledge to be president. Thank the Almighty that the country had people like himself close to the levers of power. Only a man with an eye for tactics and capable of taking the long view could keep the nation safe from the President's temper tantrums and the Vice President's liberal fantasies.

'There are two flashpoints with China, sir – North Korea and Taiwan.'

The President walked to the window and stared out at the manicured White House lawns. Griffin knew the signs. The most powerful man in the world was afraid; afraid he would be found wanting in a testing hour and finally reveal to the world that he was a blustering fool.

'We need to maintain maximum flexibility, sir. Be nimble,' he continued.

'Good idea.'

Griffin opened a thin folder. 'Here's the authorization, Mr President, so that we can take the necessary steps in real time.'

POTUS walked back and picked up his dark ink pen.

On cue, the door opened and his secretary said, 'They are waiting for you, sir.'

'Do I have to read this? I'm late for golf.'

'No, sir. It is just as we discussed,' explained Griffin. 'Confidential steps to keep China under control.'

'Good, good.' The President of the United States scrawled his name on the executive order and then hurried to the door.

'What will happen now?' he asked, his foot over the threshold into freedom.

'General Zhang will depose Juntao and China will be back in its box for the next three decades at least. Your legacy will be sealed as our greatest president *ever*.'

'Greater than Lincoln?' asked POTUS.

'Definitely, sir. Greater than Lincoln.'

The most powerful man in the world radiated smugness. 'The fake news media will have to write about that!'

'Yes, sir!' His subordinate clutched his carefully created insurance policy in a sweaty grip and watched his boss head out for a round of golf.

Jack was still lost in the past, his anxiety high and his heart racing just as it had done three decades earlier.

'You can't save this foolish Tank Man, Jack.' Xia was adamant.

'At least he'll know that someone saw what he did and gave a damn.' Jack struggled to yank his arm from Peter's grip.

'Listen to me, you can't save him and you may make it worse,' she continued.

'What do you mean?' asked Peter, desperate to stop his friend from embarking on a suicide mission.

'If they know a foreigner has seen this performance, they will *have* to kill him. Otherwise, they will lose face.'

Jack hesitated. There was a thread of truth running through her words. God knows, he thought, I don't want to make the situation worse.

'Jack, this is no time for you to come over all John Wayne. I want to help too. But this isn't our fight.'

Jack heard the hesitation in Peter's voice. He knew it wouldn't be that hard to persuade his friend to throw in his lot with the unknown protester. But did he have the right to do that? Would his desire to do the right thing cost Peter his life too?

Xia's eyes were still glued to the unfolding drama. Now she said suddenly, a catch in her throat, 'It's too late anyway.'

Jack turned back with a sinking heart, knowing what he was going to see, fearing it, but determined to bear witness. It was not what he expected.

Two men ran out from a side street on the opposite side of the avenue. Had they been holed up in some stairwell too? Who were they? He noted that both were Chinese and wearing dark clothes. They grabbed the pedestrian by the shoulders and hustled him towards the pavement.

Towards them.

Jack sensed his two companions stiffen as they saw which way the men were heading. The pedestrian was being marched forward, the expression of surprise on his face indicating that he had not been expecting outside intervention. As they got closer, Jack saw that the men were murmuring to him, urging him along. The tank commander did not seem inclined to interfere. No gun turrets swivelled to follow the men. No one leapt out from the vehicles to prevent the lone protester's escape despite the flagrant provocation he'd shown. It seemed that this Tank Man would live to protest another day.

The men who had intervened in the impasse escorted Tank Man to the side of the street. They waited silently as the tanks began their stately progress down the street again. One of them had a restraining hand on his elbow. From where they were crouched, Jack could see that the Tank Man was shaking like a leaf. Shock. The whole incident had taken no more than a few minutes although it had seemed to Jack, measuring every second in thumping heartbeats and beads of sweat, that it had been much longer than that.

In the semi-darkness of the alcove, he saw the whites of Peter's eyes. He looked worried and Jack realized that the danger was not over, for the Tank Man or for them.

As the tanks rolled out of sight around a bend in the road, there was a harsh guttural yell and the sound of fist making contact with jaw. He peered over the culvert and was in time to see the Tank Man fall to his knees, holding his face where he had been struck.

SIXTEEN

'What did you think you were doing?' demanded one of the two men.

A sense of foreboding filled Jack as, from his vantage point behind a road divider, he absorbed the crew cuts, square jaws and solid boots of the two men in otherwise civilian guise who had hurried the Tank Man away from the confrontation. These men were military. Undercover.

Out of the frying pan into the fire.

'I wanted to stop the tanks,' whispered the man.

He was slapped hard for his answer. 'You wanted to stop the tanks of the People's Liberation Army? Who do you think you are?'

'I am tired of the killing.'

'What are you talking about?'

'Yesterday – I saw them. The soldiers. Tanks shot rounds into the barricades to clear the way. But the people were unarmed. They just wanted to say their piece. To protect the youth at Tiananmen Square.'

'You sympathize with the student criminals who have embarrassed our great country with their childish pranks?'

Tank Man's voice hardened despite the blood that was dripping from his mouth. 'I sympathize with any Chinese who does not think the army has the right to gun down ordinary people in the streets of their own city.'

Jack stole another glance over the barrier. He saw that the Tank Man had a strong jaw, an unlined face and worried eyes behind dark-rimmed plastic spectacles. He couldn't have been much more than twenty-five, although he seemed older in his smart dark trousers and neat white shirt. What was his day job? A clerk manning a desk at one of the ministries? A school teacher? This was Clark Kent, not Superman. And there were no phone booths handy.

'Who are you anyway?' the Tank Man demanded, voice slurring through swollen lips.

'Who are we? We are soldiers of the People's Liberation Army. Show some respect!'

The man's chin fell against his chest as if he knew that his apparently lucky escape had been anything but. But then he dug deep and found new courage. 'Why should I respect you? You've been murdering people all night!'

'We have been fighting a war against the enemies of China,' corrected the second man, who had been silent until then. A short, squat, powerful-looking figure, he had a low aggressive voice to match.

'How did you . . .'

The soldier understood the question. 'The tank commander radioed in for assistance. We were close enough to respond.'

'Why didn't you let the tanks kill me? I expected no less.'

The tone was bitter: that would have been the preferred outcome. And maybe it would have been best, thought Jack, when Tank Man's adrenaline was running high and he'd stalled – at least for a few short moments – the forward march of the PLA. Now he would be just another corpse in a gutter.

'Kill you on a main boulevard with hotels on both sides? What if your little protest was taped? Do you think we want to make a martyr of you? Turn a weedy thing like you into a folk hero? For all we know there are foreign journalists hiding in the vicinity like rats in a sewer. The tank commander was a prudent fellow. He called in for back-up rather than gun you down on a public street.'

'So that you could drag me into this alley and kill me here?'

'Exactly,' said the squat man. He pulled a gun from his belt and thrust it at the temple of the Tank Man.

General Zhang was as pleased as a man could be who knew that there was a memo on the loose that could cost him his position and probably his life. He took comfort from the fact that the document hadn't turned up yet. It meant that this man, Jack Ford, who had killed two of his agents in Singapore and made off with the briefcase, was ignorant of what he had obtained. Otherwise, his options were limitless: do the patriotic thing and hand it over to the Americans, try and make a fast buck selling it to the press. And the final option? Attempt to blackmail him, the great General Zhang. He almost regretted that Jack Ford hadn't tried this last tactic. The general made an unconscious twisting motion with his hands. He'd be delighted to get his hands on the fellow and explain what a mistake it was for him to have crossed paths – and swords – with someone like him.

Zhang rose to his feet slowly, a gargoyle coming to life in some third-rate horror movie. He made his way to the Situation Room. His top generals were there to meet him and they all rose to their feet as he walked in. This was the advantage of being the boss of the PLA. The Secretary General-elect was a civilian without the loyalty of the men under arms in China. That belonged to Zhang. And that advantage was going to cost Juntao the top job. The general wondered whether he would have the fellow killed, an apparent suicide after his forthcoming fall from power. On the other hand, keeping Juntao on a short leash in the capital, as an example to lesser men with big ambitions, might be a good idea. Or maybe he'd send him into exile – house arrest in some village without electricity or plumbing, or a re-education camp to be cleansed of bourgeois ideas as his father had been before him. He'd make sure the wife went too, Zhang decided. On the other hand, she was a beautiful woman. Maybe she would reconsider her loyalties.

His thoughts were interrupted by the Chief of the Navy, Admiral Bo Kuangyi. 'General Zhang, it is a pleasure to meet with you. I understand that you have something important to communicate to us?'

Zhang didn't smile at the other man. In his opinion it was a sign of weakness to show levity or pleasure in front of underlings. 'Yes, Admiral Bo, you are quite right. I have received secret intelligence of a particularly threatening nature.' He paused for effect. 'I need you all, in your respective branches of the military, to work out the best manner of dealing with this existentialist threat to China.'

His words claimed the attention of those present like the icy Siberian winds from the north.

'What is it?' asked Admiral Bo.

'My sources inform me that the Americans plan to supply Taiwan with missile defence technology.'

'What?'

'How is this possible?'

'How dare they?'

The outcry from the men was immediate.

'That is the least of it,' Zhang continued. 'The Americans also plan to place, in secret, a short-range tactical *nuclear* arsenal on Taiwan. An armada carrying the weapons is steaming towards Taiwan even as we speak.'

'This is an affront to our sovereignty.' The Navy chief was apoplectic, hair standing on end and face as red as a *hong bao* packet.

General Zhang latched on to the last statement. 'That is exactly right, Admiral Bo, and do not fear – we will not tolerate it. The Americans will be stopped.'

'But why are they doing this now?' demanded General Wang, head of the PLA's tank division. 'United States ICBMs can reach mainland China already, let alone their nuclear submarine fleet. What is the use of short-range nuclear missiles on Taiwan?'

Zhang eyed him thoughtfully. General Wang was one who would bear watching. Smarter than the rest, he'd been the first to question the premise.

'Go on, Wang – what is your thinking? Why do you doubt their sinister intentions?'

'Well, it is well known that the American president is a fool. But it seems strange that he would be willing to take such provocative action with no tactical or strategic benefit.'

'Why do we care *why* they are doing it?' demanded Admiral Bo. 'All that is important is that we prevent it. Taiwan is part of China. The American imperialists need to understand this and the Chinese navy is ready to teach them the lesson.' Spittle ran down his chin as he spluttered with emphasis. 'What can we do?'

'We will blockade the Taiwan Strait,' said General Zhang.

Admiral Bo clapped his hands to show his approval. 'This will be the Cuban Missile Crisis once again.'

Zhang nodded. Bo's enthusiasm would be enough to ensure

most of these men kept their doubts to themselves and followed orders like good soldiers. But it was time to deal with Wang, who looked pained at the parade ground volume of Admiral Bo.

'Perhaps when you question their motives,' said Zhang, 'you are not taking into account the timing.'

'What do you mean, General?' asked Wang.

'The Americans are shipping the equipment to arrive around April twelfth.'

'The twelfth?' The exclamation was spontaneous from Bo. 'But that is the day of the election of our new Secretary General at the People's Congress!'

'Precisely,' said Zhang. 'What better time to do this than when we are caught up in a transition? No doubt they assume that our attention will be elsewhere and no one will notice this attempt to sneak advanced weapons technology to the Taiwanese.'

'It still seems reckless of the Americans,' muttered Wang. 'Surely the VP or the Secretary of Defence, Rodriguez, would put a stop to such foolishness?'

'It is possible that the operation is being carried out without their knowledge,' said Zhang. 'Their US military is a many-headed hydra, right now.'

'Our secret service found this out?' asked Wang.

'Yes – they have shown great initiative and ability. Without them we would not have this advance warning.'

This was no time to mention that Griffin had called him earlier to tip him off that everything was going according to plan.

'The secret service is to be commended for their access and insight,' murmured Wang.

For one of the younger members of the PLA senior hierarchy, he seemed to have an unusual willingness to speak his mind. It might be necessary, decided Zhang, to remove him from power.

'The Russians were very unhappy when the Americans deployed their weapons system in Poland,' said the army chief, General Huang.

'Yes, but did nothing to prevent it,' complained Admiral Bo.

'The Russian bear is a toothless creature now,' said Zhang. 'The Chinese dragon remains a beast to be feared!'

'So that's why they want you? They want the Tank Man?' Xia asked. 'Do you know where he is?'

Jack, dragged back to the present and their current predicament, shrugged. What did it matter? They had Fei Yen.

'Why do they want him? Now? After all this time?'

'Why do you think? It isn't to give him a bunch of flowers.'

'Will you do it?' Xia's voice was as taut as a wire. Her gaze was focused on him like a laser, searing, intense.

'Will I turn myself over to a bunch of thugs in exchange for my daughter? Is that what you're asking me?'

Jack rubbed his eyes with his thumb and forefinger. They'd tracked him down and taken his daughter to force him to talk. It wasn't a great parenting debut, that was for sure.

'I suppose,' he continued. 'It depends on whether she really *is* my daughter.'

He was making it difficult, and he wasn't even sure why. He'd known how this was going to play out from the moment Fei Yen had been taken. But now he was messing with Xia. Perhaps there was a small part of him that still wanted to hurt her, to pay her back for what she'd done to him all those years ago. A hand went to his neck, just under the collarbone. Felt the ridge of scar tissue. A bullet had grazed him on the way to killing the soldier in the dirt next to him. Not his only wound, not his only brush with death. She'd been the reason he'd taken the road less travelled through the roughest parts of the globe – looking for some righteousness to take the bad taste out of his mouth. Did that make every scar he bore her responsibility?

'Yes, she is your daughter. Do you think I would lie about something like that?'

The short answer to that question was *yes*.

Her eyes were wide, fear-filled. 'We must save Fei Yen.'

He could have said, almost said, *Who's we?* But he didn't. 'What's the plan?'

She didn't pretend to misunderstand him. 'I've been given a number to call before six this evening.'

Jack glanced at his watch. An hour to go. They'd allowed more than enough time for him to make a decision. He doubted they were worried about his readiness for the trade. More likely they'd given Xia time to track him down or vice versa. He couldn't tell Xia that it didn't matter whether Fei Yen was his daughter. She was taken because of him. She was his responsibility now, regardless of blood.

'If we don't call . . . if we don't agree by then, they say they'll kill her.' Her voice cracked like a choirboy hitting puberty mid-chorus. 'They said . . . they said they'd send me a video – that it wouldn't be quick.'

Jack didn't say anything. He considered his options. It didn't take long. He didn't have any.

'Will you do it?' she asked.

'Yup – they want me – they can have me.'

The tension eased slightly in her shoulders but her expression betrayed no surprise. She hadn't expected anything else. He supposed in a way that was a compliment.

'How did they know about Fei Yen? That she was my daughter?'

Xia shook her head – it was almost convincing. 'I've been wondering that the whole time. I never told anyone.'

'Someone knew.'

'Did you tell anyone? After you got my letter?' Typical Xia. Quick to turn defence into offence.

'I told Peter.'

'Why?'

'I asked him to find out what he could – about you, about Fei Yen.'

'You didn't believe me?'

He didn't bother to respond. She knew the history. Absolute trust doesn't just break, it fragments into a thousand pieces.

'Peter told someone, then . . .' she murmured.

'I find that hard to believe. He wasn't the sort to gossip in the mess hall.'

'They found out *some*how – and only the three of us knew.' She shook herself like a dog after a rain shower. 'I guess it doesn't matter – we can ask him later. Right now, the important thing is getting Fei Yen back.'

Should he tell her about Peter? Bottom line – she didn't need to know. Not now. There was only one mission priority.

'Call them,' he snapped. 'Arrange the exchange.'

Bring it on.

'Greater than Lincoln, eh?'

'At your next rally, sir, let's have some signs – "POTUS for RUSHMORE".'

'That's a good idea. I really like that idea.' The faraway gaze suggested to Griffin that the President was either imagining a crowd of MAGA red hat wearers waving the signs or, even more likely, picturing his head on Rushmore.

'Is there space?' demanded POTUS.

'I beg your pardon?'

'Is there space on Rushmore?'

Dear God, the ego of the man, thought Griffin.

'We will find space, even if Teddy Roosevelt has to make way. If it is what the people want.'

'If the people want it,' agreed the President.

'There is one more thing, sir.'

'What is that?'

'For this plan to work, the Chinese need to know what we're doing. So when the ships are within shouting distance of Taiwan, we'll arrange for the information to leak.' Griffin knew that the leak would happen rather earlier than that – since he'd already contacted Zhang – but the President didn't have to know that.

'What happens then?'

'Juntao loses face. General Zhang takes over. The genie is back in the bottle. We all win.'

'That's an excellent plan, Griffin.'

'It is best that we keep it to ourselves, sir. The Vice President and Secretary of Defence don't need to know.'

'You're sure?' POTUS nibbled on a fingernail and then stopped abruptly.

'Quite sure, sir. We don't want it to get crowded on Rushmore, do we?'

SEVENTEEN

'Make sure you ask to speak to her,' said Jack as Xia pressed the 'callback' feature on her phone. 'We need to know that Fei Yen is alive.'

Xia closed her eyes at his words, shutting out the thought that her daughter might be dead. But Jack didn't doubt that she recognized that he was right and would do as he asked. They had to know that she was alive before he walked into the dragon's lair. Xia held him responsible for Fei Yen's kidnapping. He knew that. It was in her eyes. She'd not said anything more because she needed him. But if anything happened to Fei Yen, Xia would probably kill him – with her bare hands. Jack felt responsible too. And, in a way, he was – but not for anything he'd done recently. The decisions of thirty years ago were coming back to haunt them both.

'I have arranged the deal that you requested,' she said into the phone immediately when the call was answered. 'I need to know where to meet to make the exchange. Jack Ford for Fei Yen.'

There was a pause and then she said, 'Yes, he is willing.'

Jack made a face, listening to Xia's end of the conversation. The bad guys were not convinced of his altruism. Xia scribbled the address down in a notebook that she had readied beforehand. Even *in extremis* she was efficient and showed foresight. What an ally she would make, thought Jack. And what an enemy.

'Wait. I need to speak to Fei Yen.'

He knew from her stiffening body that the answer had been in the negative.

'I must know that she's alive and well. Otherwise, there's no deal!'

Xia hit the speaker button on her phone so that he could hear the hurried consultation in low murmurs. The actual words were inaudible but Xia's request had provoked a discussion.

That was good. A flat denial would have left them with no place to go.

Suddenly a high-pitched female voice shouted, 'Mama – is that you?' The voice was cut off abruptly and the scream of pain suggested that Fei Yen was not being treated with kid gloves.

Xia's whitened knuckles betrayed the desperation reflected in her hoarse, half issued threat. 'If you hurt her . . .'

'Now you know she is alive. If you fulfil your part of the bargain she will stay that way, and you will see your daughter again. If you do not, you will only have yourself to blame for the consequences.'

'I will, I will! I promise. Please don't hurt her.'

An easy promise for Xia to make when he was the one who had to keep it.

She rang off and handed the scribbled address to Jack.

He looked down at it. 'Beihai Park?'

'You remember it?'

He nodded. 'The Wall of the Nine Dragons?'

'Yes, that is close to the South Gate which is the rendezvous point.'

'A public space?'

'The South Gate is right next to the Wenjin highway.'

He thought about it for a moment. Tried to picture the lie of the land. He'd been there, but it had been a long time. No highways then but maybe a road. 'Right – an open space so we can't sneak in any reinforcements without being spotted, but a quick exit route on the highway. These guys are professionals.'

'But we still don't know who they are,' she said.

Jack was silent. He thought that he had a pretty good idea who would be waiting for them next to the Wall of the Nine Dragons. There were too many clues – and they all pointed in one direction. No reason to tell Xia, though.

'Well,' he said, forcing a grin. 'Let's get Fei Yen back.'

They set off together towards the main entrance. Easily mistaken perhaps for an ordinary couple on the way home for an early dinner to be in time to put the kids to bed, thought Jack. Could it have been that way? Maybe, once upon a time. It had been his dream.

Xia put out her hand and caught his sleeve. He turned to look at her.

'Will you give him up?'

'What do you mean?'

'When we've made the trade, got Fei Yen back, will you give the Tank Man up?'

A simple question – will you give your life to protect that of another? Not kin. Someone you met just once – a long time ago. A hero.

'Dunno,' he answered, and started to walk again.

But he did. He knew exactly what he was going to do.

'Do we have any covert operations going on, Dominic?'

The Vice President was in a pensive mood. Corke could tell by her use of his first name.

'Of course, ma'am. We always do. Afghanistan, Iraq, Venezuela.'

'I meant any that I don't know about,' she explained. 'Something the President or Griffin or one of them has cooked up and failed to tell me about?'

He almost smiled. She wasn't the first vice president to worry about what might be going on behind her back that would come home to roost – especially if she ever got the top job – and she wouldn't be the last.

'I don't believe so, Madam Vice President. We don't really do that any more – not since Iran–Contra.'

'Reagan really didn't know?'

'He didn't know much of anything by then – except where the gumballs were.'

'Still no news on the mysterious Jack Ford?'

'No, he seems to have gone to ground. I'm not even sure he's alive. I tried to follow up with a reclusive contact of Peter Kennedy's in China – goes by the name Confucius – but reclusive is a good word for him, because I couldn't find him. There might have been foul play. The place had been ransacked and there was blood.'

'Ford's?'

'No. It came up negative for renegade Delta operators on the run with secret memos.'

'Any other leads?'

'A long shot. A woman. The Beijing office is on the hunt.'

'And EMPEROR?'

'He's still alive and does not appear to have lost his proximity to power – I suppose that's good news.'

'You suppose?'

'He shows no sign of making contact, which is strange given the circumstances. If he's been turned or compromised, maybe we should be the ones considering a . . . an attempt to ensure that he does not tell them what he's told us.'

'The United States does not murder people,' she said.

Corke decided this wasn't the moment to bring up the drones scattering bombs like wedding confetti on the tribal regions on the Afghanistan and Pakistan border. He supposed she meant that the United States didn't order the targeted killings of named individuals – except, of course, when they did. Morality was opaque in this office, especially under the aegis of the present occupant.

'It seems unlikely that the Chinese would let him wander around free if they had got wind of his double life,' said Corke. 'So maybe we don't have to consider taking steps yet.'

'Your best guess?'

'He's gone to ground for fear of discovery.'

'Agreed,' she said. 'But that doesn't get us any closer to this mysterious memo.'

'No, it doesn't,' sighed Corke. 'Our best bet – our only bet – seems to be to track down Jack Ford.'

'I have a suspicion that he's the sort of man who is only found when he wants to be.' She drummed glossy but clear-coloured nails on the table. 'Maybe I should just ask him.'

'Ask whom?'

'Secretary General-elect Juntao. I have a call with him later today. Apparently, he plans to make his first state visit to the United States. His protocol people have been in touch and the President told me to handle it. He's busy . . . golfing.'

'The Chinese will go over every detail to ensure that the British Prime Minister didn't get a better guest list or the Russians a tastier dessert,' warned Corke.

'You may be forgetting I was once Secretary of State, Dominic.'

'Yes, ma'am.'

'Should I ask him?'

'What happened to the memo that our spy in Beijing obtained about some top-secret endeavour in China?' Corke's voice was incredulous.

'I was planning to use more subtlety than that,' she said drily. 'Maybe ask him if there was anything important going down that we needed to know about.'

'Even if he knows, I doubt he'd tell.'

'Even if he knows?'

'Well, the factions are well and truly entrenched right now. Hardliners versus liberals. General Zhang versus the Secretary General-elect.'

'You think this might be something going on behind his back?'

'I'd put money on it,' said Corke.

'He's worried that someone is working behind his back and I'm worried someone is working behind ours. We have a lot in common, it seems. But I can't ask?'

'No, Madam Vice President. I don't see any upside but a whole lot of downside.'

'All right.'

'What will you say to him?' asked Corke.

'That he's going to have the grandest state dinner in the history of this or any other White House, of course.'

EIGHTEEN

The Nine-Dragon Wall in Beihai Park is beautiful. The carved dragons, long-scaled, serpentine creatures, cavort in the clouds. Each is picked out in a luminous colour, blue and orange predominant. Despite this, Jack ignored the wall and instead scanned the horizon for Fei Yen's kidnappers. Xia did the same. He focused on the few tourists, still staring at the wall in the fading light. None of them looked likely to be kidnappers. They were either old, overweight, engrossed or absurd. A couple of scruffy teenagers were shaking their heads in time to the music in their headphones. Lost in their own world. About a hundred yards away a man in a suit, trim, short-haired, with a phone to his ear, stood in the shadows. Jack guessed he might be part of the kidnap crew, sent ahead to make sure Jack hadn't brought reinforcements. It was what he would have done if circumstances were reversed. But he would definitely have had more than one lookout. Three, ideally. Jack guessed that the other side would have three too. They hadn't missed a trick yet – except to underestimate his ability to fight his way out of a trap. And they weren't the first to do that.

He had another look around. Wished he had a gun to follow his line of sight. He couldn't see anyone else who might be part of the exercise. Either they weren't there and these guys weren't the top of the line professionals he'd assumed they were – or the back-up was present, and he couldn't spot them. Which meant that they were the best that money could buy or nations could train. Probably the latter. Jack hoped that the meeting would go down peacefully. He had a sudden flashback to the Botanic Gardens in Singapore. He didn't want any trouble. Not when Fei Yen was in the line of fire.

Xia's phone rang. She grabbed at it with trembling hands, almost dropping it in her anxiety. Jack looked around, hard-eyed, for the caller. No one was on the phone, not even the

well-dressed guy in the shadows. There were to be no free
gifts of information, identity, anything. He hadn't expected
anything else.

Xia snapped the phone shut and turned to him. He
thought her eyes looked stricken and he wondered why.
Wasn't she just about to retrieve her daughter and dispense
with the unwanted ex-boyfriend?

'We have to go towards the highway.' She indicated the
direction of the distant humming of traffic.

Jack turned and walked in that direction with a quick easy
stride. She hurried after him.

'They will have her there – that's what they said.'

'OK.'

'That's all you have to say?'

'That's all I have to say.'

They reached the road in under five minutes. Out of the
corner of his eye, Jack noted that the man from the shadows
was sauntering after them, no more than a hundred yards
behind. He'd been right about him. The two youths – long
hair, baggy trousers and headphones – had also peeled off in
their direction. Now he saw them split up and take the flanks,
the stride more purposeful than was warranted for teenagers
with girls and drugs on their minds. It had taken longer than
usual but now he had all three observers in his sights.

There was a layby twenty yards away, and Jack turned in
that direction.

'What are you doing?' asked Xia.

'Well, they need to park, don't they? Unless you think they
can just pull over on the main highway?'

The swerving, tailgating, lane-weaving, honking madness
that was the norm on Chinese roads was evident ahead of
them. Trying to pull over on the main drag was a recipe for
disaster. They reached the layby and gazed down the street at
the oncoming traffic. A taxi driver pulled over, tyres screeching,
and Xia waved him on.

The three men who had shut off their exit routes now closed
to within ten feet. They didn't speak or gesture. Xia took a
step towards them but Jack grasped her arm and held her back.
These were the watchers. They didn't have Fei Yen. If he was

right, one of them would call in a vehicle now and then things would start to get real.

As if he'd read the script, the man in the suit reached for the phone in the inside pocket of his grey suit jacket and tapped out a message. It didn't take long, two minutes by Jack's mental clock. The windowless van must have been parked not far away, waiting for the summons. The van was black and had plates this time but Jack thought it was the same vehicle that had seized Fei Yen in the first place. He memorized the plates even though he knew it was a waste of time. What was it his selectors used to say? Make a note of everything, ignore nothing. One day, it might save your life.

Fei Yen's kidnappers had chosen a good spot for the exchange. The highway was an access and an escape. Traffic whizzed by, the drivers indifferent to any roadside action. The tourists were far away, focused on fifteenth-century walls. Any sounds they made would be drowned out by the squealing of rubber on the road and an orchestra of horns. The headlights of the vehicles were like tracers in the fading light.

A man jumped out of the passenger side of the van with lithe grace. He was tall for a Chinese, topping six feet, and had a pleasant open face. The driver remained in his seat. A quick getaway was still on the cards.

'This is Jack Ford?' he demanded of Xia.

'Hey, I'm standing right here,' said Jack, raising his hands in the air. 'Why don't you ask me?'

Xia ignored the flippancy. 'Yes, this is Jack Ford,' she said. 'He has come as you asked. Where is my daughter? Is she in the van? Let her go!' Her intonation grew steadily more agitated, her calm a cracking façade.

The three men who had followed them now closed in so that they were boxed in.

The leader, the man from the passenger seat of the van, said quickly to his confederates, 'Are they alone?'

'Yes,' was the terse answer. 'We saw no one arrive before or after them.'

'You told us to come alone. We have done as you asked. Now give me my daughter,' begged Xia.

'I'm afraid there has been a change of plan,' said the tall man.

'When I spoke to him earlier Secretary General-elect Juntao specifically requested that we postpone the military exercises in the Taiwan Strait,' explained the Vice President of the United States.

'Why didn't he ask me? I'm the President.' The leader of the free world was red-faced, wondering whether he had been dealt a slight.

'Because you asked me to deal with the Chinese over the proposed state dinner, Mr President,' she replied.

'War games exercises, Madam Vice President. Much too late to cancel. They've been in the works for months,' said Griffin.

Her narrowed eyes suggested that she didn't like what she was hearing from NSA Griffin, but the Vice President had learned over a fifty-year career to keep her powder dry until she understood all the facts. They were in the Oval Office because she had requested a meeting with POTUS and he'd summoned a collection of the top brass. Elderly men in smart uniforms that dripped medals like Walmart Christmas trees dripped baubles. And none of them respected her – because she was a woman, because she was a dove, because she wouldn't have let them play war as often as they liked if it was up to her. She despised the lot of them – with the possible exception of the commander of the United States Central Command, General Patrick Allen, who, tasked with winning an unwinnable war, had backed her Afghan pull-out to the hilt when she was Secretary of State.

VP Harris particularly disliked the head of US Pacific Command, who was speaking now. 'It would be unwise to back out of war games that have been scheduled months, even years, in advance, Madam Vice President.' General Richard Parkinson paused and then delivered the *coup de grâce* in a tone that almost managed to remain neutral. 'It would be viewed as a sign of weakness.'

Right on cue; these guys knew exactly how to manipulate POTUS, she had to give them that. POTUS jumped in. 'We can't look weak,' he said. 'We must make America great again.'

The Vice President took it on the chin although inside she was seething. Once again, these overdressed, overgrown children were accusing her of having a soft underbelly. Griffin tugged on his bow tie and continued, 'The Taiwanese would view it as a lack of will on our part to fulfil our treaty obligations to them.'

He was referring to the US commitment under the Taiwan Relations Act of 1979. 'As you know, we are obliged to provide defensive weapons and to resist any resort to force or other forms of coercion that would jeopardize the security or the social and economic system of the people of Taiwan,' added General Parkinson, as if she was a rookie learning the ropes and not the Vice President of the United States of America and a former successful Secretary of State.

'I am aware of our treaty obligations, General,' she said coldly. 'What I don't understand is how this requires that we conduct naval exercises on their doorstep with their public enemy number one, just as they are having a transition of power to a regime that may be more favourable to us.'

'It is *not* the best course of action to determine our military strategy in advance of a regime change based on an optimistic assessment about their likely engagement strategy,' replied General Parkinson.

The man should have been a lawyer, thought the Vice President. 'Is that a complicated way of saying we shouldn't be counting our chickens about this new leader yet?'

'Yes, ma'am.'

Harris had to admit that Parkinson had a point. She was banking on a new era in China–US relations once the new Secretary General, Juntao, took over. But wasn't even Dominic Corke always warning her of the dark forces at play behind the scenes in China?

'All right, then, tell me more about these *essential* war games so I can explain to Secretary General-elect Juntao.' She didn't look to see whether POTUS approved of her combative tone because she knew that he would not, and that he was too much of a coward to stop her.

'The strategic naval exercise involves two warships – the guided missile destroyers USS *Howard* and USS *Chung-Hoon*.

The intention is to test our coordinated response strategies with Taiwan in the event of a Chinese land and sea attack. If we turn them around, we will look weak,' said Griffin.

'Can't look weak,' said POTUS. 'My base won't like it.'

The man was like a pre-programmed doll, decided the Vice President.

'In the event of such an attack, we're unlikely to have warships just waiting in the vicinity,' pointed out General Allen. 'Doesn't our actual strategy for this eventuality involve the deployment of marines and aircraft from our bases in the Philippines and Japan?'

'Yes, of course,' said Parkinson.

'In other words – what you're trying to say is that this exercise has no bearing on our *actual* defence plans for Taiwan?'

'I wouldn't put it that way, Madam Vice President,' he replied stiffly. 'It is a timely reminder to both old and new leaders of China of the vast array of military might at the disposal of the United States of America.'

'Have we heard from the Chinese, apart from my conversation with Juntao, about these exercises?'

'The usual, Madam Vice President. General Zhang, chief of the general staff of the PLA – their top military leader – issued a statement through their press office strongly condemning US military exercises in the region as "unnecessary and provocative". They sent it to all Western and Chinese media.'

'But no threats of reprisals or escalation – sanctions, suspension of trade cooperation or anything like that?' asked General Allen.

'No, bottom line is that they're making the usual noises as a matter of course. We can't expect them to dust off the welcome mat for these things but they don't seem to be particularly bothered this time round. Knowing General Zhang, that means he's decided to let this one pass under the radar.'

'Patrick?'

It was bad form to go over Pacific Command's head, but she needed advice from someone she could trust.

'I think there is no harm in proceeding,' he said. 'They'll

be too busy rolling out the red carpet and polishing their boots for the new guy to pay much attention. I think our message on the military front should be "business as usual", while we also extend an olive branch politically.'

The President nodded. 'Carry on with your war games. It makes perfect sense to me.'

'I will give the order,' said General Parkinson.

'You do that,' said Vice President Harris, 'but I'll give Secretary General-elect Juntao a call and tell him we don't mean anything by it. If that is all right with you, Mr President?'

The leader of the free world opened his mouth and closed it a few times before being impaled by her steely gaze. 'Yes, you do that. Good idea.'

Xia's face drained of blood. 'What do you mean?'

'Unfortunately, we need this man's cooperation and we cannot be sure of getting it unless we keep the girl.'

'That wasn't the deal,' said Jack.

Truth was, it was no more than he'd expected. They needed him for the information he had. By now they knew he was dangerous and very, very tough. They could torture him but he might not break before he died. And that would be inconvenient when they'd put in so much effort. To persuade him to talk, they needed leverage. What better leverage was there than a man's flesh and blood? They already knew Jack valued the girl – his standing next to that stinking highway was proof enough of that.

'He will do as you ask! He will tell you everything you need to know.' Xia did not hesitate to make promises on his behalf. 'You don't need my daughter. I swear it.'

'We cannot be sure of that.'

Jack noted that Xia was biting her lip with nervous teeth. 'I will cooperate,' he said. 'Let the girl go.'

'Get in the van,' instructed the tall man.

'How do we know that she is alive?' demanded Jack. 'You expect me to come with you without you releasing the girl? Maybe it is because Fei Yen is already dead.'

Xia whimpered, a tiny sound at the back of her throat, and then rallied. 'Yes, I must see my daughter.'

'I do not have to do anything you ask,' said the leader. If it suited him, he could have both Jack and Xia bundled into the van and there was nothing they could do about it. Tall guy gestured at Jack with an angry thumb. 'You are outnumbered. Get in the van.'

'Outnumbered? Four to one? I would have called that even,' said Jack, arms hanging loosely by his side. If the tall guy could only detect the surge of adrenaline coursing through his veins, he wouldn't be so confident.

The tall guy pulled a gun. 'And now? Does this change the odds?'

'You need me alive,' said Jack.

'Then I'll shoot her,' said the man, turning the gun on Xia.

NINETEEN

'The naval exercise proceeds,' said Griffin.

He was speaking to General Zhang on a burn phone. Griffin was pleased to be the bearer of good news. It would show Zhang, if he needed showing, that he was in a position to control events in Washington.

'That is excellent news. I was concerned that your president might pull out in deference to our new leader in the wings. That would not have been helpful.'

'No,' agreed Griffin. 'The VP tried to put a spanner in the works at the request of your new guy but she failed. I saw to that.'

The NSA looked out over the Potomac and smiled to see the gleaming white Congress buildings in the vivid evening light. Spring in Washington really was the most beautiful time of year. 'It made a difference that the press statement you released was fairly low key. The Joint Chiefs of Staff read it to mean that you weren't that worried about our planned naval exercises.'

'Exactly,' said Zhang. 'We have perfected the art of speaking in Chinese whispers.' He guffawed loudly at his own humour. 'What is the schedule for the deployment?'

'As agreed. Two warships are on the way. ETA Taiwan is during the National People's Congress.'

'And you have arranged for the additional components to be on board?'

'The boats are steaming towards Taiwan carrying missile defence system parts and . . . the other things – exactly as agreed.'

'How did you manage that?'

'I have my methods.'

Zhang did not query his assertion. Instead, he said, 'It will be more than sufficient to trigger a sequence of events that someone of Juntao's disposition will be unable to handle.'

'And then you'll put your hand up for the good of China?'

'And then I will volunteer my services to deal with the threat against China's interests.'

'Sounds like a plan,' said Griffin.

'What are you going to do when we issue a press statement saying that we believe that the naval exercise is a cover to land contraband in Taiwan?' asked Zhang.

'Deny it, of course.'

'And your president?'

'He will be even more convincing in his denials, because he will believe them to be true. As far as my government is concerned, this is just a regular military exercise.'

Again, the guffaw. General Zhang was clearly in a much better mood than was usually the case.

'You seem to be very cheerful today,' said Griffin.

'Why shouldn't I be?'

'Not counting chickens before they're hatched?'

'Why should I do such a thing? What have chickens to do with me?'

'Nothing, just a figure of speech.' Note to self, thought Griffin. Leave out the idiomatic English.

'There is one small matter,' added Zhang.

'What is it?'

'The memo that was stolen by the spy EMPEROR has not been recovered – yet. It was taken from an agent of yours in Singapore.'

'And?'

'We are seeking this man – I have heard from our people in Singapore that he was identified from a thumbprint on a handkerchief. One Jack Ford, retired special forces.'

'That's right,' agreed Griffin. 'We think this man Ford is operating as an independent. I don't think anyone knows why he made off with the document. What's in the memo? Should I be worried?'

'Of course not,' said Zhang. 'It merely outlines domestic Politburo business. However, it would be embarrassing for us if it fell into the hands of your CIA.'

'What if Jack Ford brings it in?'

'We might seek your assistance in the matter,' said Zhang.

Griffin felt a cold trickle down his spine. Zhang wasn't the sort to ask for a favour. He believed in the good old quid pro quo – which was why they dealt so well together. 'Let's hope it does not come to that.'

'It won't. I believe we have the matter well in hand. Ford's return to Beijing has given us the upper hand.'

'That is good to know,' Griffin said by way of goodbye.

He stood on the spot, feeling the light breeze against his face. It cleared his mind. General Zhang was a strange ally. But what did they say? My enemy's enemy is my friend. So be it. Griffin turned and headed back to his car with an easy stride. What he was doing would smack of treason to the naive and the ignorant. The truth was that he was the only person in the entire United States government who understood the threat from China and was prepared to meet it head on. He wasn't going to apologize for that.

Xia blanched as the kidnapper turned his weapon on her.

'Go ahead,' said Jack. 'I'm here to save my daughter – not a woman I hadn't seen for thirty years before today.'

The man thought about it for a moment. He clicked his fingers at the two young men Jack had thought were teenage slobs. Xia sobbed with relief as they took steps towards the back door of the van. The captors were level with Jack when one turned suddenly and aimed a blow with the side of his cocked hand to the back of Jack's neck. Jack had been expecting a move although he hadn't been sure which of the kidnappers would initiate it. As the hand chopped down with the speed of a martial arts expert, he ducked and spun. In the same movement, he kicked the guy in the side of the leg, caught the hand, twisted it – the cracking bones were loud above the traffic – and forced the fellow down to his knees. When he was down, Jack let go and aimed a kick to his back that laid him flat on the ground. The fake teenager didn't try and get up. His colleagues didn't try and help him.

'Why don't you just show me my daughter and make this easy for everyone?' asked Jack.

The leader was livid. The white line around his mouth

indicated teeth clamped together. Jack didn't mind. An angry man was less careful, less professional than one who had his temper under control. The boss kicked the man on the ground and barked, 'Show them the girl.'

The younger man got to his feet slowly, nursing his broken hand in the crook of the other arm. He threw a baleful look at Jack that promised revenge. Jack ignored him. Punks who telegraphed their attacks weren't worth his attention. The man walked gingerly, wincing with pain, to the back of the van and flung open the doors with his good hand.

Jack took a step forward and the leader aimed the gun at his knee. 'Stay where you are.' It was convincing. There was nothing to prevent him shooting Jack in the knee. They'd probably prefer him in one piece, not threatening to bleed out while they extricated old secrets like rotten wisdom teeth. But the tall man was just angry enough to throw caution to the winds.

The leader jerked his head at Xia, who immediately hurried to the van. Her shout of delight was met by an answering youthful cry. Without a word of warning, the leader jerked her away by her collar. 'Enough,' he said. 'You have seen.'

'She's in there, Jack. Tied up. But she's alive.'

'Hurt?'

'I don't know.'

'Alone?'

'Yes.'

Xia must have seen it in the assessing look in his eyes. 'Don't do it, Jack.'

She'd guessed that he was mentally calculating the odds of taking the men down. Three against one, if he excluded the one he'd already dropped once.

'We can't risk it. They have guns.'

He'd only seen one gun, but there might well be more.

Four against one if he included the driver. Jack was fairly confident he could do it – take a gun off the first, take down the rest.

'Jack, please don't risk Fei Yen's life.'

Only one problem – if the van driver decided to drive, not fight, he might get away before Jack got to him. And then where would they be? Back to square one – except the enemy would be a whole lot more pissed off.

'I beg you. *Please.*'

He'd heard the same plea from her lips once before. Jack was transported back to the distant day when Xia had used the exact same words.

I beg you. Please.

That time, she'd said the words to stop him intervening to save the Tank Man.

He hadn't heeded her plea then.

Instead, Jack had launched himself at the two men who had the Tank Man in their custody. Vaguely, from behind, he heard Peter shout. He charged at the man with the gun. Even as he closed the short distance, he knew that this man had time to pull the trigger, kill his captive, kill the Tank Man. However, the shock appearance of Jack stayed the hand of the gunman. Instead of executing the Tank Man, he swung the weapon round to point at the charging American. That was all the time Jack needed. He grabbed the gun arm and twisted it behind the man's back. The man yelped in pain even as he tried to pull free. He was strong but Jack was fuelled with rage and a decade younger. His anger at their intended cold-blooded execution gave him strength. He twisted further and the man dropped the gun.

Jack kicked it away and then lashed out with a left to the jaw. He missed, and was rewarded with a fist in the gut that winded him. The muscular fellow packed a powerful punch. Out of the corner of his eye, he saw that Peter was in a clinch with the second man. Although taller and with greater reach than Peter, he wasn't as powerful and Peter had the upper hand. Fortunately he didn't appear to be armed, or at least he wasn't reaching for any weapon.

Jack and the first man were now grappling at close quarters, each desperate to land a blow that might be decisive. Jack ducked a blow from a hammer fist and tripped over the uneven pavement. He went down backwards and immediately the man was kicking him in the ribs with the heavy boots. He felt a rib crack, wondered if it would puncture a lung. Decided it didn't matter. He wasn't going to be allowed a slow death anyway. Not if he lost this fight. With all the strength he could muster, he jack-knifed on to his feet. He clasped his fists together and swung a full circle like someone throwing a discus. It was an Olympian effort. The squat man, not expecting such an unusual strike, took the blow to the side of his head and went down like a ninepin.

Jack rushed the man who was still valiantly fighting Peter. Two against one – the bad guy was down and out in less than thirty seconds. Jack retrieved the gun that he had kicked away and trained it on the would-be killers, both on the ground. When he realized that neither looked as if they'd offer any more fight for quite a while he slipped the gun into his belt.

'Nice work,' said Peter, leaning against the wall and panting like a dog after a run. His left eye was closing rapidly and his face was streaked with blood and sweat.

'Easy,' replied Jack, flinching from the pain in his ribs. He felt the spot gingerly. He'd need to be bound up really tight to prevent any further mishaps. He looked around to check on Xia. She was further down the street. A dog barked in the distance. As he watched her, she had a last look up and down the road as if wary of more convoys of tanks and then turned to come back.

The Tank Man was still on his knees. 'Who are you?' he asked in a whisper, finding his voice. Jack could see he was shaking from fear. He didn't blame the man; he had been a split second from death.

'We were just passing this way,' Jack answered, as he reached out a hand to help the Tank Man up and then doubled over at the pain in his ribs. 'You looked like you could use some help.'

'Why did you do it? Why did you stop the tanks?' asked Peter.

The Tank Man looked at Peter and shrugged. 'I do not know. I saw what they did yesterday on my street. A lot of people were killed. A few were taken away and no one knows where they are, whether they are alive or dead.'

'It was very brave,' said Jack. 'The bravest thing I have ever seen.'

'Those who had courage died yesterday,' the man said. 'And today they expect us to go in to work and pretend nothing happened. I tried. I was on the way to the office. But when I saw the tanks . . . I don't know what happened. I just got angry.'

'Well, it looks like you're going to get away with it,' said Jack. He couldn't prevent a broad smile from spreading across his face and he saw an answering smile on Peter's; there was even a rueful grin from the Tank Man. Nothing good could come out of this crackdown by the authorities but at least Xia was safe and they'd struck a blow for the good guys. Silver linings.

'Thank you very much,' said the Tank Man. 'You have saved my life.'

'Jack, do as they ask, please?'

The moment to attack was gone, lost as the memories came cascading down like a waterfall after heavy rains. Jack had hesitated too long and now the men were too close, too alert. One of them grabbed his arms and quickly used plastic ties to restrain him. They cut into his wrists. Xia watched with wary, troubled eyes but she did not speak or intervene.

The gun was waved in his face. 'Get in the van.'

Jack stood his ground. Now that he was safely handcuffed, his tall captor was braver. He slapped Jack across the cheek with the gun butt. Jack felt his lip split and tasted blood. Xia gave a low moan. He knew she wasn't worried about him. But any indication of brutality or loss of control from these men reinforced her fears for her daughter.

'Get in the van!'

'When will you let my daughter go?' asked Xia.

'Once this tough guy has told us what we need to know.' The tall kidnapper and spokesperson for the group smiled. 'If you do not see the girl again, you will know that it was this man's fault.'

Xia placed a hand on his arm, and Jack recoiled more than when he had been hit. 'Jack, tell them whatever they need to know. Please – I beg you.'

'I will,' he agreed.

Glancing at the leader, he decided that there was no point making them so angry that they decided to take their revenge on Fei Yen. After all, they knew his weak spot all too well. Wasn't that why he was in this position in the first place?

'All right, let's go. I'll get in the van.'

Jack smiled amiably as if he'd been asked out for a picnic on a sunny day. With his hands behind his back he stumbled getting in, but no one made a move to steady him – maybe they were afraid after seeing how he'd laid out the first guy. Maybe they just weren't the helpful kind. He clambered in and smiled at Fei Yen. She was resting uncomfortably, half propped up against the inside of the van. Her hands and feet were bound with the same plastic ties as his but her hands were in front of her body, not behind her. There was dried blood on her forehead and her cheek was bruised.

All things considered, she was not in terrible shape, yet the anger that took hold of Jack was red hot and coldly vicious at the same time.

Fei Yen's eyes widened with shock as she recognized him. 'Jack?'

'Good to see you again, kiddo.'

'I don't understand . . .' Her voice trailed off.

Jack realized she probably didn't even know *why* she was a prisoner. No doubt she assumed that this was a kidnapping for ransom. Perhaps she had been sitting quietly, hoping her mother would get the money together to buy her freedom. A captor pushed him and he fell to his knees but managed to turn over until he was sitting next to Fei Yen.

He grinned at her, almost happy to be with this girl who might be his daughter, regardless of the circumstances.

'Why are you here?' she asked.

'It is a long story, I'm afraid. A very long story indeed.'

The doors were slammed shut and Jack and Fei Yen were plunged into darkness.

The USS *Chung-Hoon* (DDG-93), an *Arleigh Burke*-class Aegis destroyer that was part of the Pacific Fleet, was under the command of Admiral Pritchard, a man who was very pleased to be out to sea again even if his mission was to play war games with Taiwan.

Looking out from the deck he could see the steel-hulled sister ship, the USS *Howard*, also a guided missile destroyer, five hundred yards on his starboard side. With an overall length of about 510 feet, displacement of 9200 tons and weaponry including over ninety missiles, the *Arleigh Burke*-class ships were larger and more heavily armed than most previous ships classified as guided missile cruisers.

The US Navy was designed to intimidate other nations to the point that they did not have to engage. The fact that they were successful meant that most of Pritchard's missions involved wearing his whites, saluting foreign dignitaries and intimidating them with details of the destroyer's fire-power. Modern warfare in a nutshell. But this time was different.

Pritchard looked out over the horizon. It was a remarkably beautiful day. Puffs of white cumulus reached up to the heavens like cotton candy. The sea was calm; only the mildest of swells suggested that they weren't docked. His crew were pleased to be out to sea again. Aside from the USS *Howard*, there was a *Los Angeles*-class submarine along for the ride, although she had submerged shortly after departing Okinawa. It was a reasonably sized task force, big enough to be taken seriously, not big enough to provoke the Chinese unnecessarily. That would probably have taken an aircraft carrier sailing up the Straits of Taiwan.

A small frown creased the brow of the leather-skinned sailor. He'd been a proud member of the United States Navy for a lot of years – and he'd never embarked on a mission as incendiary as this one. He hoped his political masters in Washington knew what the hell they were doing, or there was going to be a serious mess. It wasn't the size of his force, but his cargo – onloaded at the American base in Okinawa, Japan and apparently to be offloaded in Tsoying, Taiwan – which would cause a stir if it became known.

Tactical nukes.

Mounted on short-range ballistic missiles.

Compatible with the launch systems that the Americans had been supplying to Taiwan for years.

Capable of hitting anywhere on the Chinese mainland.

Suddenly, the day didn't seem quite so beautiful. Heavy clouds were gathering on the horizon, blotting out the sun, but they weren't just aspects of nature; they were a warning of what the future might hold.

'Jack, what are you doing here?' Fei Yen's voice was loud in the darkness of the back of the van.

'Long story, kiddo.'

Without the use of his hands, Jack had fallen heavily on his side in the pitch darkness as the van accelerated away. He wasn't hurt but he was winded. He tried to straighten up against the side of the van, pushing with his feet, shuffling backwards until he was seated, bound hands backed against the cold metal of the van.

He concentrated on the journey. They'd set off within seconds of the door closing – the driver hadn't wanted to hang about. Straight line, even speed, no deviations, doing approximately eighty. Slowing down, veering left – he could feel the pull of centrifugal forces – they were coming off the highway about two miles from where they'd been picked up. Now all he needed was a map of Beijing and some light and he could work out where they were. Another stop. Unlikely that they'd reached their destination so quickly. Another left – must have been a red light, he guessed.

'First things first: are you OK?' asked Jack.

'Yes; they haven't really hurt me except for a broken finger.' There was a catch in her throat. 'But they said they would kill me if my mother didn't do as they asked.'

'Nothing to worry about, then. She's been following their instructions to the letter.'

He sniffed cautiously. There were quite a lot of smells competing for his attention. Turpentine, paint and other things which he couldn't identify but which gave him the sense of a builder's yard. He didn't think he'd been seized by a builder who needed an extra pair of hands at a construction site. He suspected it was just more attention to detail, to disguise the men who would murder him once he had talked. Once he had talked and told them what they wanted to know – the where-abouts of the Tank Man.

'She doesn't have much money. Why did they choose her . . . or me?'

'Because of me. They want *me*.' His tone was matter-of-fact.

'I don't understand.'

'Honey' – he tried to keep his voice gentle – 'the less you know the better.'

Jack wasn't happy that neither of them was gagged. Their captors didn't mind if they communicated. Which meant one of two things. That they didn't think either of them had anything important to say to the other, or – and this was the more likely scenario – they didn't expect to leave behind any flapping lips. He swallowed a sigh. He didn't want to worry Fei Yen but right now he had no idea how he was going to get her out of there and to a safe place.

'Why do you say that?'

'Because the more you know, the more of a liability you become.'

'And the more likely they are to kill me.'

She spoke without fear and Jack felt his heart swell. He hadn't known his daughter long but he was willing to bet that she was a chip off the old block. And this could refer to her mother as much as to him, he acknowledged. Twice now he had walked away from Xia. The first time her expression had been undiluted rage. This time she had been stricken. Third time lucky?

'That's right,' he agreed. 'Knowledge is dangerous for you right now.'

His eyes were getting accustomed to the darkness. It was not pitch and he could make out the silhouette of Fei Yen.

'They wanted you?' she asked.

'Yep – I'm a popular guy.'

'And they kidnapped me to get you?'

They were skirting close to deep waters now. 'Yes,' he agreed.

'Why would you give yourself up for me?'

That was the crux of the issue and she'd got it within two minutes. A fine legal mind.

He tried for levity. 'Hey, I'm the sort of guy who rescues kittens from drains. You were a no-brainer!'

'This is a rescue?'

'Eventually. We need to take the long view on tactics,' he said, smiling in the darkness. She was still showing spirit despite her ordeal.

'Seriously, no one gives themselves up for a complete stranger.'

'My – so young and already a cynic.'

Jack was buying time, changing the subject, trying to decide what she needed to know, if anything. A small part of him was desperate to tell her who he was. He wondered how she'd react if he slipped it into the conversation. *Oh, by the way, I'm your father.* He knew that would be a mistake. Too much emotional pressure for the girl to take when he needed her brave, alert and ready to take her chances. She might feel a sense of responsibility for him, or anger, both of which might affect her willingness to follow his commands. Besides, he wasn't likely to make it out of this fix alive and he didn't want to leave the girl with a legacy like that. Let Xia sort it out once Fei Yen was safe and sound.

Two quick rights and another left. Jack wondered why he was bothering to follow the journey of the van on a mental map. Even if he could retrace his footsteps, that would just take him back to that damned park. The van stopped again. More lights? It went over a hump quickly and he winced. His shoulder was bruised. He hoped it wouldn't slow him down. He wasn't that worried. It wouldn't be the first time – although it might be the last time – that adrenaline would have to carry him through. The van was descending at an even slow pace. In a few seconds, it began to take a wide spiral downwards.

'We're almost there,' he said.

'How do you know?'

'I'd guess we're driving down a car park ramp. We're on a slope and the turns are gentle.'

'Wow! You could figure that out from in here?'

He wondered where she'd learned her Americanisms. Her

speech patterns were so different from the stilted careful pronouncements of her mother.

'Just gotta pay attention,' he said.

The van came to a halt. Jack could hear doors opening and then two quick successive slams.

'All right, honey. This is it. Be brave and follow my lead.'

TWENTY

They searched Jack for weapons and relieved him of his wallet but not the memo, folded neatly and slipped into the inner lining of his jacket through a slit near the armpit. Confucius had done this, and Jack was once again forced to wonder about the man's antecedents. He had a knack for espionage.

Jack considered his options – which, he had to admit, seemed limited. He was shackled to a chair which was bolted to the floor. The room was windowless, lit with fluorescent tubes, with a white tiled floor. It reminded him of nothing more than a rather large toilet from which the ceramic utilities had been removed. Of Fei Yen, there was no sign. They had taken her somewhere else despite his protests, which he stopped only when the leader hit him across the mouth with his semi-automatic. Jack ran a tongue over a couple of loose molars. His cheek was swollen, narrowing his left eye, though not enough to impair his vision. He tugged at the bonds that tied his hands behind the chair but there was no way of pulling free. These guys were not amateurs.

The door at the far end, heavy and metal – like the door to a safe – opened smoothly and quietly. Two men came in: the tall guy from the van, still in civilian clothes, and a man dressed in the working uniform of a colonel of the PLA.

'My name is Colonel Guo Feng,' he said, as if this was a friendly occasion. Jack half expected him to whip out a business card.

'I don't care who you are. Let the girl go. Let me go.' Jack contemplated the gun on the other man's hip – if he had a free hand, he might be able to take it. Use one of the men as hostage. Find Fei Yen – get out of there. If he had a free hand . . . *there's the rub.*

'You've given us a lot of trouble,' said Guo Feng.

'You came after me. I was minding my own business. Just another tourist in Beijing.'

'Ah – but you see, we need something from you.'

'You could have just asked me nicely.'

The colonel smiled thinly but his eyes remained as cold as ice. 'Your reputation precedes you, Jack Ford.'

Jack's heart sank. Any sliver of hope that he was just unlucky, and mixed up in a whole load of aggravation through no fault of his own, went out the window. Or would have if the room had had a window.

'But you're right,' said Guo Feng. 'Perhaps that is what we should have done. Very well, I will give you a chance. I will "ask you nicely", as you suggest. If you tell me what I need to know, you and the girl can go.'

The tall guy shifted slightly at this. A man's body sometimes revealed the truth in a nervous twitch while he concentrated on keeping his face a mask. Jack knew that he was not walking out of there. They'd let him see Guo Feng in full uniform – now he knew this was official, not a rogue element or gangsters. The Chinese government was involved and it was impossible to know how far the rot had spread within. Which meant he couldn't be allowed to live. That didn't bother Jack all that much. He hadn't liked his odds from the moment Fei Yen was taken. His role was to improve *her* odds.

'Go on, then. What do you want to know?' As if he didn't know.

'Where is the Tank Man?'

Thirty years earlier, the Tank Man shook hands with Peter and Jack. The two soldiers who had seized him were out cold on the ground. Jack kept a sharp eye on them. He didn't want any seconds.

'You're safe now,' said Peter.

The Tank Man nodded his gratitude.

'I wouldn't speak too soon,' said Xia.

She had come up on them quietly and now they turned to her in surprise. Her words and cold tone were at odds with the good spirits of the three men. Xia trained a gun on the Tank Man. A standard-issue PLA handgun. Where had she got it? It was a duplicate of the one Jack had stuck down his trousers.

'What are you doing?' demanded Jack.

'I am sorry, Jack. I need to take this man with me.'

'Xia! What's going on? Where do you need to take him?' It was Peter with the question this time.

She didn't answer.

'Xia?' Peter hobbled closer, staring at her. She waved him away with the gun but his expression remained puzzled, not worried.

Small clues burst through Jack's mind like mini-fireworks. Xia had been unrestrained while the other students were in cuffs on the military truck. The colonel had released her to him after she'd said something to him in Mandarin that Jack hadn't understood. He remembered her awkwardness when he'd asked her what had happened the previous evening. Her denial of any massacres. Her discomfiture when he'd insisted that he'd seen killings with his own eyes. Her reluctance to intervene to save the Tank Man. Jack pushed the thoughts away; what he feared was unthinkable.

Except that she had a PLA-issue gun pointing at the Tank Man. Student rebels didn't tend to be armed with anything except their words, and maybe a cudgel. Jack looked at Peter, whose mouth hung open.

'This isn't the time for jokes, Xia,' Peter said. 'We need to get this guy to safety.'

'Unfortunately, I cannot let him leave.'

'What are you saying?'

'His act of bravado is likely to turn him into a focal point for the protesters,' she replied. 'Especially if anyone has made a recording of it. This street has many hotels where the foreign journalists stay.'

'But that's a good thing, right?' Peter's confusion was apparent on his face. 'He is the hero the Chinese people need.'

'I must turn him over to the authorities.'

'Xia, that's a death warrant! You saw what they were going to do? They were prepared to kill him in cold blood on a street corner.' Peter turned to Jack. 'What's going on? Talk to her, Jack!'

'Haven't you figured it out, Peter?'

The other man shook his head.

'Xia is not the brave student leader and rebel . . . she's a government spy.'

'I have no idea what you're talking about,' insisted Jack. 'Who is the Tank Man?'

At a slight nod from Colonel Guo Feng, the tall guy took a step forward and stamped hard on Jack's left foot with his heavy boot. The pain exploded in his head like an IED.

'Hey,' he complained, trying to keep his tone level. 'I thought we were going to be nice.'

'Where is the Tank Man?'

'I have no idea what you're talking about.'

The other foot this time. Jack knew it was coming, but the cuffs around his ankles prevented him from dodging it. At this rate, he'd struggle to walk out of there as and when he figured out an escape plan.

'Where is the Tank Man?'

'You might as well ask me where Batman or Iron Man is,' said Jack. 'I don't know that either.'

The tall guy loosened a tooth on the other side of Jack's mouth with a blow that made his ears ring. He would have matching black eyes now. Jack blinked as his eyes watered with the pain of the blow. Guo Feng stood with his arms folded, resting easily on his heels. The floor was speckled, Jackson Pollock-style, with Jack's blood. His attempts to rile the man with a smart mouth had failed. The colonel was a professional.

'We know you are the American agent who assisted the Tank Man to escape,' he said. 'Now we need him back.'

'Why would you think something like that?' he asked. 'I was in Tiananmen Square. I've seen the video of that man every year on the anniversary of the massacre. But why in the world would I know anything about his whereabouts? He must be dead by now.'

'We *know* you know.'

'How?' Jack asked.

'Xia,' he said. 'Xia, your old lover, who led us to you using your daughter as bait.'

*   *   *

'Xia here is not the brave student leader we thought she was – she's a government spy.' There, he had said it. Jack waited for her to deny it, to find some plausible explanation that would relieve him of the enormous burden of knowledge that threatened to bring him to his knees.

'Xia? Is that true?' Peter's voice cracked on the question.

She shrugged, gun still pointed at the Tank Man. 'This protest movement is a threat to the stability of China. I did what I had to do. I have always done my best for my country. I am a patriot.'

Peter stepped across until he was between the Tank Man and Xia, his hands in the air, but his gaze was firm despite the painful limp. 'You can't mean it, Xia!'

He'd given Jack time and a split second outside her line of sight to pull his gun and turn it on her, and he did not waste the opportunity. He held the gun steady although his heart was racing. Now she had Peter and the Tank Man in her sights. And he had her. All four were as still as marble statues.

'You did your best for your country?' shouted Jack. 'That's between you and your conscience. But just so you know, this guy's not going anywhere.'

She lowered her gun slightly. 'Jack, please don't make this difficult. I have no choice in this matter.'

'I'm making it difficult? You're a traitor!'

'And you're a CIA spy. Both of you.'

Jack felt as if he'd been kicked in the stomach by a mule.

'You've used me and spied on me and reported back to your masters. I did the same. What is the difference between us?' she continued.

'It isn't like that, Xia. I've been on your side – what I thought was your side – from the very beginning.'

'How did you find out?' asked Peter.

'The Chinese government had you followed back to the embassy. You were not very careful.'

It was a fair accusation. They had taken sufficient precautions to fool a student leader, not someone with the machinery of government behind her.

'The students trusted you!' Jack was desperate to find a way to get through to her but she was as hard as granite.

'I trusted *you*,' she said.

Jack felt a fist grip his heart. His limbs grew cold as his vision blurred. He tried to breathe regularly, to focus on a single spot on the far wall, to fight the panic attack that threatened to overwhelm him. He was drowning in memories. Once Guo Feng sensed his weakness, it would be over.

'I don't believe you,' he said.

'You trust this woman, Xia? Has she not already betrayed you before? Are you such a fool?'

Jack closed his eyes. It was as if he was back on Chang'an Avenue, pointing a gun at Xia, begging her to reconsider, to betray her masters instead of the man who loved her. To betray her masters instead of the Tank Man, who deserved their help.

'She would not betray her daughter,' he whispered, hoping, praying, believing it was true. *Chaos is come again.*

His words were slurring, he couldn't prevent it. Too much damage to his mouth. Or too much adrenaline pumping through his blood.

'Well, I might not have been entirely honest with her about that,' said Guo Feng. 'You know how it is. Best laid plans and all that.'

The full realization of the mess he was in had the unexpected effect of calming Jack down. He felt his pulse steady and he slowed his breathing. He tried to piece together the puzzle methodically. Xia had told this man that Jack knew where the Tank Man was; she had then used her daughter, Fei Yen, to entice him to China. It had worked like a charm. Once a gullible fool, always a gullible fool. Xia must have banked on that. When they came after him and failed to seize him at Confucius's tiny residence, they had decided to use Fei Yen instead, without Xia's knowledge or consent – although she must have guessed soon enough that her daughter had been seized to bait a trap.

'Is she mine?' he asked. 'Is Fei Yen my daughter?'

*   *   *

'I will kill you if I have to – it is my duty – but you will not be able to do the same.'

Thirty years ago, Xia had the same indomitable will. And was sure that she could make Jack Ford do her bidding; that she was the stronger of the two.

'You underestimate me, Xia.' Jack steadied his gun hand until the weapon was pointing directly at her heart.

'You said you loved me.' Her voice cracked. 'And although I guess it is hard to believe me in the circumstances, I care for you too. Are you going to let this stranger come between us?'

'The person I loved . . . doesn't exist,' said Jack, despair seeping through the hesitation in his voice. He didn't need Xia – this Xia with the hard eyes and firm hands – to sense weakness, but he could not hide it. 'She was just a creature of my imagination.'

'You know that's not true. I want what is best for China – that is all.'

'Then put down the gun. Let him go.'

'No.'

'Xia, I beg you. Please.'

'Is Fei Yen your daughter? I suppose so. Would you abandon her if she was not? That is not what your record says. You too want to be a hero like this Tank Man.'

Jack was gutted that they had his service record. Information was power in these situations. But he did his best to hide his chagrin from Colonel Guo Feng and his sidekick.

'Why do you want him anyway?' asked Jack. 'Tying up loose ends? A bit late, surely.'

'Actually, the opposite. We want to make this man a hero.'

'He's already a hero,' snapped Jack. 'He was from the moment he stood in front of your tanks.'

Tall guy stepped forward but Guo Feng put up a hand. Jack was relieved and despised himself for it. He didn't want to be suckered by the good cop.

'Well, you will be pleased to know that I – and, more importantly, the Secretary General-elect Juntao – feel the same way. We wish to rehabilitate this man – present him to the citizens of China as a hero and a patriot.'

Jack eyed him thoughtfully. 'And why would you do that?'

'It's complicated. But the new guy is a reformist. Wants to make China more democratic, make power more accountable. He needs a symbol – someone like the Tank Man – to demonstrate his intentions to the people, persuade them to support him.'

'Yep – I can tell you're the good guys,' said Jack. *Et tu, Brute?*

Guo Feng shrugged. 'Would you have believed us if we had come to you in good faith and told you we wanted to rehabilitate this man in the eyes of the public?'

Probably not. 'Maybe,' said Jack. 'I certainly don't believe you now.'

'Where is the Tank Man?' asked Guo Feng.

'OK, look – simple answer, I don't know. I helped him get away – yes. But after that he was on his own.'

Guo Feng sighed. 'I could pull out your fingernails, toenails and tongue,' he said.

'I'd struggle to tell you anything then, wouldn't I?'

'Unfortunately, I am working to a tight timetable. I could, of course, break you – but I am in a hurry. Thus, you leave me no choice.'

He jerked his head at the tall guy, who hurried from the room. Jack felt a cold hand close around his heart when he reappeared a few minutes later with Fei Yen.

The convoy was making good progress, steaming towards the Gulf of Taiwan, careful to stay out of the territorial waters of the various countries of South-East Asia. Or, at least, the two destroyers were careful. The submarine – largely undetectable to the inadequately equipped nations in the region – went where it pleased. Admiral Pritchard felt a shudder run down his spine – sleek death lurking under the waters. He was a ship's captain, had never aspired to be a submarine commander. He'd never told anyone, but he suffered from terrible claustrophobia. His idea of hell was to command a nuclear submarine.

Pritchard raised his binoculars to his eyes. He could see the faint grey of land in the distance. The Spratly Islands. Most of the countries in the region claimed sovereignty, hoping to get their hands on the oil reserves under the waves. It was absurd that a few rocks in the middle of the ocean gave a nation hundreds, even thousands of square miles, of extra territory. It skewed the incentives. The admiral was giving them a wide berth. He wasn't looking for confrontation – he had enough already. Delivering tactical nukes to the Taiwanese seemed to him to be the height of recklessness. But he was a navy man, following orders. And that was that.

Pritchard stared out across the water. The slate grey sky matched the angry seas. The weather was turning. The next few hours would be rough – even on a ship as big as his. He looked over to the starboard side and spotted his sister ship. She was already riding the bigger waves like a rodeo star. Pritchard licked his lips and tasted salt and rain. The taste of tears. Not long to go now.

TWENTY-ONE

Jack was proud of her. Fei Yen's pupils were dark pools of fear but her chin was still up. She gasped when she saw him – he must look in worse shape than he'd realized – and tried to escape the grip of the tall guy to rush over to him. She was rudely dragged back and forced into another chair that a flunkey brought into the cell. About the only thing that could be said about her chair was that it wasn't shackled to the floor. This was apparently a 'one victim at a time' torture chamber.

'I'm all right, Fei Yen,' he said quickly, trying to head off any further acts of rebellion. He tried a small smile, but judging by her shocked face it didn't look quite right.

'Enough conversation,' snarled Guo Feng. 'Now talk. Where is the Tank Man?'

'I can't do it. I can't betray him.'

'She is your daughter!'

There was a gasp from Fei Yen. If it was possible, her eyes grew even bigger.

'Is that true?' she breathed.

She didn't sound enthused by the proposition. He couldn't blame her. Things weren't looking so good for the family right now.

'It is a good story,' said Jack.

He was rewarded with a slap. The ring on Guo Feng's finger – some sort of heavy signet – cut his cheek and he felt the sting followed by the warm blood welling up.

'Where is the Tank Man?' demanded the colonel.

'I can't tell you.'

This time it was Fei Yen who was hit. The tall guy used a closed fist and her head snapped back. Tears formed and trickled down her cheeks but she didn't say anything after the first yelp of pain. Jack comforted himself that he was going to see the man dead before he left the building. *Vengeance is in my heart.*

'Where is the Tank Man?'

'Who is that, Jack?' It was probably too early for her to call him Dad.

'A dissident,' said Guo Feng. 'I want you to understand that your father will not save you to protect a criminal.'

'A brave man,' said Jack. 'He doesn't deserve to fall into your hands.'

'Does your daughter deserve to die?'

Fei Yen whimpered and the tall guy smiled. Jack had seen so many of these sadistic types who were drawn to power, improperly exercised, because it gave them a chance to live out their fantasies about hurting the innocent. He'd killed a lot of them in his time. He was looking forward to adding another notch to his belt.

Colonel Guo Feng nodded at the tall man, who produced a pair of pliers from a cavernous pocket. He walked over to Fei Yen, making sure that he kept Jack's line of sight open. Fei Yen's arms were tied down to the arms of the chair. She tried to yank away her hands. Jack could see the red marks forming around her wrists and elbows. The plastic cuffs were effective. There was definitely no escape that way. Jack was processing information – focusing on movement and reaction, trying to keep the big picture in his mind. But it wasn't working.

Tall Guy grabbed one of her hands. Left hand. Held a finger steady. Reached down with the pliers. Guo Feng watched him, not the girl. Jack remembered the Tank Man – tall, gawky, brave, grateful. He looked at his daughter.

Tall Guy yanked; Fei Yen screamed. Jack strained at his cuffs, not even knowing what he was doing, screaming at them to stop. Tall Guy reached for another finger. Fei Yen was sobbing. Blood was oozing from the index finger, now without a nail.

Guo Feng turned to Jack. 'Would you like to change your mind?'

Jack was crying. Staring at his daughter. Her whole life ahead of her until he had come to China carrying secret memos and looking for a past that should have been left for dead.

The memo. Could he trade that for Fei Yen?

'I have something you might want,' he said, voice hoarse with fear for the girl.

'I know that,' said Guo Feng.

'No – I can't give you the Tank Man – but there is something else.'

'You're trying to buy time, and it is not going to work. Unfortunately for you, the National People's Congress starts soon. We need the Tank Man.'

'A memo,' said Jack.

'Why would I care about a memo?'

'A memo that I recovered from an American agent just before he was killed in Singapore by Chinese agents.'

He'd caught the other man's attention. Jack could tell from the sudden stillness.

'You're obviously the go-to guy for the dirty work,' said Jack. 'You must have heard of the memo.'

Guo Feng didn't deny the accusation. 'Where is it? What's in it?'

'I'll tell you if you let Fei Yen go.' He didn't bother to bargain for his own life. That wasn't going to happen. He knew too much.

'Not going to happen.' Could this guy read his mind?

'The girl is delivered to her mother, I tell you where the memo is.'

'How many fingernails will your daughter have to lose before you tell me everything I need to know?'

'You're going to kill us anyway.' The truth hung in the air between them. Jack could feel the document against his side, inside his jacket lining. He hoped Guo Feng didn't think to search him again for something other than weapons.

Jack turned to Fei Yen. 'Honey, listen to me. I know you don't understand what I'm doing. The truth is – we're not going to make it out of here if I tell them what they want to know.' His voice broke. 'I'm so sorry.'

'Touching,' said Colonel Guo Feng. But Jack could see the worried crease between his eyes. A tiny part of him was afraid that Jack wouldn't talk. Or wouldn't talk on time.

'We mean the Tank Man no harm.'

Jack spat out a tooth. 'I'm convinced.'

As panic constricted his throat, Jack was drawn back to the only other time in his life he had been so afraid. It seemed that he only felt these extremes of terror when he feared for the wellbeing of Xia or her daughter. In a sense, there was a certain symmetry to the two parallel experiences.

He remembered the way his heart beat in his chest like a battering ram as one of the men who had tried to execute the Tank Man stirred. He was coming round, and he wouldn't be a happy man when he did. Once the two soldiers recovered consciousness, the odds would begin to stack up against Jack and Peter.

Jack knew that if he wanted to get the Tank Man away safely, he would have to act quickly. Which meant shooting Xia.

He couldn't bring himself to do it.

She seemed to be having the same difficulty – he knew that because he was still alive. Maybe she had cared about him just a little bit. Maybe she just didn't want a gunshot reverberating down the street. Either way, time was running out.

A Mexican stand-off.

It had always seemed like an implausible situation on television. Now he was living it.

'The problem is you never understood what those kids were fighting for,' he said. 'The ones you betrayed.'

'We don't have time for this, Jack.'

'In the US, we call it freedom.'

Peter was looking at him now, expression questioning. Jack didn't doubt he was on the alert, looking for a sign. He knew Jack too well to believe the small talk.

'Some people think that means making money – you know, pulling yourself up by your own bootstraps. Some think it means defying authority, like this guy here. Others just wanna go to a game and drink a whole lot of beer.'

Xia had noticed the men on the ground stirring too. That was why she was listening. She needed to buy time until she had back-up. If that meant putting up with his stories, so be it.

'I was hoping to take you for a football game sometime back home. You'd have been impressed. It looks rough but it's all tactics. Quarterback throws for the line . . . running back is ready for the catch. Next thing you know, the defensive line has tackled the guy and it's all over bar the shouting.'

'I like American football,' said the Tank Man suddenly, as if he had been genuinely paying attention despite the fact that his life and freedom were in the balance.

'It's just like life,' said Jack. 'Quarterback makes the throw and everyone reacts *immediately*.'

On cue, Peter rushed Xia. She saw him coming out of the corner of her eye. Despite her training, the gun in her hand wavered ever so slightly. Jack saw his opportunity. He too charged at Xia. She shot Peter just as he hit her around the knees. She went flying, the gun looped into the air and Jack caught it with his free hand. One of the men on the ground sat up and Jack knocked him out again.

'Touchdown,' he said.

'Good call,' agreed his friend, trying to rise to his feet and then collapsing back down, his face contorted with pain. A hand over his leg rapidly turned bloody. 'I wasn't sure what you were on about until you mentioned defence,' gasped Peter.

'Well, yeah. Only the quarterback's capable of coming up with a game plan. You guys are just the brawn.' He tried to smile but his heart wasn't in it. He might have won the day – saved a man's life – but he'd lost an alternative universe.

'How bad is it?' he asked, kneeling by his friend and moving his hand to look at the wound.

'I'll be fine,' said Peter, and Jack could see that the bullet had exited the wound without hitting bone or the femoral artery.

Jack pressed a hand down on the wound to stop the bleeding and tied a tourniquet around it.

'What about him?' asked Peter, nodding at the Tank Man.

Jack cast a wary eye at his former girlfriend, now sitting with her back against the wall, her expression sufficient to curdle milk. He barely recognized her – could hardly believe the hard-faced creature was, had been, the love of his life.

He turned to the Tank Man. 'There's only one place you'll be safe, my friend. Let's get you there.'

*   *   *

'His name is Confucius.'

'Are you trying to be funny?' shouted the tall guy, the one Jack had marked for death.

'No,' said Jack. His face was drawn, his jaw was throbbing. Bursts of pain kept going off in his cheek. Was this the worst thing he had ever done to a fellow human being? Quite possibly. He hoped Confucius had done as they agreed and left his tiny residence.

'Go on,' said Guo Feng.

From the gleam of interest in his eyes, Jack's guessed the colonel knew more than he was telling. It didn't surprise him. Despite his smart uniform and mild manners, he sensed that Guo Feng was a very dangerous man. There was restrained power in the minimal movements.

'That's the Tank Man's alias now. He lives in Beijing. Runs a teahouse in a *hutong*.'

'That was the man you went to see,' remarked Guo Feng.

The tall guy had fallen silent now that he realized that there was stuff going on that he knew nothing about. His eyes moved from one man to the other, trying to figure it out.

'Yes, I thought he might help me. He owes me, after all. A long time ago, I saved his life.'

'Our information was that this man, Confucius, was a friend of the dead agent. We had him staked out waiting to see if you showed.'

'You think I was making the rounds of Peter's friends? Peter stayed in touch with the Tank Man – more or less since Tiananmen.'

'But Xia said Peter didn't know where he was. Only you did.'

'You should know by now that you can't believe everything Xia tells you.'

'The Tank Man has been in China all this while?'

'Yep. He went into hiding for a few years. Worked as a farmer, apparently. Then turned up in Beijing one day and settled down.'

'A brave man.' The colonel was still sceptical.

'Yes.'

'You saved his life thirty years ago?'

'He was a brave man then too.'

Guo Feng walked up to Jack and his fist flew so fast that Jack didn't even have the time to jerk his head away, lessen the blow. His neck cracked back as if he'd been rear-ended in a car at high speed.

'I don't believe you.'

Jack thought his nose might be broken.

'Are you all right?' whispered Fei Yen.

'Never better,' said Jack. He felt like hell.

'I don't believe you,' continued Guo Feng, 'because I think that you are a brave man too. I do not think you would give him up so easily.'

'Easily? You have my daughter, you bastard!' Jack's glance flickered over to the girl and then back again. 'It's true,' he said. 'I took him to the US Embassy that morning, looking for help. Peter was in hospital – Xia had shot him – so I was on my own. I told them at the embassy what he had done. Defied the tanks. They refused to have anything to do with him. They cleaned us up, put us back out on the street. Apparently they didn't want to be seen provoking the Chinese.'

He fell silent, lost in the past. The memories were still bitter. The clear day. The terrified man. The bureaucrats. He'd yelled and shouted. At the back of his mind thinking of Xia, wondering where she was, where she had gone after he left her tied up on a street corner, why she had done it. A day of betrayals. As fresh as yesterday. *True is it that we have seen better days.*

'What happened?'

'I had a few friends. I looked for back-up. Spirited him out of the city in the back of a cattle truck. We had to give him to the Chinese underground. Anyone seen with a Westerner was a target.'

'He got away?'

'Yes. When the footage broke, the embassy was all over me – they realized he might be a useful propaganda tool and they wanted him back. I refused to give him up – didn't trust our colleagues any more. Wouldn't even tell Peter. I walked away from the agency.' He didn't mention that he'd decked the station chief. He had form that way. 'Peter stayed in – but there was a black mark on his file. He never got past the rank of senior paper pusher. Much later, I told him about Confucius.'

'And he stayed in touch with the Tank Man, alias Confucius?'

'Yes.'

'And that's your story?'

'Yes.'

'It should be easy enough to find out whether you're telling the truth.'

He barked a few instructions at the other man, who set off at a quick trot, a big grin on his face. Licence to create more mayhem, no doubt. Another innocent about to pass through his hands. Jack wondered whether he would ever forgive himself for giving up Confucius. The finest thing he had ever done – saved the Tank Man from certain death even though it had cost him Xia – was all for nought. But Jack would never forgive himself either if something happened to Fei Yen.

Colonel Guo Feng ambled towards the door. When he got there, he turned around, taking in the scene. 'I hope for your sake you're telling the truth, Jack Ford. Otherwise' – he paused, and his voice grew as sharp and cold as an icicle hanging from the eaves – 'what your daughter has been through so far will be nothing compared with what happens next.'

The Great Hall of the People was ready for the transfer of power. It would be a peaceful transition between generations in China. General Zhang walked along the dais, staring out at the hundreds of empty seats. The place was spotless, shining, decked in red flags, each emblazoned with the large yellow star and four smaller ones representative of the people under the benign guidance of the Communist Party. The brass bands of the PLA with their green uniforms and gold braid were ready to perform. The National People's Congress would convene the next day. On the third day, the product of all the horse-trading and backstabbing – Juntao – would be elected Secretary General.

The people, as represented by their Congress, would also elect – or was rubber-stamp a better word? – twelve new members to the Politburo and three to the Standing Committee. The balance of power was fragile between hardliners and reformists, liberals and conservatives, the honest and the corrupt, the princelings and the paupers, those from the coasts and those from the heartlands. Zhang had lost the post of Secretary General to Juntao by a whisker and it still grated. He had as many enemies as supporters and thus had lost out to a man who had hardly any of either. It was true that water found its lowest level. Zhang pulled back his lips to reveal the sharp yellow teeth, stained from years of drinking tea. It had been better in the old days when the paramount leader had nurtured and then nominated a protégé. That was the way to select strong leaders. Now, weakness was written into the Communist Party's DNA.

General Zhang clasped his hands behind his back. He was reasonably confident that, once Juntao was thoroughly discredited, the Party leaders including the populists and the princelings would fall in behind him and accept his leadership as the price for stability and control. He glanced at the watch on his wrist – Rolex, probably his only indulgence. He expected to hear from Guo Feng any moment. The minute he was confident that he had neutered Juntao's grand plan to produce the Tank Man before the people, he would be ready to put into action the final part of his own masterpiece. And his prize would be China.

His phone rang on cue. Sometimes he thought that faggot, Guo Feng, could read his mind.

'Yes? Have you found the whereabouts of the hero of China?'

'We are currently acting on a tip. We should have him in custody soon.'

'You have done well, Guo Feng.'

'I will accept your praise as my due when the task is complete, General Zhang.'

Zhang grunted his approval of this self-restraint. 'Is that all?' he asked.

'Everything is under control.'

'And how is the boyfriend?'

'He is well, General Zhang.'

Zhang pressed the 'end call' button with a stubby thumb. He allowed himself a smile. Things were going to plan. The

Tank Man was almost within his grasp. The American convoy
bearing the latest weapons was steaming towards Taiwan. Only
the memo was still missing. He dismissed it. If it had fallen
into the hands of anyone with the wit to use it, the contents
would have been made public by now. Most likely it had been
binned somewhere in Singapore. Knowing that tidy little town,
it had probably been recycled.

They were alone in the room. Two people bound to their chairs.
Jack strained against his bonds. His eyes darted around the
room, looking for weaknesses. Fei Yen sat with her head
drooping like a rosebud without water. Blood dripped from
her finger on to the floor.

'I'm sorry,' he said.

She didn't respond.

'Fei Yen, I can't tell you how sorry I am that this is
happening.'

She looked up and he could see that her cheeks were streaked
with tears. 'This Tank Man – he was the guy who stood in
front of the column of tanks right after Tiananmen?'

'Yes.'

'You helped him escape?'

'Yes.'

'But now you've given him up.'

'I couldn't let them hurt you any more.'

'I didn't know things like this actually happened. I thought
it was just the movies.'

'Sometimes it's real.'

'Who were those men?'

Jack would not have been surprised if the room was bugged.
Indeed, it was the least he'd expect of a smooth operator like
Guo Feng.

He smiled at Fei Yen, did a theatrical one eighty with his
head and said, 'The less you know the better, Fei Yen. They're
more likely to let you go if you don't have enough information to be a threat to them.'

Her eyes grew wide as she realized the room might be
bugged. He just hoped there wasn't a camera as well.

'But you've given them what they wanted!'

He shrugged and she nodded a slow understanding. They might not keep their word. He tugged again at the restraints around his wrists and ankles; he'd scraped off the skin and his wrists were smarting almost more than his nose was throbbing and his jaw was aching. He tried to yank the chair from the floor but it was bolted firm. Hers wasn't, though, and she dragged it a few inches towards him.

He grinned. 'Nice to see that one of us is on the move.'

She smiled back, some of her spirit returning. 'Not a lot of places to go, unfortunately.'

'How's your Shakespeare?' he asked suddenly.

She looked puzzled but she answered. Maybe she thought he was humouring her. Maybe he was. 'I did the plays as part of my English course.'

'*Macbeth* is my favourite,' he said. 'Especially that bit where Macbeth is staring at something floating before him.' *Is this a dagger which I see before me?*

Who said a literary education wasn't useful?

'If we had what he had, we'd be out of here.'

Fei Yen considered what he was saying. Without another word, she began the slow process of inching her chair across the floor to him. Every now and then she would teeter on the edge of rocking over. His heart was in his mouth each time. She would never be able to get upright if that happened. At last she was close, and he had an answer to one question – there were no cameras in the room. When at last she was right up to him, she swivelled around so that they were back to back.

Almost inaudibly, she muttered, 'Safety pin.'

'Where?'

'Side of my waistband.'

It took him what seemed like an eternity with his bound hands, almost numb from a lack of blood flow, to unhook the pin until he held it between thumb and forefinger. He began to poke at the plastic cuffs methodically, hoping against hope that they would fray – and that they would fray in time.

General Zhang called a press conference in the Great Hall of the People. He stood at the dais, the microphones from the world's press before him, camera lights flashing in his eyes. Everyone was there, CNN, the BBC, Al Jazeera and the Chinese press, of course. He had told his spokesperson to indicate that something important was in the wind. Now, he waited until the hubbub had died down and faces were turned to him expectantly. He was in full dress uniform and flanked with the leaders of each branch of the military, all standing to attention like waxworks. The civilian leadership of China was absent. He had not told them of his plans.

'I call you here today to inform you that the United States of America, under the leadership of President Warmonger, has sought to take advantage of the peaceful democratic transfer of power in China.' He read from a script, his spectacles perched on his nose. Now Zhang looked up over the reading lenses and saw that he had the attention of the crowd. TV cameras were rolling as well and he wondered whether programmers had already realized it was time to break into regular broadcasting.

'It has come to our knowledge that the United States, under the guise of a naval exercise in the Taiwan Strait, intends to deliver missile defence technology and short-range tactical *nuclear* missiles to Taiwan, China.'

The audience broke out into exclamations of surprise and scepticism and General Zhang waited until the shock had died down and the room was silent again.

'This would give Taiwan, China first strike capability to reach any part of the Chinese mainland. This act of war will not be tolerated. The Chinese government insists that the American ships be turned back forthwith or *all* necessary action will be taken to prevent the delivery of their cargo to Taiwan.'

He paused and took off his glasses. 'Are there any questions?'

He was besieged.

Finally, Jack felt the bonds fray. He did his best to wrench his hands apart, ignoring the pain as the thin cord bit into his wrists.

'Jack, are you all right?'

He didn't answer. Instead, he flexed his arms again and this time he felt the bonds snap. He held up his hands, still clutching the safety pin between finger and thumb. 'I am now.'

After that, it didn't take long to free himself. He used the pin on his ankle cuffs. It was much easier when he could see what he was doing, although the pin itself was now blunter than a chopstick. He sat for a moment, massaging his hands and feet, allowing the blood to circulate freely, wincing at the agony of blood flowing into his starved extremities.

He could see Fei Yen was impatient but she didn't ask him why he was just sitting there. Maybe she realized that if he stood too soon, he'd end up on the floor. At last, he felt confident enough to get to his feet. He stood, flexed his ankles, took a deep breath. He raised a finger to his lips and was rewarded with a scowl that suggested she wasn't dumb enough to give the game away at the eleventh hour. She was Xia's daughter all right – missing a fingernail but not the plot.

He knelt down by her chair and, using the pin, picked the lock of the metal handcuffs around her ankles. Her eyes widened but she remained silent. He wished that he could have told her that this was a fairly poor effort by his standards because his fingers were numbed. Jack managed to untangle the knot that held her to the chair. She stood immediately and stumbled. She would have fallen if he hadn't caught her. She lay against his chest and he could feel the quiet sobs. He held her tight for a few seconds – his daughter. Even before he could release her, explain that there was no time, she pushed away from him and stood steady. Her eyes demanded to know the next step.

Jack pointed at the chair he had been bound to, the one bolted to the ground. She sat down again, albeit with a reluctant expression on her face. He immediately retied the knots loosely and arranged the handcuffs so that it looked as if she was still wearing them. Her eyes showed her panic and she would have spoken, maybe screamed, if he had not pressed her hand in reassurance. He cupped her face, forced her to look at him. Touched his heart. *Trust me.* He hoped she understood. It would buy him a couple of seconds of hesitation when the next captor came in. He had a quick look around – was there anything he could use? The room was as bare as the proverbial padded cell – without the padding. No windows, a single door that opened inwards. Jack examined the door. There was a lock, but he knew from the sounds earlier that it was bolted from the outside. He felt the metal. Too heavy to shift. No one made those doors that could be kicked in any more. It was a damned shame. Kicking down a door would have impressed Fei Yen, and it would have felt good too. Nothing for it. Jack moved the other chair so that it was within reach and took up his position next to the exit. He could feel Fei Yen's eyes on him as he stood loose, ready and waiting for the next person that came in. *There is a tide in the affairs of men.*

'What the hell is going on?' demanded Harris as she stepped into the Situation Room.

She was the last one in; the President, Joint Chiefs of Staff and various functionaries were already seated at the large conference table. She took her seat. A slim folder was in front of her. The Chinese statement was replaying on the big screen on one wall: General Zhang fielding questions an hour earlier. The sound was off but the ticker tape translation across the bottom repeated all the necessary information: 'act of war', 'nuclear first strike', 'all means necessary', 'withdraw immediately'.

'General Zhang, head of the PLA, has accused us of shipping nuclear weapons as well as missile defence technology to Taiwan,' said Secretary of Defence General Alberto Rodriguez. 'He has demanded that we send the naval force currently sailing towards the Taiwan Strait back to Okinawa at least.'

'Why would Zhang think we would do something like that?' asked General Parkinson.

'He will not reveal his evidence,' said General Allen.

'That's because he hasn't got any,' insisted Rodriguez.

'This is all nonsense, isn't it?' asked Harris. 'We are not shipping nuclear weapons to Taiwan, are we?'

'Of course not, Madam Vice President.' Rodriguez looked genuinely taken aback by her question.

'All right, then. What are we going to do?'

'Deny their claims categorically. We are drafting the statement,' said Rodriguez.

'And?'

'And what, madam?'

'Are we pulling back the ships?'

'That would look weak, as if the United States can be bullied,' said NSA Griffin sharply.

'We don't change mission at the order of the Chinese government,' agreed General Parkinson.

'We can't look weak,' said the President, sitting up straighter in his chair.

'Sir, we are not taking into account the power struggle in China. It is not a coincidence that Zhang made the statement and that the Secretary General-elect is nowhere to be seen. This is a power play by Zhang, and he is using us. If we give in, it will strengthen his hand versus the new guy.' General Allen was, as always, the voice of reason in the room.

'It might be the opposite,' pointed out Vice President Harris. 'What if he wants to escalate this confrontation so that the new guy looks weak? We play right into his hands by refusing to back down.'

There was silence except for the rustling of paper and the screen image of Zhang looming large over the gathering. Harris caught the eye of the CIA director, Dominic Corke, who sat in rigid silence. Why hadn't they had a heads-up from EMPEROR? She refrained from asking the question out loud.

'What do you think we should do?' The President once again turned to his most trusted adviser, NSA Griffin.

'We release the statement of denial but also insist we are *not* going to back down and pull the convoy back.'

VP Harris knew that Griffin had echoed her words with intent and that now the President saw withdrawal as not just 'weak' but also the preferred outcome of his despised vice president. She had been too forthright, given the tensions.

'Let's do that,' said the President, unable to keep the relief out of his voice that a decision had been made for him.

Griffin spoke, his voice loud in the quiet room. 'It is time for the Chinese to put up or shut up.'

* * *

Guo Feng hurled a heavy glass paperweight across the room and enjoyed the satisfaction of seeing it shatter into pieces against the wall. It was childish and he knew it. But General Zhang with his threats and insinuations provoked that sort of response. It beggared belief that he was actively assisting the bastard to ascend to the top of the Chinese pyramid. The colonel sighed. Did he have a choice, he asked himself? It was always the same question and it was always the same answer. But he owed it to his conscience to look for a way out once in a while. To seek an escape from Zhang and his demands. He'd sent his men to corner Confucius. When he finally had his hands on the Tank Man, he would not do as he'd promised Juntao and have him ready for the Congress. Instead, he would turn him over to General Zhang. No doubt the man would disappear again – this time for ever.

But the American had mentioned the memo. And despite his natural caution, he had eschewed the safe option and kept the information from Zhang. Which meant that, for the first time since agreeing to betray the Secretary General-elect to his rival and enemy, Guo Feng had an extra string to his bow. And he needed it now that Zhang seemed determined on a path of all-out war with the Americans. His phone rang.

'Guo Feng?'

'Yes, Secretary General-elect.'

'What the hell is going on? What is Zhang doing? Is it true? Are the Americans arming Taiwan? Why was I not briefed?'

'Sir, General Zhang acted on his own without going through normal channels.'

'He's trying to start a war and he hasn't bothered to inform me in advance? What in the hell is he thinking? This will undermine me before I even begin as Secretary General.'

'I believe that is his intention,' said Guo Feng. Juntao knew very well what was afoot with the general's bombshell announcement. He was just taken aback at the sheer effrontery of the man. Guo Feng had to admit he was taken aback as well.

'What is your advice, Colonel Guo Feng?'

'Try and set up a backchannel with the Americans, sir. If possible, try and take control of the issue.'

'I will call the VP. She is not as reckless as the rest.'

There was a silence as both men tried to game out the next few steps in their heads.

'Do you think there are nukes on those ships?' asked Juntao.

'It is hard to credit that the Americans would be so provocative, sir. Arming Taiwan with nukes would be an act of war and would play straight into Zhang's hands. I do not see what the US has to gain from such an action.'

The sigh was audible down the line. 'I hope you're right, Guo Feng. I really hope you are right!'

TWENTY-TWO

'**N**othing from EMPEROR?'

'Not a squeak.' The CIA director looked morose and his expression matched that of the Vice President of the United States.

The two of them were in her office. He sat across from her. Unlike the *Resolute* desk of the President of the United States, the desk of the Vice President was covered in paperwork and files and the secure laptop was open. However, she was not interested in any of the material before her. The official response of the United States had been released through the Department of Defence by General Rodriguez. The VP held a copy in her hand with the care of someone handling a poisonous snake. She read it aloud.

'"The United States has not supplied and does not intend to supply Taiwan with nuclear technology. This would breach the long-standing commitment of the United States to disarmament and to commitments pursuant to the non-proliferation agreements. However, the United States will not be told by other governments when and where to sail its navy in international waters and rejects any threats from the government of the People's Republic of China. The joint naval exercise with Taiwan will continue." How come the statement is from Rodriguez, not POTUS?' she asked.

'A way of acknowledging that the threat from China did not come from the civilian leadership, and that we are not going to escalate,' replied Corke.

Harris nodded approvingly. That must have been Rodriguez or Allen showing restraint. POTUS would have gone for one of his missives with the exclamation marks and capital letters. Her phone rang and she reached for it and then raised a finger at Corke to indicate it was of interest to both of them.

'Put him through,' she said. And, after a pause, 'Secretary General-elect Juntao, what can I do for you?'

She heard Juntao's voice at the end of the line. 'I call concerning the armada that you have sailing towards the Taiwan Strait, and about General Zhang's accusation.'

'Yes, Secretary General-elect.'

'I urge you to use your influence in the government to have it turned around.'

'The US government does not see the need because, as I am sure you know, we are *not* shipping nuclear weapons to Taiwan.'

'Are you quite sure of that?' Juntao asked.

'One hundred per cent.'

'Nevertheless, I ask that you withdraw the ships to avoid any unnecessary tension.'

'The President and his advisers do not believe that is justified. They do not wish to send a signal of weakness just as you are to be installed as leader.'

Corke's phone beeped and he glanced at the screen, frowned and held it up for the VP to see. She read it as she listened and her eyes widened.

'I would consider it a signal of an intention to work with China for global peace and prosperity,' said the Secretary General-elect.

'I would not disagree, but I am afraid the President has just made his feelings on the subject crystal clear.'

'A tweet?'

'Yes.' She read it out, wishing that the pinnacle of power in the United States was not in the hands of someone with kindergarten-level language skills. '"The Chinese do not tell America what to do. NOT NOW NOT EVER!!!! Your favorite President will not be pushed around. MAKE AMERICA GREAT AGAIN!!!"'

She swallowed a sigh. 'I understand, and will make every effort to advise the President of your position, Secretary General-elect. But for now, the ships are bound for Taiwan.'

'Your efforts are appreciated, Madam Vice President.'

The Standing Committee of the Politburo was a collection of old men, hardliners and reformers, but most of all survivors. Right now, they were angry old men, gathered in a small dining room without windows and with only one double door, which was firmly shut. Aides had been banished. Food dishes were on a side table covered in gleaming silver, but none of those present ate anything and the delicacies had grown cold. The only appetite appeared to be for cigarettes. Smoke filled the venue as if it was a waiting room for the fires of hell.

'How dare you do such a press briefing without consent, General Zhang?' demanded the Secretary General-elect. 'You have placed me in an invidious position.'

'This was a military matter, and it was urgent. I took matters into my own hands.'

'You have made it impossible for that cretin, the US president, to pull back now. You know he fears to look weak.' This was from one of the reformers, red-faced and perspiring. 'You saw that ridiculous tweet.'

'The Americans assure me that there are no nukes on board those ships. Why would you even suggest such a thing?' Juntao tried to give the impression of a man with equal access to information, but it was obvious to all the men in the room that he had been outfoxed by Zhang.

'They are lying,' said Zhang, chest puffed out and arrayed with medals. 'I have it on good authority that there are tactical nuclear weapons on board one of those ships, the USS *Chung-Hoon*.'

'Do you have proof?' demanded Kai Pin.

'None that I am prepared to share with a leaky bunch of old men,' grunted Zhang. 'When we board the ships, you will see that I am right.'

'What do you propose we do now?' asked Liu Qi, his scrawny neck sticking out of his collar. 'You have backed the Americans into a corner.'

'*They* have backed themselves into a corner,' responded General Zhang, unable to hide a smile that Liu Qi, rather than Juntao, had asked him the question on next steps. His fellow hardliner was delivering when it counted, although he was still the fool who had lost the memo to some damned spy. Perhaps he was trying to make amends. Good for him, but Zhang would still have him purged from the Politburo at the first available opportunity.

'We too are backed into a corner, thanks to Zhang's provocative stance,' said Juntao. 'Surely you do not intend that we *board* American navy vessels?'

Zhang stood up suddenly and slammed two fists on the table. His face was mottled red but his lips were pale in contrast. 'How dare you question me on military matters, Secretary General-elect?' He enunciated the word 'elect' with disgust that was apparent to all in the smoke-filled room. 'The provocation is from the Americans. If they really do not plan to supply weapons to Taiwan, China, why continue with this pointless exercise?'

There were nods around the table; he had a point.

'We are a sovereign state. This action is an affront,' insisted one of the hardliners. 'The Americans have no right to come sailing into our waters causing tension.'

'That is correct,' said Liu Qi. 'What do you intend to do, General Zhang?'

'I will teach these American cowboys a lesson that they will not forget,' said Zhang.

'How?' demanded a few voices in unison. Even Juntao looked at him for the answer although he did not embarrass himself by joining in the question.

'We have imposed a naval blockade at the entrance to the Taiwan Strait.'

Confucius had gone underground. That was the message that came back from the team Guo Feng had sent to apprehend him. The old man's teahouse in the narrow *hutong* in Old Beijing was trashed, equipment destroyed, the place abandoned in a hurry; impossible to know if the damage was self-inflicted or if Confucius had enemies – or other enemies, to be precise. Guo Feng was not surprised to hear the bird had flown the coop, although he was disappointed. After all, two secret servicemen had gone missing there before when they had gone to apprehend Jack Ford. The writing had been on the wall for Confucius from that point onwards. If he stayed put, more men would follow. And if he really was the Tank Man, as Jack Ford insisted, he was a man who knew how to run and hide. He had been doing so effectively for thirty years.

The colonel was confident his men would track Confucius down but the situation was urgent and he was not sure they would find him in time either for Juntao's election or for Zhang's takeover – depending on where, in the end, he delivered his prey.

Colonel Guo Feng considered his options. It was possible that Jack Ford had been lying about the identity of the Tank Man, in which case he should beat further information out of him. Alternatively, the American might have some idea where the man had gone. They must have cooked up some plan for this sort of eventuality. If, on the other hand, Confucius had gone to the US Embassy, then the gig was up and Guo Feng would have to tell his bosses of the outcome. Somehow, the colonel doubted it. The Tank Man aka Confucius had not sought support or assistance from the Americans since his initial escape three decades ago. It seemed unlikely that he would be prepared to trust official channels after all these years.

The military man continued to walk towards the cell in which he had imprisoned Ford and his daughter. Jack Ford had mentioned a memo. He had felt it was important enough to trade for his life and that of his daughter instead of the identity and whereabouts of the Tank Man. He could have been bluffing, of course, desperately buying time. But Guo Feng was running out of options and needed a win to palliate the Secretary General-elect as well as that blackmailing madman, General Zhang. The head of the PLA was out of control. He had just announced, with great fanfare, a blockade of the Taiwan Strait. The news was everywhere. Egged on by their absurd leader, the Americans continued to sail towards their destination. The low key naval military exercise between Taiwan and the United States had turned into a game of chicken between China and the Americans. A game of chicken between two nuclear powers.

If this memo was important, it might be worth finding out the contents even as his men continued to hunt for Confucius. Perhaps it would give him some leverage over General Zhang. Still deep in thought, Colonel Guo Feng unlocked the door to the cell and pushed it open, leaning in as he did so since the door was heavy. He stepped into the room.

'You will tell me more about this memo, Jack Ford,' he

said, just before being struck across the face by the American, who had been waiting behind the door.

EMPEROR was livid. He had provided the Americans with the ammunition to contain the threat from General Zhang and, instead of using the information as planned, they had lost the memo to some rogue element named Jack Ford. And now, to heap insult upon injury, the general had told him that the man, some ex-special forces soldier, had returned to Beijing from Singapore – with the memo. The fact that, despite Zhang's best efforts, they had not been able to track down the renegade gave EMPEROR some hope, but not much. This Jack Ford was either an idiot or a traitor. Either he did not know the value of what he had or he had plans to sell it to the highest bidder.

In the meantime, Zhang had triggered a global confrontation and looked set to depose Juntao from the top spot. The Secretary General-elect had been caught off guard and looked weak, unable to contradict the line Zhang had taken in public without undermining China, unable to rein in the head of the PLA in his confrontation with the Americans without undermining the PLA. As it stood, General Zhang might succeed in taking over China and rejecting democratic and economic reforms – or, in the worst-case scenario, he might trigger World War Three.

EMPEROR's decision to betray his country and spy on behalf of the Americans was made in order to ensure that the Chinese leaders did not use their young men and women as cannon fodder while they pursued personal or national interests without counting the costs. Yet here he stood now, on the verge of achieving the precise opposite. Even a non-nuclear skirmish in the Taiwan Strait would cost the lives of many. And if the situation got out of hand, there was no limit to the potential fallout. The children of many nations stood to suffer if this stand-off persisted.

EMPEROR picked up a black and white photo of his son taken when he graduated from military college. Yongkang was in full regimental gear. The boy looked so proud; he was evidently trying hard not to smile, but the slight curve at the

corners of his mouth revealed his delight. The silver frame
was as heavy as the old man's heart.

'Yongkang, my son. Everything I have done, I have done
for you . . .' he whispered, his eyes wet with unshed tears.
'But it seems that I am unable to avert the greatest tragedy
of all.'

He turned back to the television, which was carrying General
Zhang's statement in a continuous loop on every channel,
interspersed with angry, tailored responses from the 'man on
the street' as well as prearranged 'spontaneous' flag-waving
by groups of children.

> Acting, therefore, in the defence of our own security and
> of the continued sovereignty of the Chinese nation over
> ALL of its territory including Taiwan, I have directed
> that the following initial steps be taken immediately.
>
> To halt this offensive buildup, a strict quarantine on
> all offensive military equipment under shipment to
> Taiwan, China is being initiated. All ships of any kind
> bound for Taiwan from whatever nation or port will, if
> found to contain a cargo of offensive weapons, be turned
> back. This includes, but is not limited to, the naval vessels
> of the United States which are currently on route to
> Taiwan, China with their dangerous and unacceptable
> cargo of short-range nuclear weapons.
>
> I speak also to the people of Taiwan, China. These
> new weapons are not in your interest. They contribute
> nothing to your peace and wellbeing. They can only
> undermine it. But China has no wish to cause you to
> suffer. We know that your lives and land are being used
> as pawns by those who deny your freedom. Stand with
> us against the tyrannical Americans.

TWENTY-THREE

Colonel Guo Feng went down like a ton of bricks but he came up fighting. His nose was bloody and broken where he had been struck by the chair, swung like a baseball bat by Jack Ford. As the two men grappled, punched and rolled, gasps of pain and gasps for air punctuated the silence. Fei Yen cowered and watched, came closer and then retreated, unable to decide whether and how to intervene. A cut above his eye bled into his vision and his foot was unstable underneath him, but Jack fought like a man possessed. Guo Feng began to tire, his kicks were less precise, his fists missed their target and whistled past Jack's jaw. With one last heave, he pushed Jack away and went for his weapon. The American was in time to grab his wrist, to prevent him shifting the gun to aim at his opponent, and now they battled over an object rather than with each other. Jack bent the gun in Guo Feng's hand backwards until he heard the trigger finger crack. The colonel yelped but did not weaken his grip.

At last, the colonel seemed to lose focus and sagged against the other man, one eye swollen shut, blood splattered down the front of his uniform. As Jack followed in to take advantage of the weakness, Guo Feng head-butted him with all his might, aiming for Jack's chin. The weakness had been a feint. It worked. Jack went down backwards, unable even to try and break his fall. The colonel shifted the pistol from his right hand to his left. On his back, thinking fast but not fast enough, Jack noted the gun was as steady in the man's left as it had been in his right. He had to admire the colonel. Fei Yen saw her chance, or maybe she realized there was no option: it was her turn to swing the chair against her captor's back. He must have sensed the movement because he turned in time to catch the blow to his arm. Even as he stumbled, Jack spun on his back and took Guo Feng's legs out with his own. Again, Guo Feng went down. This time Jack rolled over on top of him and punched him once, twice, three times – left, right, left. The colonel was an elite member of the PLA, a martial arts expert in peak physical condition, but it would seem that he was no match for a man fighting to save his daughter's life.

The colonel was out cold. Jack picked up the gun and rose to his feet. Fei Yen rushed to him. They hugged, although the retired soldier kept one arm free and his gun hand trained on the man on the ground.

'Are you really my father?' she asked.

'Are you always in this much trouble?' he responded.

The Chinese ambassador was adamant. 'My government seeks your reassurances that you will not test our blockade of the Taiwan Strait. Under no circumstances will we allow nuclear weapons on Taiwan, China.'

'We do not have nuclear weapons on those ships. I don't know how much clearer I can make myself.' General Rodriguez was no longer able to contain his impatience.

'Then my government seeks your cooperation in allowing us to board your ships and see for ourselves before you reach our line of control.'

'The Chinese military will never board a US Navy ship!' POTUS raised his voice and for once received general nods of approval from the other US personnel in the room.

'If you have nothing to hide, why won't you let us conduct an inspection?' demanded the ambassador. A graduate of Harvard and MIT, he spoke perfect English. Usually he would demand an interpreter anyway as a means of insisting on a separate cultural identity, but he had abandoned the pretence that day.

'Because it is an American naval vessel and you have no right or jurisdiction to board our ships.' Griffin had his hands on his hips, his tie was loosened and his pepper and salt hair and moustache were more dishevelled than usual. 'In fact, you have no right to blockade the Taiwan Strait. You are in breach of international maritime law.'

'It is not a blockade, it is a quarantine,' said the ambassador. 'And in any event, you are in breach of international non-proliferation rules,' he continued.

'For the last time, there are no nukes on those ships.' Rodriguez was red-faced with anger.

'*For the last time*, that is not our information.'

'We seem to be at an impasse, then,' grumbled the Secretary of Defence.

Although it was Rodriguez who had spoken, the ambassador addressed his response directly to the President of the United States. 'Mr President, China does not see an impasse, she sees a hostile act by the United States of America that infringes the sovereign right of China over all its territory, including Taiwan. I am asked to convey to you that China will not stand idly by and allow this international criminal act to go unpunished.'

'*Who* in China says so?' asked the Vice President. It was the first time she had spoken at the meeting although she had listened with the utmost care for every nuance.

'The Chinese government speaks with one voice, Madam Vice President.'

'That is not my understanding,' she murmured.

'What are you going to do?' asked Griffin. 'If we cross your line of control, what will you do?'

'Every single Chinese man, woman and child will rise up against the invasion by your forces, sir.'

'You wouldn't dare,' said POTUS.

'Do not test the Chinese dragon, Mr President.'

'No secret mirrors, no microphones?'

Colonel Guo Feng shrugged. 'Sometimes interrogations do not need witnesses.'

He was tied, with a belt and Jack's shirt ripped into shreds, to the chair that had originally held Jack. They had tied him up while he was still out cold and waited while he slowly regained consciousness. The colonel scowled as he became aware of both his pain and his quandary. He looked around, trying to focus in the white empty room. Jack had the gun trained on the PLA soldier. He sat on the other chair while Fei Yen was on the floor, leaning against a wall, dark circles under her eyes and the bloodstained nails visible on her clasped hands, the only evidence of recent trauma.

'You cannot escape. This is a secure facility,' remarked Guo Feng.

'I'll take my chances,' said Jack.

'Why are you still here, then? Should you not have tried to flee?' He turned his head to the door and noted that it was closed again. From the outside, it was possible that all seemed normal.

'I need some answers,' said Jack.

'I think you will find that I am relatively cooperative,' said the other man. '*I* am not the hero type.'

'How did you find out about the Tank Man?'

'Xia told me. She worked as a liaison between the PLA HQ and the office of the Secretary General-elect and got wind of our interest in him.'

Fei Yen's face crumbled at this but she made no sound. Jack did not want to contemplate what the revelations were doing to her faith in her mother.

'Why do you want him? Why do you want the Tank Man?'

'I told you: our new Secretary General-elect is a reformer. He was going to use the Tank Man as a symbol of change and hope.'

'By kidnapping him?'

'By getting a chance to explain our plans to him and allowing him an opportunity to support the democratization of China.'

'You used Fei Yen as bait to get me to Beijing?' Jack took two steps towards the other man as if he wanted to hit him again. 'So that I could be forced to tell you his whereabouts?'

'An excellent plan, hatched by Xia.'

The reminder that Xia had been involved in the plot served as a damper on Jack's temper. What was the use of being angry with an official like Colonel Guo Feng, who was only following instructions, when a mother was prepared to use her daughter as a means of betraying, yet again, the man she had once claimed to love?

'Is Confucius the Tank Man?' Guo Feng asked the question this time, his tone one of genuine curiosity.

'Didn't you ask him?'

'He . . . he . . . errr . . . wasn't there when we went to get him. His place was abandoned.'

Jack felt a sense of profound relief rain down on him like a warm shower. He almost smiled. His betrayal had not yet caught up with Confucius. And where there was freedom, there was time, there was life – and a future of almost infinite possibilities.

'It doesn't matter anyway,' said Guo Feng. 'It is too late.'

'What do you mean?' asked Jack warily.

'General Zhang has successfully sidelined the new Secretary General-elect. It is only a matter of time before he is officially deposed.'

'How has he done that?' Jack's body had grown as still as a jungle cat catching a whiff of prey downwind.

'Triggered a confrontation with the Americans,' said Guo Feng. 'Although the way things are escalating, General Zhang might just have triggered World War Three.'

'What are we going to do?' shouted POTUS. 'You got me into this mess, now get me out of it.'

The President was back in the Situation Room with his military and civilian advisers.

'We cannot back down, Mr President,' insisted Griffin.

'Neither can they,' said General Allen. 'Are we really going to war over this nonsense?'

'What's the status of our ships?' asked Secretary of Defence Rodriguez.

'About two hundred and fifty nautical miles from the blockade,' said the Secretary of the Navy. 'We will be within hailing distance—'

'You mean *boarding* distance,' growled Rodriguez.

'. . . within boarding range in approximately six hours,' continued the other man.

'They wouldn't dare board us,' said the President. 'Would they?' he asked in a more plaintive voice.

'We are gaming out every option, sir,' said General Parkinson. 'Trying to anticipate every variable.'

'Do any of your variables *not* end in World War Three?' asked the Vice President.

General Allen looked rueful. 'Runaway escalation in a tit for tat encounter is a real risk.'

'Why is this happening?' demanded POTUS.

It was a rhetorical question but Harris took the opportunity to answer it anyway. There was no harm in the leader of the free world making slightly more informed decisions than was his usual habit. 'It is basically an internal power struggle,' she said. 'Hardliners against reformers.'

'What has that got to do with us?' demanded POTUS.

'General Zhang, leader of the hardliners, is using the confrontation with us to imply that Secretary General-elect Juntao is too weak for the top job. He has seized the moment and whipped up a patriotic fervour in China against the US and Taiwan.'

'Does that mean if Zhang secures victory in this internal conflict, he will back down?' asked Rodriguez.

'Possibly. If he can find a face-saving way to do it.' This was Griffin. 'We should consider what that might be. Shall I open backchannels to the hardliners?'

'That would reward Zhang's behaviour in this coup against the Secretary General-elect,' said the Vice President.

'That is the least of our problems, Madam Vice President,' said Griffin. 'In any event, it is my view that US interests will be better served if the hardliners under Zhang gain control in China.'

'And I believe our interests will be best served when China becomes a full and democratic member of the community of nations,' retorted Harris, 'as proposed by Juntao.'

'Difficult to see how that's going to happen, ma'am, with our ships steaming towards their blockade.' General Allen had a point.

Harris leaned back in her chair looking around the table at the men, in uniform and out, and at their Commander in Chief, who was looking from one speaker to another with an air of barely suppressed panic.

'I have an idea,' she said.

TWENTY-FOUR

'World War Three?' asked Jack, a sense of foreboding growing like a mushroom cloud.

'Part of General Zhang's attempt to overthrow Juntao. The hardliners are determined to stop the elevation of Juntao and his democratic reforms even though he is the Secretary General-elect. Which means the Tank Man is about to become sadly irrelevant again,' responded Guo Feng. 'And now Zhang has provoked a confrontation with the US to make Juntao look weak.'

'A confrontation about what?'

'Untie me and I'll tell you.'

'Let me guess,' said Jack. 'Nuclear arms shipments to Taiwan?' The memo was burning a hole in the lining of his jacket.

'How in the hell did you know that?' Guo Feng pulled against his bonds, strained to break free, but to no avail. 'You've been in here since the news broke!'

'What's the status now?' asked Jack, ignoring both the frantic struggles and the question of the other man.

'China has blockaded the Taiwan Strait. The US Navy ships that Zhang accuses of supplying nuclear weapons to Taiwan are a few hours away, at most. Neither side is backing down.'

'Jesus.'

'I warned you,' said Guo Feng. 'You had your chance to side with the good guys and you blew it.'

'You're working for Juntao?'

'Yes. I am his military attaché. He asked me to recover the Tank Man, which is why' – his lips thinned at the irony – 'I had you and the girl taken. But now the so-called Tank Man has done a runner and you have turned the tables on me – so the hardliners win.'

Jack looked at him sharply. Colonel Guo Feng was PLA

and General Zhang commanded the loyalty, almost without exception, of PLA troops. Once burned, an infinite number of times shy. 'You work for the Secretary General-elect? Great – so what is your relationship with General Zhang?'

Guo Feng managed to curve his cut lips into the semblance of a grin. 'It's complicated.'

A chartered helicopter with private markings unloaded a television crew from CNN and Sky News, the two news teams who had been able to mobilize immediately. The crew disembarked, set up and began to broadcast 'live' as a second helicopter with United Nations (UN) markings landed on the designated spot on the deck of the USS *Chung-Hoon*. A team of men and one woman got off even as the rotors continued to turn, and the chopper lifted off almost immediately. The ships were now three hours from the blockade but Vice President Harris's idea was being implemented: International Atomic Energy Agency (IAEA) inspectors had been rushed over from North Korea, where they were kicking their heels waiting for Kim Jong-Un to keep his word and let them inspect facilities, to verify that the US naval vessels were not carrying nuclear weapons to Taiwan.

The Vice President had offered the deal to Secretary General-elect Juntao: the US would allow international nuclear weapons inspectors to board the US ships before they reached the blockade to confirm that there were no nuclear devices on board. This would be broadcast 'live' on television by reputable networks. If General Zhang was mistaken, the blockade would be removed and the US vessels allowed to proceed.

'What if weapons are found?' asked Juntao.

'They won't be,' explained the VP. 'You know very well that Zhang made this whole thing up to try and get you out.'

This time, the American top command watched the reformer, Secretary General-elect Juntao, hold a press conference laying out the terms of the deal. 'I have been able to negotiate this inspection with the US government, and thank them for their commitment to a peaceful resolution of this dispute.'

The press was camped outside General Zhang's office as

well but he had not yet made a statement on the sudden intervention by the reform faction in China.

On a split screen, the arrival of the weapons inspectors was being broadcast 'live' on CNN and every other channel.

'This was a good suggestion,' said General Allen. 'We give Juntao a way of blaming Zhang for this whole fiasco. We don't look weak by allowing Chinese military to board and inspect if we allow the IAEA to do it. Well done, Madam VP.'

'Where are POTUS and Griffin?' she asked. 'Sulking?'

'They're on their way, ma'am,' said Rodriguez. 'Something came up.'

'I won't gloat, even if we have taken the wind from Griffin's sails,' she muttered semi-audibly to Dominic Corke, who sat next to her at the big table. 'This has been too close to a conflagration.'

On the screen, the weapons inspectors were greeted by Admiral Pritchard with a smart salute and then a warm round of handshakes. He introduced a young officer who, as the breathless CNN reporter – hovering in the foreground as the wind whipped his hair about – announced, would lead the inspectors through the cargo hold. Sensitive handheld Geiger counters would soon clarify whether there was radioactive material aboard.

'You said we had to support the hardliners and then you let that woman get away with her weapons inspectors,' complained the President of the United States to his National Security Adviser.

Griffin refrained from pointing out that, of the two of them, he was not the one with the top job.

'It was a good idea and a way to save face for the Chinese,' said Griffin. 'It will also allow Juntao back in the game.'

'Which we don't want, according to you.'

'Which we don't want.'

'So now what?' demanded the President.

'Now we wait for the pendulum to swing back,' said Griffin. 'Don't worry, sir. We have it covered. Everything is going exactly according to plan.'

'Whose plan?'

'Our plan, sir.'

* * *

In the Situation Room the Vice President, CIA director and military brass all watched the giant screens that carried the live feed of the weapons inspection.

The President of the United States and Griffin watched the television set up in the residence. The former ate crisps from a plastic packet and the latter drank from a cold glass of water.

General Zhang watched in his office. He was being given a wide berth by his subordinates, who feared the explosion of his temper when his devious plan to seize power from Juntao blew up in his face.

Secretary General-elect Juntao, his wife and other reformists watched developing events in an audio-visual room at the Great Hall of the People. Outside, delegates filed in to take their seats in the main hall after walking through metal detectors, having their bags searched and being patted down. It was a massive venue that would soon seat thousands to celebrate the appointment of Juntao to the office of Secretary General. A press conference had already been called for later that day so that the newly appointed Secretary General could claim credit for the peaceful resolution of the dispute with the United States and heap blame squarely on General Zhang for the fiasco. Juntao intended to use the goodwill to press ahead with his reforms, with or without the Tank Man. He would have General Zhang arrested, decided Juntao. He had pushed his luck too far and with the wrong man and it was time the PLA chief got his comeuppance.

They were all watching when the Geiger counters held by the weapons inspectors began to buzz wildly as they approached a series of stacked containers in the hold of the USS *Chung-Hoon*.

'What is in these containers, please?' The Frenchman in charge of the IAEA weapons inspectors on the ship was polite but firm.

The young naval officer held the inventory lists on a portable electronic device and now he held it and scanned the barcode on the first box. The Geiger counters continued to chirp.

'According to this, the material in here is for upgrading work on the Taiwan Air Force F-16 squadron. As you know, the United States and Taiwan signed an agreement last year to upgrade their fighters.'

'Nuclear material?'

'No, just guidance systems parts, advanced radar equipment, that sort of thing.' He was still scrolling as he spoke, trying to find an explanation for the radiation detected.

'This is Anderson Cooper from CNN on board the USS *Chung-Hoon*. Radiation detection equipment used by the IAEA has detected above-normal levels of radiation. We expect the boxes to be opened so that the IAEA inspectors can check inside. The United States has denied having any nuclear technology on the ship but there must be some explanation – an innocent explanation, I'm sure – for the readings.'

'Open the container, please.'

The camera zoomed in as the colonel fiddled with the locks. The locks could be heard snapping open and the officer carefully opened the lid so that they could see what was within. The watching world as well as the men around the crate stared at the contents.

A gleaming sleek missile in silver with a maroon nose cone, approximately twelve feet long, was stored within. The device had a guidance tail kit at one end and a control panel on the side, which remained shut. The only sound in the hold of the ship was the Geiger counters hitting their maximum readings. The CNN cameraman panned up and down the missile and then widened the angle so that half a dozen identical containers were visible.

'Colonel, would you like to explain why you have B61 munitions on board this ship?' asked the senior IAEA inspector, his voice shaking a little as he stared at the contents.

'Sir, what is the B61?' demanded Anderson Cooper, sticking the microphone under his nose. 'What is this?'

'It is an American-made *nuclear* gravity bomb designed to be delivered by fighter jets.'

'Which fighter jets?' asked Cooper.

'The stealth bombers, in future the F-35 . . .' said the US colonel, who seemed to be speaking his inner thoughts out loud.

'And the F-15s and F-16s,' said the IAEA inspector, 'currently supplied by the United States to the Taiwan Air Force.'

TWENTY-FIVE

'What in the hell?' demanded the Vice President. No one heard her because of the ruckus that broke out. As some of the military men present leapt to their feet in concerted horror, someone overturned a glass of Coke and the dark liquid spread across the surface. No one noticed. Voices, metallic, terrified, disbelieving, crashed like waves around them.

'B61s?'

'Who authorized that?'

'Are they real?'

'Is that a plant?'

'My God, what have we done?'

'Gentlemen!' VP Harris's high-pitched voice broke through the hubbub and there was a sudden silence as all eyes turned to her. 'General Rodriguez, why are there nukes on that boat?'

'I don't know, ma'am.'

'Does anyone know?'

There were head shakes around the table. Some of the most powerful men in the world looked as if they'd collectively wet their pants.

The actual most powerful man in the world was not there.

'Where's POTUS?' demanded Harris.

The door was pushed open by a marine in dress uniform and the President walked in, closely followed by the National Security Adviser, Griffin.

'We need to turn those ships around,' said the Vice President, turning to face the President and targeting her remark at him, the man with the authority to put the pin back into the grenade. 'Sir, there are nukes – unauthorized nukes – on board that ship!'

Griffin stepped forward to his seat but remained standing. POTUS walked around to the head of the table and sat down. He motioned with his hand and everyone returned to their seats, some with the careful, deliberate motions of people in shock and others flinging themselves back as if hoping for a safe haven.

'Sir?' Only the Vice President had the balls to ask again.

'We are *not* turning back,' said POTUS.

'But there are nukes on that ship!'

'I know.'

Griffin, still standing, spoke up. 'There are nukes on that vessel because I ordered them to be put there. They were loaded at Okinawa before the ships departed for Taiwan.'

'Who the hell gave you the authority to do something so goddam foolhardy?' Rodriguez was beside himself with rage, standing up and leaning forward, fists on the table.

'Who gave me the authority?' echoed Griffin. 'Let me tell you who gave me authority, General Rodriguez.' Griffin's head turned in a slow arc until he had made eye contact, in turn, with each person around the briefing table, including the Vice President.

'The *President* of the United States of America gave me the authority,' he said.

'We have to do something,' said Jack.

'What do you mean?' asked Guo Feng.

Jack removed the memo from its hiding place in the lining of his jacket and held it out for Guo Feng to read.

The military man's face turned progressively whiter as he read through the document.

'My God. This was all planned?'

'A coup against the reformist camp is well under way. Zhang and his American allies planted the nukes and now we have come to this.'

'I thought General Zhang wanted to undermine Juntao, not depose him. Or start World War Three.' Guo Feng tested his bonds. 'How did you get hold of that memo?'

'Long story.'

'We need to stop him,' said Guo Feng.

'We?' said Jack, with a wealth of disgust in his voice.

'You can't do it alone,' pointed out the other man. 'I can get you in to see the Secretary General-elect. He must be at

the Great Hall of the People for the People's Congress and
his election. Zhang intends to disrupt his election.'

A phone rang and they all reacted like startled deer. The
sound was from the briefcase that Guo Feng had been carrying
before Jack assaulted him. It lay by the door now.

'You have to get that phone,' said Guo Feng. 'It might be
about Confucius.'

'You're not in any position to be making demands, Colonel,'
said Jack.

General Zhang read out what he called the Five-Point
Declaration to the waiting thousands in the Great Hall of the
People, as well as the press. He was in full uniform, as befitted
someone stepping in to save the day from the feckless leaders
who had betrayed China.

'Today, before the eyes of the world, the United States
of America demonstrated that they are seeking to supply the
traitorous Taiwanese government with nuclear weapons.
Even as we speak, their ships continue to sail towards our
blockade.

'At the request of the Politburo and as Chief of the People's
Liberation Army I have, in this national emergency, stepped
in to manage this threat.'

Huge cheers rang out but Zhang remained stony-faced. 'As
a patriot, I stand here before you ready to do what is right
and necessary for China.'

'We want President Zhang!' the crowds shouted.

'We want President Zhang!'

'We want President Zhang!'

EMPEROR sat huddled in the wings watching General Zhang
make his statement. The pain from his ulcers would usually
have had him doubled over but today he barely noticed. Juntao
was with him but the former Secretary General-elect was under
armed guard. Zhang had wanted him to watch his failure and
defeat in person.

'How did you let it come to this?' asked EMPEROR in a
tortured whisper.

'I have been outmanoeuvred,' said Juntao. 'I did not

anticipate that General Zhang would risk nuclear confrontation to gain power.'

'You are a fool, then. He has been planning this for months.'

'Why do you care? You are a hardliner. Presumably you support this unlawful coup just so you can keep the Chinese people from their rightful place in the world.'

EMPEROR remained silent. He could hardly believe that he had smuggled out the memo to forestall this moment and the Americans had messed up to the point that the memo was still missing and nothing was standing in Zhang's way.

'How did you know this was his plan, anyway? How did he do it?' asked Juntao.

'He conspired with some in the US government to set up this nuclear stand-off. Zhang would obviously be better prepared for this than you since he knew in advance.'

'I have been speaking to the US VP, discussing my state visit and our vision for a new world order in which the US and China are both democratic powerhouses. She did not give any sign of this.'

'She doesn't know,' said EMPEROR. 'The US government has as many factions as we do. This was the NSA, Griffin, I believe.'

'How do you know so much?' demanded Juntao.

'It's a long story,' said EMPEROR. This time he felt the wash of acid regurgitate into his throat. The taste of failure was bitter.

Jack handed the phone to Guo Feng. He pointed the gun squarely at the other man and beckoned Fei Yen over to translate.

'One false move and you're dead,' said Jack.

'Yes?' said Guo Feng into the receiver after Fei Yen had put the phone on speaker.

'Sir, we have the man known as Confucius.'

'Well done.'

'What do you want us to do with him?'

Guo Feng and Jack made eye contact. Guo Feng nodded to show that he had understood the unspoken message. 'Bring him to the Great Hall of the People,' he said. 'I will meet you there with some other high-value prisoners. The Standing Committee will be pleased with our work today.'

'Brief them,' said POTUS.

It was obvious to everyone in the room that the President was pleased with himself.

Griffin stayed seated. 'I arranged for the weapons to be placed on board the USS *Chung-Hoon* in Okinawa. I did this with the full *authorization* of the President.'

'To what end?' demanded Rodriguez.

'To ensure that General Zhang is able to depose the new guy, Juntao, and take over power.'

'Why?' asked Harris. 'Surely it is in our interests if China reforms?'

'The President and I disagree. We do not believe that US interests are served by a free and democratic China. This will lead to instability in China and greater competition abroad. Better that the Chinese remain under the iron control of the hardliners.'

'How do you know General Zhang will succeed?' asked Rodriguez. 'We are on the verge of a nuclear confrontation! My God, man, do you not understand the risks?'

'My backchannels have informed me that once Zhang has taken over, he will deal with us to remove the threat. This should happen in the next hour or so – *before* we reach the blockade.'

'We will pull back the ships then? What happened to not looking weak?' General Parkinson was livid and it showed on his blotchy face and in his high-pitched voice. He ran a finger between his collar and sinewy neck. His uniform was suddenly too tight.

'We won't look weak because, in exchange, General Zhang will give us something that we have been wanting for a long time,' said Griffin, radiating smugness. 'It's what I like to think of as a win-win situation.'

'Win-win,' echoed the President, puffing out his cheeks. 'Win-win – I like that.'

When Griffin told them what he had been promised in return,

everyone in the Situation Room, except the Vice President and Corke, cheered and clapped.

Guo Feng's official car was parked outside. They jumped in, Fei Yen at the back, Guo in the driver's seat and Jack Ford in the passenger seat, pointing Guo's own weapon at him.

'No funny business,' he warned.

'The funny business is happening at the Great Hall of the People,' retorted Guo Feng.

Jack handed the phone to Fei Yen. 'Call your mother. Tell her you're safe,' he said.

'Nothing from EMPEROR?' asked Harris.

Corke and the VP were back in her office, shocked by what they had just heard.

'Nothing.'

'Do you think the President had any idea what Griffin did *before* today?' she asked.

'I'd bet my house, no,' said Corke. 'But he's going along now. This is going to be his big foreign policy victory.'

'At the expense of democracy in China,' she said.

'There are many who would argue that American safety is more important than that.'

'Do you?'

'I don't see the two objectives as incompatible,' said Corke.

'We are in a minority of two without any leverage,' said Harris.

A head poked around the door after a quick knock. It was her secretary, a tall black woman with impeccable grace. 'General Zhang is on the air,' she said.

They switched on just in time to hear Zhang's announcement that he was taking over during the national emergency.

The general stopped for the waves of applause and yells.

'We want President Zhang!'

'We want President Zhang!'

'We want President Zhang!'

Zhang continued, 'I have ordered the arrest of Secretary General-elect Juntao, who allowed this situation to escalate and failed to take the necessary steps despite warnings from our security services. He is nothing more than a lackey of the Americans who did not believe the word of our Chinese intelligence services that there were weapons on board the US Navy vessels until they showed it on CNN!'

The delegates booed and hissed. Juntao had fallen from grace in an instant.

'I will insist the Americans turn back from the blockade and warn them of the consequences if they should ignore my wishes. They will soon understand that no nation may threaten China with impunity; if we have to, we will board those ships and seize the nuclear devices. Taiwan is China and China is Taiwan.'

Huge uninterrupted cheers greeted this pronouncement.

'We want President Zhang!'

'Wait for me here, comrades. I go forth to demand an American withdrawal. When I return victorious – only then will I accept *your* demand that I assume leadership of the Communist Party and Mother China.'

Guo Feng was driving like a madman. In this, he was indistinguishable from the rest of the drivers on the road. He screeched to a stop at a traffic light, almost wiping out a collection of elderly men on bicycles.

'Fei Yen, get out here. Find your mother.'

'I'm coming with you.'

'It's not safe.'

'I don't care.'

Guo Feng didn't wait for the family dispute to be resolved but set off with spinning tyres the split second the lights turned green. It did not take them long to reach the first roadblock outside Tiananmen Square.

He showed his ID to the guard, who looked at it and waved them on.

'They didn't ask about us?' Jack Ford was still pointing the gun at Guo Feng, only now it was hidden by his folded arms.

'They know me around here.'

Knowing, from watching the television along with the rest of the world as the Chinese coup played out in real time, that

General Zhang was likely to call, the team at the West Wing gathered in the Oval Office. The Vice President and Corke joined them, although no invitation had been issued to them. Rodriguez nodded a welcome and Griffin decided he didn't mind that these two whom he despised would be watching his moment of triumph.

The phone rang. The President let it ring a few times, took a deep breath and picked up.

'General Zhang, I was expecting your call. I am putting you on speakerphone so that my team can hear you too.' He pressed a button and put down the receiver.

The general's words came through, clear, loud and confident.

'Mr President, I call on a matter of national emergency.'

'Yes, what is it that you want?'

'I want you to withdraw your ships heading towards our blockade.'

'The United States does not back down,' said POTUS.

'Neither does China,' retorted General Zhang.

'This is Defence Secretary Rodriguez. Are you the one with authority to deal with us?' Rodriguez asked. 'Where is the Secretary General-elect?'

'Both former and future Secretary Generals are under house arrest for betraying China,' said General Zhang.

'You're the man in charge?' asked POTUS.

'I am,' replied Zhang.

'I am sure you understand that a sudden withdrawal will make us look weak,' said the President. 'And that is not acceptable to my great country. The United States does not turn tail and run.'

'That is why I have a sweetener to offer you,' said Zhang.

All eyes turned to Griffin, who shrugged and held out his hands palm upwards in an I-told-you-so gesture.

'What is your offer in exchange for our withdrawal?' asked POTUS, grinning broadly.

'How do we do this?' asked Jack.

'You will have to appear to be my prisoner.'

'No way.'

'Security is not going to let you march into the building otherwise,' said Guo Feng.

They stopped at a second checkpoint.

In Mandarin, Guo Feng asked, 'What has happened so far at the Congress? Anything interesting or just the usual windbags?'

The answer was in such a flood of language and body language, Jack couldn't follow.

'We live in interesting times,' said Guo Feng as they were allowed on their way.

'What's happened?' demanded Jack.

'General Zhang has deposed Juntao. He has seized power at the General Assembly.'

'So we are too late? We must turn around?'

'No,' said Fei Yen from the back seat of the car. 'This is my country. I will not allow General Zhang to do this and take China backwards again. We go on until we are dead or imprisoned or we win the day.'

Jack's heart swelled with pride and fear. It seemed the courage and conviction that he had once believed were in her mother's character had found expression in Fei Yen. Unfortunately, these attributes were now likely to get them all killed.

TWENTY-SIX

'Pursuant to the hostile act by the United States, China has agreed to supply North Korea with long range intercontinental ballistic missile technology,' said General Zhang. 'We intend to give Kim ICBMs.'

'What?' The reaction of Rodriguez matched the expressions in the Oval Office. 'That will allow North Korea to reach the US mainland with nukes!'

'Perhaps you should have thought about that before trying to plant nuclear weapons on the Chinese territory of Taiwan.'

'But . . .' Griffin started to speak and then trailed off. He looked as if he had been punched in the gut.

'If, however, the United States withdraws her ships before reaching the blockade,' continued Zhang, 'we will put the technology transfer to North Korea on hold. You have approximately forty-five minutes to turn the ships around. Otherwise, the Chinese military will board and seize the ships and we will promptly supply North Korea with the advanced military technology they need. You do not have to call me with your agreement. We will know that you are compliant if the naval vessels turn back.'

He hung up. The President and the others listened to the beeping of the disconnected line without saying anything. Their expressions ranged from shock to anger, from disbelief to fear.

'That isn't what we agreed,' said Griffin.

'Make America great again?' asked the Vice President. 'More like make China great again.'

Confucius was waiting for them, hands bound behind his back, two burly men in uniform holding an arm each. The long-haired, long-robed man appeared serene despite his arrest.

'They got you too, Jack?' he asked, as Guo Feng walked in with the handcuffed man and girl.

'I'm sorry, Confucius.' Jack was devastated to see that his betrayal had consequences.

'I'm sure you had no choice. And I would imagine this is the reason?' Confucius smiled at Fei Yen, who was also bound. She tried to smile back but her heart was not in it.

'You are our famous renegade, the Tank Man?' said Guo Feng. 'Our leaders will be delighted to make the acquaintance at last of China's symbol of rebellion.'

'Is that what Jack said? That I'm the Tank Man?' Confucius looked pleased. 'That was clever, Jack.'

'Are you denying it?' demanded Guo Feng. 'Are you denying that you are the Tank Man?'

'Of course.'

'He would say that, wouldn't he?' pointed out Jack.

'There's only one way to find out,' said Guo Feng. He reached into his pocket for his phone and made a call. 'Xia, I have the Tank Man. Meet me at the Great Hall.'

'What the hell have you done, Griffin?' demanded General Allen.

'That's not . . . that's not what he agreed,' repeated the National Security Adviser. He looked as if he was about to throw up.

'This is your fault, Griffin! You said he would give us Kim Jong-Un!' raged the President. 'Instead, North Korea is going to get weapons technology to reach us right here in Washington, DC. Kim Jong-Un is getting ICBMs!'

'This may be the moment to consider our first strike capability,' said General Parkinson.

'What? Are you completely mad?' demanded Corke.

'We have the ability to take out the North Korean nuclear facilities. Maybe we should proceed to eliminate the threat before they obtain ICBMs.'

'Has something changed since we last considered this?' asked VP Harris, her voice dripping with sarcasm. 'You know as well as I do that we cannot be certain of success. They have scattered and buried their facilities. North Korea will retaliate against the South and Japan if we attack. Millions might die.'

'What choice do we have?' demanded Griffin.

'What choice do we have?' Harris's voice was like ice. 'We turn the ships around. That's what we do.'

'China and the world will see that as a Chinese win. Everyone will know that the US is weak. The Chinese will expand further into the South China Sea. The Russians will seize Ukraine. We cannot risk it.' General Parkinson bit off each word.

'China won this confrontation the minute we put nukes on those ships,' said Harris.

'Wait here. When the woman Xia arrives, bring her to me.'

The security at the main entrance saluted smartly in response to Guo Feng's demand. 'Yes, sir. Where will you be, sir?'

'Where are General Zhang and former Secretary General-elect Juntao?' barked Guo Feng.

'They are in the conference room adjacent to the Hall, sir. The delegates in the Great Hall await General Zhang's return after he has delivered his ultimatum to the Americans.'

'Then that is where we are going with these public enemies,' said Guo Feng. 'General Zhang's cup of happiness is about to spill over.'

'I'm not turning back the ships,' said the President.

'How long before we reach the blockade?' asked Harris.

'At present speed, forty-five minutes,' replied Rodriguez.

'Slow them down.'

'What?'

'Slow the goddam ships down. We need more time to figure this out.'

It was a mini-convoy of people now. Guo Feng pushing Jack and Fei Yen ahead of him into the building. The two men who, still gripping Confucius by each arm, followed the colonel. A couple of extra security men whom the colonel ordered to come along trailed in their wake.

'Where are we going? Where are you taking us?' demanded Jack.

Guo Feng gave him a hard shove in the back and the American stumbled forward and almost lost his footing.

'Prisoners do not ask questions. Especially American traitors.'

'Everyone get out,' said POTUS. 'Except you, Griffin.'

As soon as the room was cleared and the door shut, the President turned to his National Security Adviser. 'What have you done? You said the hardliners would give me Kim Jong-Un! That's why I backed you up!' He was shouting, red-faced, with the white rings around his eyes as clear as the rings of Saturn.

'Sir, you backed me up. You signed an executive order agreeing to this precise strategy.'

'You and I both know that you misled me about the contents. I did *not* know about the nukes.'

'On the contrary, I *told* you it was the plan to boost the hardliners. You decided to play golf rather than read the detail.'

The two men glared at each other. Both trapped; both eager to blame someone else; both aware that options were running out rapidly; and both stuck with covering for each other if they did not want to be outed as failures and traitors.

'Zhang played you,' said the President.

'General Zhang played *us*, sir.'

'Their ships have slowed down, sir,' said General Wang, on a secure line from the Chinese equivalent of the Situation Room.

'What is the ETA now?' asked General Zhang.

'At this speed, another hour, sir.'

'They're buying themselves some time to decide what to do. They will soon realize they have no choice but to turn back.'

'What are your orders if they do not turn back, sir?'

'Prepare to fire a warning shot across the bow of the USS *Howard*. Make sure boarding parties are ready.'

'Aircraft?'

'Ready to scramble – armed with torpedoes.'

'What about the other ship, sir?'

'That one has nukes on board, and I would prefer not to detonate them accidentally. We will use our ships to form a physical barrier so that they cannot pass without ramming a Chinese naval vessel. Then we will board the US ships if they do not surrender.'

It was quite a tableau. Four members of the Standing Committee of the Politburo, including Liu Qi, all hardliners, sat on sofas under chandeliers in one of the waiting rooms next to the Great Hall.

General Zhang was on the phone, looking as smug as the cat who had ordered a lifetime of cream to be delivered daily and had the family dog arrested.

Former Secretary General-elect Juntao sat in a hard chair, handcuffed and with two men standing to attention next to him. His wife sat close by. She was unshackled, but weeping softly.

A sharp knock on the door caused a few heads to turn.

General Zhang hung up and nodded to one of his men to open the door. He did so, had a brief conversation outside and returned.

'What is it?' asked Zhang.

'It is Colonel Guo Feng, sir. He says he has captured the man you wanted.'

General Zhang cracked a smile that no one in the room had seen for multiple decades. 'Send them in,' he said.

Guo Feng walked in with his prisoners.

General Zhang sauntered over. The colonel saluted smartly and indicated Confucius. 'At your request, we have appre-hended the criminal known as the Tank Man.'

'Guo Feng! What are you doing?' The outburst was from Juntao. He got to his feet despite his bound hands and took two steps forward; at that point he was restrained by the guards.

'My apologies, Secretary General-elect. In light of the circumstances, it seems prudent to inform you that I work for General Zhang.'

'You filthy coward!'

'Are you the Tank Man?' asked General Zhang of Confucius.

'Yes, sir.'

'He is not!' shouted Jack. 'I lied. Of course I lied.'

'And who is this barbarian?' asked General Zhang, looking at the American as if he was a single cell amoeba under a microscope.

'This is the American I told you about – the one who assisted the Tank Man to escape all those years ago. He identified this man under duress.'

'Duress?'

'This is his daughter.' Guo Feng yanked on Fei Yen's arm so she was forced to take a few quick steps forward to maintain her balance.

'You have outdone yourself, Colonel Guo Feng. There will be much for you to do in the new China.'

'I depended on you, Guo Feng.' Juntao sounded like a broken man.

'How can we be certain this is the Tank Man?' asked Zhang, prudent to the last.

'The only other person who can confirm his identity is on her way here, sir.'

'We withdraw the ships, but at the same time launch a surgical strike at the North Korean leadership and nuclear facilities.' General Parkinson was pointing at the various targets on a large map on screen.

'What happens if we don't get them all?' asked General Allen.

'If we have killed Kim Jong-Un, that will buy us time to come to terms with any new leadership in North Korea,' said Griffin.

'We had years to come to terms with *this* leadership and you blew it with your stupid stunt,' said Corke.

'What if we don't get Kim?' asked Allen. 'We know he has prepared for this eventuality with underground facilities.'

'It is unlikely he will become aware of the strike in time,' said Parkinson.

'Unless the Chinese warn him,' said Harris, her words cleaving the heavy silence like an axe.

'What do you propose?' demanded POTUS.

'Withdraw the ships.'

'And get nothing in return?' shouted Griffin.

'If Zhang keeps his word, at least the North Koreans will not get ICBM technology,' said the Vice President.

'Do you trust General Zhang's word?' demanded Griffin.

'No more than I trust *yours*,' snapped the Vice President.

'Sir?' said General Allen in a tentative tone, looking directly at his Commander in Chief.

'Yes?'

'We have twenty minutes at most before we are in range of their blockade. From satellite images, it would seem their ships are preparing to fire on us and have boarding parties organized. In addition, fighter jets have been scrambled at the southern Chinese bases.'

'Why do you want the Tank Man?' asked Liu Qi.

'I don't,' explained General Zhang. 'It was the former Secretary General-elect who requested that he be tracked down.'

'Why did you want him?' asked Liu Qi, turning to address Juntao, who was back in a chair but slightly closer to the action. 'Surely not to settle old scores?'

'Of course not. He was to be the symbol of our reform movement.'

'Unfortunately for our naive former would-be leader, he trusted the colonel here, who was working for me the whole time.' General Zhang looked like a man without a care in the world – which, all things considered, he probably was, thought Jack.

'How long do the Americans have to turn back before we engage?' asked Liu Qi.

'Twenty minutes.'

'If they don't?'

'We fire. Then we board.'

'People will die,' said Liu Qi. 'Young men and women. Patriots.'

'It is their duty to die for China.' General Zhang's words cut like a whip.

'For China, not for you.'

'Are you getting cold feet, Liu Qi? You have not been the

same since we lost the memo. Do not worry. As you see, it has not become an issue.'

Jack looked at his daughter and then at Guo Feng. He had no idea what to do. He was only bound loosely, he could break free, that had been the deal with the colonel. But there were several armed guards and Fei Yen might be caught in the crossfire. He wasn't sure he could overcome them all without Guo Feng's support. And the colonel seemed to have changed sides yet again. Jack certainly didn't trust him an inch.

'What memo?' asked Guo Feng.

'It is no longer important,' said General Zhang.

Liu Qi's phone rang and he picked it up. He listened to the person on the other end and then rang off. All at once he was shaking from head to toe, as if he had sudden onset Parkinson's disease.

'What's the matter?' asked Zhang.

'The Americans plan to launch a multi-pronged nuclear strike against North Korea.'

'You can't be serious.' Harris was irate, her tone harsh and grating. 'We *cannot* become the only country in the world to use nuclear weapons against an enemy for a third time! Surely Hiroshima and Nagasaki were enough?'

'We cannot let this gangster, General Zhang, trample all over us.' This was General Parkinson.

'I agree – and we will have to find a way to get the upper hand again, but not by starting a nuclear war!'

'It's a surgical strike,' insisted Griffin.

'There is no such thing!' yelled Harris.

'How much time do we have?' asked Rodriguez.

'Decision to strike has to be made in the next seven minutes.'

'They will not be so reckless,' said General Zhang. 'I do not know who your sources are, Liu Qi, but they are unreliable.'

'I just spoke to the Vice President of the United States and Dominic Corke, CIA director,' said Liu Qi. 'They intend to launch in approximately six minutes.'

'What? Someone is pulling your leg, old fool,' growled Zhang.

'They called to ask me to stop you from triggering this nuclear confrontation. They are going behind their president's back to try and prevent war.'

'Why would they call *you*?'

'Because I have been an American spy since your actions caused the death of my son in Tibet.'

'An American spy?' Zhang bellowed his disbelief.

'My codename is EMPEROR.'

'You told me EMPEROR was dead.'

'It seemed expedient at the time. I was trying to smuggle the memo out of the country, which would have revealed your plot to the Americans and the world. And the Secretary General-elect would have had his chance to transform China.'

'Colonel Guo Feng, arrest him! Arrest the traitor!'

'Sir, we need to prevent this strike on North Korea.'

'Why?'

'Thousands will die, sir.'

'Then the world will see the Americans for what they are and the Chinese century will dawn under my leadership. I will leave events to take their course.'

'I cannot let you do that,' said Guo Feng regretfully.

The nuclear codes were entered and verified.

Vice President Harris said, 'Mr President, I hereby resign as your Vice President.'

'And I as your Defence Secretary,' said General Rodriguez. 'I urge the rest of you to do the same. This attack is not justified.'

'Kim Jong-Un has been asking for it,' said POTUS.

'That may be,' said General Allen. 'But the rest of the people of the Korean Peninsula and Japan did not. I too resign.'

'Get out, then. There is no room for weakness in my administration,' replied the President. He was apoplectic, but determined. History would not forget his tenure as President of the United States.

Guo Feng turned his gun on General Zhang. The security men pulled their weapons and aimed them at Guo Feng, Liu Qi and Juntao.

The three other Politburo members remained sunk in their sofas, mouths opening and closing like landed fish.

'I will shoot you,' said Guo Feng. 'Do not doubt me, General Zhang.'

'Then my men will execute the traitors – including you – and China will be in nuclear crisis and without *any* leadership. Our country will implode.'

'I am a patriot,' said Guo Feng.

'So am I,' said Jack, and launched himself at the guard who had his gun on Guo Feng.

All hell broke loose.

'Call the Americans. Ask for time. Tell them that Juntao is fighting back,' shouted Confucius, tripping a soldier who was running to attack Jack.

Shots rang out.

Liu Qi dived behind a sofa and reached for his phone but he had dropped it on his way down and now it lay out in the open. A bullet ricocheted next to it in a puff of marble dust. Fei Yen, pressed against a wall, saw the problem and fell to her knees. She crawled towards the phone and pushed it to Liu Qi just as a soldier spotted danger and shot at her.

Fei Yen screamed.

Jack turned at the sound and saw red. He knocked out the soldier he had brought down with a hard right to his chin. He rose to his feet and launched himself at another. Colonel Guo Feng and General Zhang were grappling for a gun.

'Mr President!'

'What?'

'I have just heard from EMPEROR. Juntao is trying to seize back power. He asks that you wait a few minutes, please.' The Vice President was not ashamed to beg.

'How do we know he is not compromised?' demanded Griffin. 'I thought EMPEROR was compromised.'

'Do not launch, sir. Please do not launch yet. Give them ten minutes.'

General Zhang was the stronger of the two. Or maybe it was because Guo Feng had lost a fight to Jack Ford earlier in the day and was still carrying the knocks. Either way, Zhang slowly overpowered the colonel until the gun was pointing at him. He began to squeeze the trigger. Across the room, around ten yards away, Jack hit a soldier, grabbed his gun, swung him around, still holding him – and shot the general.

A few scant moments after that, Jack and Guo Feng were in charge. The soldiers were all down for the count. Zhang was clutching his shoulder and breathing fire. Fei Yen was down.

The door opened and Xia rushed in. She looked around at the chaos, spotted Fei Yen and dashed over, fell to her knees by her side.

'Is she all right?' asked Jack, his voice shattering with the fear he felt.

'Yes, I'm OK,' said Fei Yen, and Xia nodded.

'I spoke to the Americans but I am not sure what they will do,' said Liu Qi aka EMPEROR.

'I have the memo that proves the whole thing was a plot by the general,' said Jack, pulling it out of a pocket and waving it at the others.

'You have the memo?' EMPEROR was stunned and General Zhang, still on the ground, turned his head, flabbergasted.

'What is your name?' he breathed.

'Jack Ford. My name is Jack Ford.'

The whole world watched as Secretary General-elect Juntao took to the microphones for a live broadcast.

'. . . uncovered a plot by General Zhang *and* senior members of the US administration to provoke a confrontation between the US and China. In the ensuing chaos, the criminal Zhang hoped to seize power. He almost succeeded, except for the brave intervention of various individuals from both countries to thwart his plans. We have acted in conjunction with the Americans: we have ordered the removal of the blockade and they have authorized the withdrawal of the USS *Howard* and the USS *Chung-Hoon*. Today, the world took a step away from the brink of nuclear war and we are grateful that common sense and good will prevailed.'

*   *   *

'Mr Griffin, you are under arrest for conspiracy against the United States,' said General Rodriguez, a note of pure satisfaction in his voice.

'I have a signed order here from the President of the United States authorizing my actions. I was merely following orders,' replied Griffin, pulling the executive order out of his breast pocket.

All eyes turned to the President.

'I'll make a deal,' POTUS said to Harris, his eyes watering. 'I will resign in exchange for a pardon.'

'Is this the Tank Man?' Colonel Guo Feng asked Xia, gesturing at Confucius.

She stared at him for a moment and then shook her head. 'No, definitely not.'

'I could have told you that,' said Confucius.

'You protected him till the end?' asked Guo Feng.

'Yes,' said Jack. 'You have no right to use him as a political pawn, whatever your motives.'

On a small island just off Taiwan, a man cast a line out to sea from a jetty. He had a serenity that radiated outwards like ripples on a pond. He took a newspaper clipping out of his pocket and read the headline. *Identity of Tank Man Remains a Mystery*. The man smiled to himself.

Liu Qi, formerly the American spy known as EMPEROR, lit joss sticks at an altar for his son. Tears streamed down his face. He emptied a pile of pills into his hand and swallowed them all with the help of a cup of tea. He bowed his head in prayer and waited to join Yongkang in that hinterland after death. He had done his duty and achieved his revenge. It was time.

Confucius pulled Jack aside. 'I have the DNA results. I have Fei Yen's DNA results.'

Jack looked across at Fei Yen, who was on her feet leaning on her mother and shaking hands with the Secretary General. She had a makeshift bandage on her arm where she had been grazed by the bullet.

'Thank you for your courage,' said Secretary General Juntao to the young woman. 'China has a bright future, with young people like you.'

She smiled in response. The smile became a grin when she saw Jack looking at her and she winked at him.

'I don't need to know if she's my daughter,' said Jack to Confucius. 'I don't want to know.'